SECRET
~ OF ~
LITTLE BEAR CREEK

BOOK ONE OF THE
BRADLEY CHRONICLES

D1739077

BY

THOMAS K. MATTHEWS

ANDALUSIA
PRESS

Tom K Matthews 2021

Little Bear Creek is an actual place, or was, until flooded to create Little Bear reservoir. To look out across the vast, flat water, I imagine the remnants of my Father's past, sleeping below the surface.

~ TKM ~

PAST ~
Birmingham, Alabama – 1942

Steam roiled from the idling locomotive, waiting to leave Alabama. While passengers huddled on the platform, August fulfilled her promise of a sweltering farewell. The wood-sided, faded train station looked tired in the sweltering sun as The Bradley family climbed aboard. Robert sat by the window, surrounded by his seven siblings. Each wore an array of expressions, from expectation to fear. His family had never come close to boarding a train before, let alone riding one from Alabama to Michigan. Robert's younger sister, Sarah, hid her face in her mother's arm and wept.

"Hush!" His father barked. "Not a sound."

"Harley?" His mother whispered. "Ain't Mr. Cunningham gonna' come after us for runnin' out on our contract?"

"That man will never find us, 'specially out of state," he said.

"But som'a what you sold t'get these tickets was his," she whispered. "That's stealin', and some of it was pretty 'spensive."

Harley hissed back, "That man was neva' fair on the deal we struck. Anythin' I sold, and any cash I took was due me. 'Specially for the likes a' his kind."

"I'm just worried," she said.

"Worryin' 'bout nothing," he said.

Robert touched his bruised cheek, his hand wrapped in a makeshift bandage. He took some pride in that his father also wore bruises from their fight. Having worked with his father in the fields for two years, Robert was strong enough to fight back.

When each child reached the age of ten, they toiled alongside their father. Of the eight children, five boys and three girls, Robert stood tallest of his siblings. His younger brother, Matthew, was already proving to be a large specimen, even at the tender age of four. He and his twin sister, Sarah, would be the only members of the brood to escape cotton-picking.

"But what about the law?" His mother asked.

"I didn't do nuthin' that any God-fearin' man wouldn't do to protect his family. Dammit, Liz, I said to shut the hell up about that. They ain't gonna come up North 'bout anythin' like that. Stop yer fussin'."

Elizabeth knew better than to push, so she set a tight lip and prayed the train would hurry up and leave.

"Daddy?" Sarah asked quietly. "When we goin?"

"When the train's good an' ready. You best be happy we ain't drivin' north like them other fools. Two days on the road to Detroit with a buncha' screamin' kids. No suh."

More passengers climbed aboard the crowded train. Robert's mother nodded to a woman she knew from church. Robert looked at the others on board. Flies settled on heads and faces, then shooed away by waving hands.

In the car ahead, Folks wore fine shirts and clean hats. Folks with money. The multitude in their car looked ragged and frayed. His mother did her best to make them look presentable, but there was nothing left for luxuries after purchasing the tickets. He took some solace because other families looked dirty and wore no shoes. She also insisted on baths for all and bought each child a pair of second-hand shoes - the first they ever owned. Robert felt a sense of pride in them, though they felt foreign on his feet.

"We won't be looked on as trash," she said.

The door between the cars opened, and a fat black porter in a dark uniform opened his frog-like mouth and called for tickets. He walked the aisle, punching the paper tickets and counting heads. Robert watched as the barefoot children looked nervous. The porter stopped and demanded their tickets, and the father feigned surprise.

"I had 'em," he said and patted his dusty shirt. "I swears I did. Had 'em right heah."

"Suh, I need to see your tickets," the porter rumbled.

"Now, just a minute. I paid good money fo' my family to ride dis train. If'n I misplaced 'em, I'll find 'em before we get whe' headed."

"Sorry, if you can't show me tickets, I'll haf'to ask you to get off now. We're on a schedule."

"Now, you jest–"

"Don't make me call the bulls," the porter said.

"Damn stealin', unbelievin' good-for-nuthin' nigga! C'mon, let's get off this dirty ol' train."

Then the family hurried off while the rest of the travelers waved their tickets to be punched.

"That was the Hendersons," Robert's mother said.

Harley shook his head. "That man neva' did have no sense of pride. Besides, the likes of him wouldn't do no good workin' for General Motors."

"How long will it take us to get to Michigan?" Robert asked.

"I told you, boy, hush!"

"The boy deserves an answer, dear," his mother said.

"Till tomorra' this time. Now, hush!"

Minutes felt like hours, and some children began to cry. Everyone fidgeted. Sweat stains bloomed under every arm. When the whistle sounded and the locomotive lurched forward, a collective sigh went up.

Robert looked back at the platform and spied the Henderson's standing in a tattered clump. An expression of longing and sadness replaced Mr. Henderson's gruff attitude. As the train gained speed, his mother handed him an apple.

"Don't eat it all at once," she said. "Gotta' make that last."

He took a bite and watched the station and the platform slowly shrink in the yellow haze of the August air. Robert thought of the life they were leaving. He hoped this new life offered better. Despite that, some would be missed.

"Harl?" Elizabeth asked quietly.

"What?"

"What if your cousin can't get you a job? We'll be –"

"I'll get the job," he snapped.

"But there's so many. How'll you–"

"They need men to work the factories. We gots 'nuff money for a damn house, and I'll get that damn job. This family won't go hungry, and we won't be on no street."

"Daddy? But what if –" Robert began.

"Hush!" His father raised his hand. Every child went still and silent as the dead.

"Ya' want another?" His father warned. "I don't wanna' hear nuthin' 'til we get to Michigan."

Just you wait, Robert thought. *Things will be different there.*

The train lumbered along, the apple ignored in Robert's hand. Every stop brought on more people, and soon the car was standing room only. The air became rank with perspiration.

Robert wished he could open a window. He hoped Michigan was a better place than Alabama. He prayed his father got the auto plant job, and it paid enough that they could all eat and be happy. If his father were happy, then maybe he'd be more kind.

As sharecroppers, they often went hungry. Now the future was like a cloud of doubt, and the past pursued them like a demon. Fear was always a part of their lives. His stomach growled, so he took another bite of the apple.

His mother said, "Not alla'once. Save some. We gots a long way to go."

"You best be happy for it," his father said. "Remember what I always say."

"Yes, daddy."

His father often reminded them.

You can't eat cotton.

PRESENT DAY ~
San Diego, California

Hannah MacAllister watched her father's coffin lowered into the ground. Her husband, Kyle, dabbed at his eyes while her children looked agonizingly disinterested. Not that she blamed them. Evan, her eldest, knew his grandfather more as a business than an emotional relationship. He occasionally helped around his ranch for extra spending money. Her daughter, Gwen, knew him from awkward hugs and cash stuffed cards on Christmas and birthdays.

The divide between the generations was too broad to span and too cold to fathom. Hannah suspected her husband's overt emotion more out of confusion than any other reason.

"Ashes to ashes, dust to dust," the priest droned.

Hannah closed her eyes. That about summed it up. Ashes of the burned relationship built on forced respect, then later driven by sickness and need. Add the dust of a long-dead family that Hannah never knew. Nobody from her parent's family attended.

She tried, but she had no luck finding them. As far as she knew, all the Bradley's were dead.

Hannah and her three brothers, each dumbfounded by lack of grief, stood struggling to understand the soul of the man who raised them. Her only sister, Rebecca, did not attend.

"I have an audition," she said. "It's a great part. This could put me back on top."

Always the drama queen. The exact reason Beck became an actress. Experts say, to be happy in a vocation is to do what you know. Rebecca knew how to act like anybody but herself.

"Just tell everyone I'll be thinking of them," she said.

That made Hannah chuckle. Rebecca had one agenda, herself.

When the coffin hit the bottom of the grave, she and her brothers each tossed a single red rose into the hole. Hannah dropped another in Rebecca's name. The soft fall of the flowers might have gone on forever into the dark and bottomless hole her father withered in. Parkinson's disease slowly tore him down until he was no more than a fearful shell.

In the end, he struggled against padded restricting gloves, there to keep him from pulling out his IV. His illness had him in a state of trembling fury, his suppressed emotions spilling out in trapped, feral intensity. When he finally collapsed in surrender, he gave Hannah a vacant expression and uttered one sentence.

"I want to go home."

She put her hand on his forehead and whispered, "You are home, dad."

"Where's your mother?"

"Right here," she said.

9

He passed an hour later. Hannah felt sympathy and relief that her father was out of pain, but no grief or loss. When she signed the papers to release his body to the funeral home, she felt only relief.

Father Ward's voice snapped her out of her reflection. His eyes and hands raised to the heavens, he called the congregation to join in his elation.

"Now we offer Robert Lee Bradley to God and to rest beside his beloved Mary. Reunited in the kingdom of Heaven."

Hannah fought a smile. Despite what these people thought, her father had been distant, brooding, and swift with the belt. Not with her or Beck, only the boys. Her mother, distracted by work, always looked the other way. That was where the money was. Her husband's university salary would not suffice. Like Scarlett O'Hara, Hannah's mother shook her fist at the sky and declared never to go without, *whatever it was,* again – no matter the cost.

"Now, Hannah MacAllister, the oldest daughter, has some words to share," Father Ward said.

She stepped up and faced the crowd. Made up of her father's former university colleagues, neighbors, and her mother's business associates. They all shed tears for the man, the father, and the husband they believed him to be. Hannah gathered her false grief and addressed the crowd. These people were there to mourn a much different man than she knew.

"Thank you all for coming out today. It is wonderful to see the faces of all who knew my father. Over the years, you've all shared how much you respected him, what a good man he was, and how lucky my siblings and I were to have him as a father. Those words offered comfort, and I know every one of you knew my dad in your own way."

She paused. At the back of the crowd, a woman stood with lowered eyes. Hannah knew her well. They all did. Ten years before, her father embroiled himself in an extramarital affair with her. Debra Henderson, another teacher at the college. Hannah's mother put a stop to it with a call to Debra's husband. Not another word was spoken, and life went on as it always had.

Hannah continued, "My father was a great teacher and a very driven man. He prided himself on doing the best he could with what he had. He once said he'd been teaching in the same room at the same university with the same books for thirty years. Only the faces changed. Many former students told him, and us, that he was the best teacher they'd ever had. Even the best man they ever knew."

Because they didn't know him, she thought.

Hannah finished by saying, "Please join us in the reception area for some refreshments. There will be a receiving line, and we have asked that in place of flowers, donations be made to the South Marvin University Social Services. These donations will help underprivileged families. Thank you all for coming."

Then Hannah and her brothers, Otis, Leigh, and Clem, stood and shook each hand of the attending well-wishers. When the crying stopped, the noise became a loud crashing of laughs and words, all fighting for attention.

"Can you believe this shit?" Otis yelled over the noise.

"No," Hannah yelled back. "I really can't."

Leigh sauntered over with a plastic cup filled with what looked like Chardonnay. "This is too much. These people actually liked this asshole. I don't blame Beck for canceling."

"Good old sis," Otis said. "Remember Mom's?"

"Oh yeah."

"After all her friends got done saying all those great things about her, I thought – *this sounded like a wonderful woman, I wished I'd have met her*. How many autographs do you think Beck sighed that day?"

"Too many," Leigh said. "And what about home-wrecker Debbie sobbing in the back?"

Hannah nodded and said nothing.

Clem maneuvered through the crowd carrying four opened, long neck beers. He handed each of them an ice-cold bottle.

"To Dad," Clem said. "May Saint Peter stop him at the Pearly Gates and ask he explain it all."

"To Dad," Hannah said. Then they clinked the bottles like musketeers with their swords. "And now we get to split up the spoils of Mom's obsessive nature."

"By the way," Leigh said, "Thank you for handling this."

"Hey, what're big sisters for?"

"You always were the protector," Otis said.

Clem leaned in. "How long we have to wait to divide the cash?"

Hannah laughed. "He's barely cold, and you want to talk the sordid topic of coin?"

"Hey, it'll come soon enough," Otis said. "How much are we going to get after we sell that mausoleum of theirs?"

"You guys are unbelievable," Hannah said. "But the house was appraised at one million six hundred thousand. No mortgage and no taxes."

"Sweet," Clem said. "But, really, how long do we have to wait for the cash?"

"Thirty days," Hannah yelled over the rising voices. "Be patient."

That brought chuckles.

"Easy for you to say, you're the executor of the estate," Clem said. "How long do we have to hang around this farce?"

"Not long," she said. "We have to be out of here in an hour."

Hannah's phone buzzed. A text from her husband.

"I have to go to rescue Kyle."

"Ok, Hanny," Otis said.

"Really?" she said. "I hated that name when I was twelve."

"At least our loving parents didn't name you after a toothless redneck," Otis said.

"You don't know Uncle Otis was toothless," Leigh teased.

"We didn't know Uncle Otis at all," Clem said.

"Of course not," Hannah said. "Dad would never have allowed it because he *was* a toothless redneck. Now I have to extract my family from this insanity."

She pushed her way through the milling crowd. Women called out to her, and men patted her shoulders. A large woman chattered at Kyle, oblivious to his aggravation. Hannah gave him a sympathetic smile. The noise sounded like a swarm of crazed savages in Hannah's ears.

She finally reached Kyle. "Had enough?"

"More than enough," he said.

"I'll make an excuse," she said. "Head to the exit, and I'll meet you in ten minutes."

"In this crowd, that sounds like a lifetime."

"Be right back." Hannah found the pastor. "Excuse me. The emotion and the day got the best of me. My brothers will stay, but my family and I are leaving now. Thank you for the lovely service."

The pastor nodded and said, "Your parents are in a better place. They are with God."

Lord help me, she thought.

"We can only hope," Hannah said and broke free. She found Evan talking with his cousin.

"Hey," she said. "Dad and I are going. Are you coming home, or do you want to stay and get a ride home with your uncles?"

"I'll stay."

"Where's your sister?"

He pointed. "Gwen's over there."

"Be good."

She found her daughter standing with some other teens and looking bored. When she caught her mother's eye, she came to meet her.

"Dad and I are going. Staying or coming?"

"Oh God, coming with you."

The car ride home was a hysterical session of, *"could you believe that?"* and *"can you imagine?"*

Gwen laughed in the back seat while Kyle egged her on. Hannah wiped tears from his eyes and coughed up a laugh as they pulled into their driveway. Her phone rang. Rebecca.

"Perfect timing," Hannah said. "Probably calling to see if anybody asked about her. I'll take it out here. You guys go in."

"Say hello for me," Kyle teased.

"After last year's Christmas party? She'll probably never talk to you again."

Kyle and Gwen headed in. Hannah tapped her phone. "Hey, Beck. How'd the audition go?"

"Hannah, it's Andrew." Rebecca's boyfriend. His voice sounded weak.

"Hello, Andrew. Is everything alright?"

"I," Andrew's voice was rough with emotion. "Hannah, I–"

"Andrew, what's wrong?"

"Rebecca's in the hospital."

"What happened?"

In a shaky voice he said, "She came back from her audition. I could tell she was upset like when she doesn't get a part. She went to take a shower. The water ran a long time, so I went to check on her."

"What's wrong?"

"I found her lying on the floor. She took a whole bottle of Valium. I called 911. She wasn't breathing when they got here, but they were able to bring her back."

Hannah closed her eye. "Jesus. Where is she now?"

"Cedar Sinai Hospital."

"When did this happen?"

"An hour ago."

Just after we put Dad in the ground, she thought.

"Okay, I'm coming up there. I'll call you when I get close. Stay with her."

"I will," he said sadly.

"I'll be there as soon as I can. Call as soon as you know who I need to talk to."

"Okay."

"Andrew? This isn't your fault," Hannah said.

"I–I know–"

"Are you okay?" she asked gently.

"I–" He lost his voice in sobs. Hannah waited. "I'm sorry."

"Don't be."

"They won't tell me anything because I'm not family."

"Just stay there," Hannah said.

She hung up and stared at the front of the house. Rebecca did not try to kill herself because she didn't get the role. She swallowed a bottle of pills because of too much hurt and pain.

Pain caused when the last people who should have cared left her alone. Over the years, Beck stayed in touch with only her. In their conversations, she shared what her therapists said, what she felt, and often asked questions she hoped Hannah could answer.

"You're the oldest. You remember better than I do," she would say.

"Yes, Rebecca, but you were his favorite," she reminded.

"Then why was he the way he was with the boys?" she nearly begged. "Why didn't Mom do anything to stop it? Why did he spare me? I have a lot of guilt about that."

"He never hit me either" Hannah said. "I also felt guilt that he treated the boys like that."

"Why did he hate them?" Beck pleaded. "And why didn't Mom doing anything to stop it?"

Hannah could only shrug. "Our parents were broken."

"Why?" Beck begged.

"I don't know. They never talked about it."

As the older sister, Hannah often acted as a guardian between her father and her siblings. Is that why Rebecca tried to take her own life? Because she failed her brothers? That was bullshit, and she knew it. The blame had nothing to do with failure. Andrew hadn't failed Beck. Her career hadn't abandoned her. It was not the future that drove her to hopelessness. Simply put, it was an unresolved past that seduced her to take this desperate act.

When Hannah came through the door, Kyle was pouring a glass of wine.

"Did she call to give you more lame excuses why she didn't come to the funeral?"

"She's in the hospital," Hannah said seriously.

"What happened?"

"She tried to kill herself. I have to go to Los Angeles."

Kyle came to her. "Oh, my God."

"She took a bottle of pills. I have to take care of this. I better call my brothers."

"Should I come with you?" Kyle asked.

"No," she said. "Evan is still not home."

Kyle hugged her. "Are you okay to drive and handle this? After the funeral?"

Hannah nodded. "I'm okay. I'll call you when I get there."

"I'm so sorry. Please be careful driving."

"I will."

Hannah fought a growing and too familiar pattern of calm control after drama and crisis. She thought of Rebecca's flight from the family. Her escape to the craziness of Los Angeles.

L.A. was Just like her, Hannah thought. *Beautiful at first glance, draped in mystique and glamor, but with a dark side where the human psyche lurked in ignored abandonment.*

As was always the case, the drive took longer than Hannah expected.

When she pulled into the hospital parking garage, she drew a breath of relief. She called Andrew. "I'm here. Where are you?"

"Intensive care," he said miserably. "I can't get in because I'm not family."

As she walked the concrete bridge to the main entrance and wondered who she might see today? Movie stars? Rock stars? Influencers? All smiling and holding seeping wounds or injured souls?

"Jesus," she whispered to herself, "listen to me."

Hannah took in the view. Cedar Sinai Hospital occupied an entire city block just east of Beverly Hills, catering to the most affluent in the city. It represented the excess of the whole Los Angeles philosophy. Walking in the entrance was like entering a medical cathedral. She followed the directional signs and eventually found the intensive care unit. At the central nurse's station, she waited for a young Tom Selleck lookalike to finish on the phone.

"I'm here for Rebecca Bradley?" Hannah asked.

"And you are?"

"Hannah MacAllister, her sister. Bradley, before I got married."

"May I see some identification?"

She flipped open her wallet, and he gave it a close look.

"Thank you. Could you step in front of the camera, please?"

"Camera?"

"Just there. I have to print and access card."

The nurse activated a mounted digital camera, typed into a keyboard, and a moment later, a plastic I.D. badge, complete with Hannah's name and likeness, emerged from a small, squat printer.

"Please wear this at all times. I'll call for an attendant to take you in."

"Some security you have here," she commented.

"A necessary precaution."

An East Indian nurse dressed in a green pantsuit approached and asked her to follow. Like most hospitals, the hallway was cluttered with supply closets, numbered room entrances, and nurse's stations along the way. But unlike the community hospitals she was used to, this place gleamed. They finally came to a corner room.

"If you need anything, there is a button by the bedside."

"Thank you," Hannah whispered.

Nothing could have prepared her for the sight. Only four hours had passed, and the space overflowed with flowers, balloons, and cards. Rebecca was pale and thin. A respirator fed her oxygen, an I.V. supplied fluids, and monitors of every description tracked her bodily functions. A digital screen above the bed gave a running update of respiration, blood pressure, and heart rate. Hannah leaned down and looked closely at her sister's ashen face.

"Hello, Beck," she said, then turned to the nurse. "I understand that Andrew Hutchinson is waiting to visit?"

"Yes, he is in the lounge just down the hall."

"I'll be right back." Hannah found him sitting in nervous agitation. He jumped up when he saw her. "Hannah, thank God. I've been going crazy here."

"Come with me."

Andrew followed and then went to Rebecca's bedside. "Oh my God. How is she?"

The nurse calmly said, "The doctor is on his way."

"I'm here now," Andrew whispered at Rebecca's side.

"Mrs. MacAllister?"

Hannah turned to meet the doctor. "Yes."

"I'm Dr. Kellerman."

"How is she?"

"Straight to the point," Kellerman said.

"I have family waiting to know."

He looked at his clipboard. "Your sister flat-lined, and paramedics were able to revive her. We have no idea how many pills she took, but we know she was already taking three medications for anxiety and depression. Her blood test showed she was already intoxicated."

"Oh, God," Andrew whispered.

Hannah nodded. "What are her chances?"

"We're not sure how long she was without a heartbeat," Kellerman said. "She is breathing on her own, but we're giving her oxygen as a precaution. We'll know more when we get our reports back."

Andrew asked, "Do you think she'll come through this?"

"And you are?"

"Boyfriend."

"All we can do is wait." The doctor excused himself and left.

Andrew sat slowly into the chair by Rebecca's bed and began to cry.

Hannah said, "Why don't we get some air."

"I'd rather stay here in case she wakes up."

"She isn't going to wake up anytime soon," Hannah said. "Let's get some coffee."

"But I –."

"Andrew, I need to get some answers. I promise we'll come right back."

He pulled himself from the chair as if struggling with enormous weight. They returned to the small sitting room and sat at the same table.

"Coffee?" Hannah asked.

Andrew shook his head. "I'm jumpy enough as it is."

Hannah poured herself a cup and sat down. The expansive windows looked down on the city, undulating in continuous motion ten stories below.

"Tell me exactly what happened," she said softly.

Andrew struggled to tell the story.

He finally found his voice.

"She came home from the audition, and I could tell she was upset. I didn't ask. I knew she didn't get the part. Then she said she was going to take a shower."

Andrew paused and swallowed hard. Hannah waited.

"A long time passed, so I checked on her," he wept. "There she was."

Hannah felt torn between wanting to shake him or hug him. "Then, you called 911?"

All Andrew could do was nod. Hannah suggested they return to her sister's bedside.

"I have to talk with the doctors," she said. "Will you be okay by yourself?"

He nodded. Hannah returned to the nurse's station. "Mr. Hutchinson will be acting as my liaison regarding my sister. How do I make sure that is official?"

"I have a standard form," she said.

Hannah signed it and went back to the room. "Andrew, you have full access. I have to get heading home. Call me with any updates."

"Thank you, Hannah," he said. "I'll probably be here all night."

Her heart went out to him. They parted with a hug. Then, she extricated herself from the hospital. She liked that word; it meant *to free or remove from an entanglement or difficulty*. What could be more complicated than this? She had a missed text from Kyle to call when she was free.

Hannah dialed.

"Hey there," Kyle said softly. "How's it going?"

"Well, I'm out," she said. "Beck is in a coma. She was already intoxicated and on three behavior meds when she took an unknown quantity of Valium. It's bad."

"I'm so sorry," he whispered.

"I'm just leaving. If I run into the same kind of traffic, it may take me a while to get home. What a great ending to an already great day, huh?"

"Just drive carefully. You want me to stay on the phone with you?" Kyle asked.

"That's probably not a good idea. I better focus on my driving. Do the kids know?"

"Only Gwen. Evan is still out. He's getting a ride home later. He doesn't know."

"Probably a good thing."

"Be careful. I love you."

"Me too," she said.

When she arrived home, she heard raised voices. Hannah walked in on his drunken nineteen-year-old son, yelling at his father.

"Evan!" Hannah exploded in anger. She could not calm down until the police arrived.

DETROIT 1939 ~

Set outside the teeming population of Detroit's downtown, Michigan Central Station welcomed Robert Bradley and his family to the North. He stood with his head back and stared into the tangle of iron and cable above his head. Behind him, the train sat idling while it unloaded its human cargo. The diesel engines broiled in the lowered track and sounded like an angry monster. He forgot his throbbing cheek and his scabbed hand hanging at his side. Simultaneously awe-inspiring and frightening, the massive structure was almost impossible to behold.

"Glory be," Robert said.

"Tha's sumpin', ain't it kids?" Harley said.

"Sho' is," Elizabeth whispered.

A man in a suit smiled at them. "She's a beauty, alright. Those are bronze doors with mahogany trim. There are marble pillars, ticketing offices, a huge main waiting room, and that arched ceiling is 65 feet high."

"Ya' don't say?" Harley sneered.

The man gave them a contemptuous smile, then said, "Careful looking up like that son, you'll get a stiff neck."

Harley watched the well-dressed man stride away. "Damn city slicker, thinks we's a buncha' hayseeds. C'mon, we gotta' find Cousin Lenny. He said he'd meet us outside."

only gawk. The walls reached to high ceilings covered by tiled vaults and divided with broad coffered arches.

It was overwhelming.

The waiting area offered marble floors, bronze chandeliers, and large Corinthian columns. Three enormous arched windows flanked four smaller ones, ornamented with lovely wrought iron grilles.

"This place looks like a damn castle," Harley said.

Robert took it all in. Maybe this was a vision of things to come. Perhaps this fantastic structure would inspire his family to embrace their new life and find a way to be like the well-dressed people coming and going. But one thing was for sure; those same fancy people gave them, and the other ragged arrivals, a glance of disgust.

Harley caught a sideways look. His mood suddenly soured. "C'mon. let's go."

"A soul could get lost in all this," Elizabeth whispered.

The family stayed in a huddled group while making their way through the station. Other ragged families looked lost, some overwhelmed. One group sat on a bench and cried. Robert watched the city folks become more irritated with the bumbling bumpkins. Robert feared that a better life seemed unlikely. There were too many of them, and the locals resented their invasion.

"C'mon," Harley said and pushed on. They found a long ramp that took them to the exit doors. "Here we go."

"Lord 'almighty," Elizabeth gasped.

They found themselves in another heaving mass of people. Streetcars and taxicabs moved slowly past the curb while other cars motored through at dangerous speeds.

"Harley!" a voice called from the chaos.

He nudged his wife. "Thea' he is."

Elizabeth urged the kids to move ahead and all, but Sarah obeyed. She stood glued to her mother's leg. Elizabeth picked up her frightened daughter and hurried to the waiting car.

Lenny tipped his hat back on his head, "Geez Louise. Look at all these kids. Good thing I got this Oldsmobile wagon. C'mon, let's get everybody in so we can get outta' this madhouse."

"Whea' Ginny?" Harley asked.

"She's waitin' at home. I figured, with the whole family, we'd need all the room we could get. Harley, you sit up here with me. Liz, you get in here, and I'll put the little ones in the back."

Lenny opened the heavy rear drop door, and the kids piled in. Sarah refused to leave her mother, so Elizabeth held her in her lap. Robert sat beside his mother.

"Like this car?" she asked him.

"Yes'm. S'pecially the wood sides."

Lenny slipped behind the wheel. "That's why they call it a Woody."

"Is this bran'new?" Harley asked.

"Nope. She's a '38. Real beauty."

Lenny popped the clutch and threaded the car through the traffic like a needle through burlap.

"Ever'body okay back there?"

They all said they were.

"So," Harley said tentatively, "what 'bout this job?"

"Done deal," Lenny said. "Boss says if you're half the worker I am, he'll be proud to have you. I gotta' tell ya' cuz, we got so many comin' up and lookin' for work. Hundreds every day. The city ain't got room for 'em all. People are buildin' shacks in the alleys and backyards and rentin' to the Southies."

"Southies?"

"That's what they call us. But I found you a nice place. I put the deposit down, and it's waitin' on you. You'll sleep with us for a couple days. They're throwin' the niggers out, and we'll get you in to see the boss. It'll all get squared away."

Lenny drove back into the city. Everybody stared at the towering structures and crisscrossing power lines, streetlamps, and crowds of people on foot. The trip through downtown was an assault on Elizabeth's senses.

Sarah clutched her, while the rest of the kids stared in overwhelmed amazement. Harley turned to give his family a toothy grin.

"Welcome to yer new home," he said. "Robert, watcha' think?"

"It's big," he managed.

Thirty minutes later, Lenny motored down a tree-lined street to a small house with a steep yard and a one-car garage in the back.

Harley said, "Sure ya' got room fer us all?"

"We'll make room. C'mon. Liz, you take the kids in, Ginny's waitin' on you."

"Thanks, Len."

She gathered up her tired children and walked to the front door. Lenny's wife nearly squealed with delight.

Lenny held Harley back. "Jest a sec."

"Was'sup?

"Need to talk t'you."="

""Bout what?"

Lenny put an arm around Harley's shoulder and lowered his voice. "Ginny don't like drinkin' in the house. She's got Jesus hard as nails, and she don't abide any liquor."

"Okay."

"Another thing, these folks up here are not too happy about havin' the likes of our kind here. Don't get me wrong, they like us better than the niggers, but we got to try and fit in. 'Specially on the plant line. Try and listen to how they talk and try to sound like 'em. They'll take you more serious if you don't sound like a Southy."

"I'll do m'best."

"C'mon then, supper time." They walked to the house.

CHAPTER TWO ~

To Hannah, the office exuded calm and confidence, just like the woman sitting across from her.

"Hello, Hannah. Nice to meet you in person."

"Thank you for seeing me, Dr. Gregory."

"Oh, call me Karen," she said. "You were referred to me by Paula Keller?"

"Yes. She said you helped her through her divorce. You came highly recommended."

"I hope I can live up to her praise. Coffee or tea?"

Hannah felt uncertain. "Are you having any?"

"Just finished a cup," Karen said. "Feel free, though."

"I'm fine."

Hanna glanced around. If Karen was a crisis counselor, the office betrayed her vocation. Calm colors and delicate touches gave the room a feeling of a parlor. The two chairs facing one another cradled them in comfort.

Karen put on her glasses and looked at her notes, then folded her hands in her lap. "Before we start, what do you do for a living?"

"I'm a writer."

"Books?"

"Magazine articles, mostly," Hannah said. "Golf, fitness, nutrition. I have always wanted to write a novel but haven't had the time to commit to that length of a project."

"Do you intend to now?"

"I want to," Hannah said. "I just have to come up with the right story."

"What does your husband do?"

"Advertising, promotion, and graphic design," Hannah said. "He's also a writer."

"Creative family."

Hanna nodded. "He brands and promotes a lot of craft beer companies. You've probably seen his work. Half the small breweries in San Diego have used him."

"He works from home?" Karen asked.

Hannah nodded. "One of the perks of the creative life."

"I can imagine," Karen said. "I ordered a copy of the report from family services. I want to go over that night again. Do you feel up to it?"

"Of course."

"First, I want you to leave any shame or guilt you feel out of it. I find discussing these events pragmatically helps eliminate any blocking caused by remorse."

"I can do that," Hannah said.

"Before we start, how old are you?"

"I'm forty five."

"You must take great care of yourself," Karen said. "I wouldn't have guessed that."

Hannah gave her a grateful smile. "Thank you."

Karen leaned slightly forward.

"I mean that sincerely, you look great."

Hannah could only smile.

"How many years married?"

"Twenty-five."

"Congratulations," Karen said. "And your kids?"

"Evan and Gwen."

"This altercation was with your son?" Hannah nodded. "Was alcohol involved?"

"He was drunk, not me."

"How old is he?"

"Nineteen. Gwen's seventeen."

"Is that what the argument was about?"

"Initially."

"Then what happened?"

"Doesn't the report state that?"

"It does. But I'd like to hear it from you."

Hannah gave her a questioning look.

"Here's what we're going to do," Karen said. "Close your eyes, take a deep breath and then sit quietly for a few seconds. When you open your eyes, just tell me the story."

Hannah followed the instructions and then shared her father's funeral events, the weary anger, her trip to Los Angeles, and unanswered questions about her sister's suicide attempt. Then the long drive home from Los Angeles to find her drunken son in an argument with his father.

"When I walked in, the entire family was fighting. I tried to intervene, and Evan stepped over the line. I exploded."

"And that's not like you." It was not a question.

"No. The neighbors must have called the police because they came knocking."

"How did that feel?"

Hannah looked down. "I felt ashamed. That's not me. Even my family gawked at me."

"How was it resolved?"

"One of the officers was a woman," she said. "She pulled me aside and explained she wouldn't take action if I promised to see somebody about this. She warned me she had to file the incident with family services. But, if I took action, the incident would be dropped."

"I hope you take that seriously. Then what happened?"

"I burst out crying. The kids went to their rooms. Evan was freaked out."

"He'd never seen you like that before?"

Hannah shook her head. "None of them had. Not even my husband. We all went to bed. In the morning, Kyle urged me to see somebody as soon as I could."

"Was he understanding?"

Hannah smiled and nodded. "My husband is a good man and knew that was not me."

"But it *was* you," Karen said. "That part of you that you try so hard to hide and control. I call it *"the beast,"* and we all have one inside us. It's fierce in mean. But we have it. I consider it part of our old D.N.A., flight or fight on steroids."

"I just feel so ashamed."

Karen took off her glasses. "Hannah, I am a pretty good judge of character, and I can see you're a good woman. Married that long and with pride in your voice when you answered about the kids. I want to know what could have possibly taken a good and loving woman and had that experience triggered?"

Hannah looked down. "I usually have so much more control, but life has been tough lately."

"I understand," Karen soothed her. "We all have a breaking point. We'll look at the whole scenario."

"After dealing with my sister's situation, I felt angry and sad and tired and lost in grief."

"Then you came home to your intoxicated son?"

Hannah nodded her head.

"Does your son drink a lot?"

"Not that I know of," Hannah said. "I think it was the memorial, and he was with his cousins, and everybody else was drinking."

"So, he just took advantage."

Hannah nodded.

"Have you ever lost your temper like that before?"

"Not with my family."

"With who?"

"My father. But that was years ago."

"What happened that day?"

Hannah sighed and said, "My mother learned about my dad's first affair. She left the house, and my brothers all ran for cover. My sister confronted him. When he tried to defend himself, she called him a liar and a cheat. Dad raised his hand, and I reacted."

"And what does that mean, exactly?"

"I got between them. My voice was so loud it seemed to rattle the windows. If Rebecca hadn't pleaded, I don't know what I would have done."

"Scary stuff," Karen said. "How tall are you?"

"Five ten."

"How tall was your father?"

"Five eight and 145 pounds soaking wet."

"So, you looked down on him," Karen said. "And you were defending your sister?"

Hannah nodded.

"And this time, you were defending your family from your son's verbal attack."

"Yes, I was."

Karen leaned forward, her expression pure compassion. "Hannah, was your father violent with you and your siblings?"

"Not my sister and me. Only my brothers. For me, it was silence and dismissal."

"Did you ever provoke him?"

Hannah nodded. "When I saw he was on the warpath and looking for an excuse, I would distract him with mindless chatter. That way, he wouldn't hit my brothers, and I knew he wouldn't hit me. Then it all ended, and the house was silent and tense, most of the time."

"How old were you when it stopped?"

"15."

Karen made a note and then asked. "Are your brothers as tall as you?"

"Clem is almost my height. Rebecca was tallest, almost six feet."

"I know. My husband and I saw her in several movies," Karen said. "You girls were never hit?"

"No."

"Until that day," Karen said.

She blinked. "What?"

"You said you got in front of your father because he raised his hand to your sister."

Hannah nodded slowly.

"So, did the physical abuse end after that day?"

Hannah shook her head. "No, that ended years before."

Karen cocked her head. "I'm sorry, I'm confused. Can you clarify that?"

"My mom told my father if he ever hit my brothers again, she would leave him. After that, it was more emotional and psychological. He ignored us and looked for reasons to get angry. His favorite was ruining holidays and special events."

"Your mother never tried to change things?"

Hannah shook her head. "Too busy. She made a fortune in network marketing."

"Tough business," Karen said.

"She became a superstar and was always at conventions and coaching seminars. She prided herself on her tenacity and her numbers."

"But the emotional stuff didn't bother her?"

"That didn't leave any marks."

Karen raised her eyebrows. "That's a powerful statement. Did he continue to cheat on your mom?"

Hannah nodded. "Yes. We counted three affairs that we knew of over the years. By then, my mom was so focused on her career she paid no attention. Just before she died, she was on the cover of the company's annual report."

"Not very nurturing." It was not a question.

"Once we were off the nipple, we were on our own."

"What did your father do professionally?"

"He taught Mathematics."

"That explains a little."

"How so?" Hannah asked.

"Numbers are absolute, they don't lie, and they are rather static," Karen explained. "Math is hard and ridged."

"Hard and ridged is right," Hannah said, "Let's say we all became pretty self-sufficient."

Karen said, "You know none of this was your fault."

"That's what I told my sister's boyfriend."

"Are you taking your own advice?"

"I wasn't that day," Hannah said.

"His passing left you pretty well off, didn't it?"

"It did," Hannah said. "The liquid assets payout in about a week."

"Does that help take to angst out of all this?"

Hannah cocked her head. "No, not really."

"Thank you for being honest," Karen said. "We're almost out of time, but I want to be sure you're okay."

"As well as I can be," Hannah said.

"So, where do things stand with your sister?"

Hannah folded her hands in her lap. "She had an advance directive not to resuscitate or attempt heroic measures. From here, I go oversee her life support disconnected."

"And you didn't think to bring that up today?"

"Oh, I meant to. But, once we started talking about everything else, it slipped my mind."

Karen raised an eyebrow. "Disconnecting your sister from life support *slipped your mind?"*

"When you say it that way, yeah, it sounds crazy."

"Will your brothers be with you?"

"No," Hannah said. "She assigned that to me in her directive. I didn't think to ask them."

"And did they ask to be a part of it?"

Hannah cocked her head.

"No."

"Why noy?"

"That's the Bradley way. Don't ask, don't tell, and don't think you should. We learned that from our parents."

"I have come to understand that," Karen said. "Okay, then. Call me after the hospital duty if you need to talk. If I don't hear from you, I'll see you next week."

"Thank you, Karen."

*   *   *   *   *

Forty-five minutes later, Hannah pulled into the parking garage of Cedar Sinai Hospital, then walked the hallways to intensive care for the last time. Security was tight. All cell phones were collected at the door. In the days after the news broke on Rebecca, the paparazzi became ravenous. The Internet became a festival of whispered rumors and speculation.

Beck would have loved this, she thought.

She called her brother Leigh. "I'm here."

"Are you alright?"

"Yeah. I have a question for you."

"Shoot."

Hannah looked at her shoes and said, "Did you want to be here for this? I didn't think to ask."

There was a brief silence. "Shit, sis, that's a loaded question. I, uh –"

"No, I'm serious," she interrupted him. "It's not intended to accuse you of anything. I realized I didn't even consider if this was something you guys might need for closure. I figured I better ask, so you didn't think I hadn't thought of your needs?"

"My needs?" Leigh laughed nervously. "Hanna, I'm so happy you're handling this crazy shit. No, I don't feel like I have to be there. I know that sounds messed up, but–"

Hannah cut him off. "Hey, no worries. Beck asked me, and I'm handling it. What about Clem and Otis? Did they say anything?"

"Yeah, they said they were glad you were handling it, too."

Hannah laughed out loud. "Okay, I get it."

"It's not that we don't care," Leigh said.

"No worries. I'll call you later."

She approached the reception desk, presented her I.D., then clipped on the plastic pass. Some of the visitors hanging around the lobby looked conspicuously inconspicuous. Probably reporters or paparazzi hoping for a shot.

Luckily, Beck kept her family life sequestered from the fan-based world, so nobody knew her from Adam. Besides, instant fame through tragedy usually trickled down to the parents. Without that connection, tracking down siblings would take longer. She took the elevator and found Andrew sitting in the waiting room. He looked like hell.

"Hello Andrew, how are you holding up?"

"They said I had to wait for you," he said.

"Well, I'm here."

After a short, whispered meeting, the doctors agreed as long as Hannah exonerated them of any responsibility. If it led to any security leak or images, she had to agree not to implicate the hospital for breaching their protocol.

"Trust me, we won't sue you," she promised. "Come on, Andrew."

He gave the doctors a sideways glance.

They walked in silence to Rebecca's room. A doctor, a nurse and the hospital priest waited with grim expressions. Andrew went to Rebecca's side.

"Did she ever regain consciousness?" he asked.

"I'm afraid not," the doctor said without emotion.

Hannah broke the tension. "So, how does this work?"

"On your word, we will remove her breathing tube, disconnect her I.V., and we wait."

"Andrew, are you ready?"

"I –" He could not finish. He wept by Beck's side.

Hannah looked at the doctor. "Give us a minute."

Beck's complexion looked mottled, and her eyes squinted as if in pain. In the days since her admittance, she seemed to have aged a decade. Andrew stepped back. Hannah put an arm across his shoulders to offer emotional and physical support.

"Are we ready?" the doctor asked.

"Yes," Andrew whispered.

The priest administered the last rites and stepped away. The nurse disconnected Rebecca's I.V. while the doctor removed her breathing tube. There was a burbling exhalation, and she flinched. When she stopped breathing, the monitor beeped, and the nurse shut off the alarm. Rebecca twitched, her heartbeat slowed, and soon she was gone.

"Now she's with God," the priest offered.

Andrew wept quietly. Ten minutes later, Hannah and Andrew left the I.C.U. The elevator ride down was silent and sullen. On their way out, the loitering visitors gave them raised eyebrows.

"Vampires," Andrew said.

"That they are."

Once outside, Hannah waited for Andrew to collect himself.

He loved her, she thought. *Despite her flaws and drama and insanity, he really loved her.*

"You going to be okay?" She asked.

"Yeah, I guess... I dunno," he said sadly. "I have to go home and start going through her stuff. What about you? Are you alright?"

"I'll be okay," Hannah said. "Take care. Call if you need anything."

Andrew nodded and walked away. Hannah realized Andrew genuinely saw something more in Beck. Or, maybe he was just as neurotic as she was. She wondered if losing a tragic soul mate was the worst thing that could happen to a damaged person.

Her walk to the car seemed twice as long, and the whole ordeal began to weigh on her. Once in the car, she dialed Karen. She got her machine.

"Well, it's done, Hannah said. "I'm feeling flat. I know that will pass. When it does, I'll probably be a mess. I just wanted to reach out."

Once on the freeway, Hannah clicked on the radio heard it announced that troubled actress and model, Rebecca Bradley, passed away at Cedar Sinai Hospital.

"Sellouts," she spat. "The nurse probably sold the information to one of the assholes in the lobby. Wonder how much she got?"

She called Kyle, and she put him on speaker. "Hi."

"Hi there," he sounded worried. "I just heard about Beck on the news, and it's all over the Internet. Are you okay?"

"Yeah, I think so."

"Talk to me."

Hannah looked inside herself.

"No," she admitted. "I was going through the whole ordeal, wrestling with my demons and finding a way to come home and leave the worst of this behind."

"Do you need me to stay on with you?"

"No," she said. "Karen is calling me back."

"Drive careful. I love you. Call if you need me."

Hannah answered Karen's call. "Hello, thanks for calling back."

"Of course. Talk to me."

"I'm feeling kind of flat."

"That's not unusual," Karen said. "Hannah, I want to ask a delicate question. What did you feel when you witnessed her passing?"

"I'm not sure."

"Because it feels foreign or because you felt nothing?"

Hannah thought for a moment. "Both, I think. I felt for her boyfriend, and I even felt for the doctor. It was almost like I wasn't there. Does that make sense?"

"More than you know. I want to share something."

"Sure."

"When I first sized you up and thought, *here's another angry woman facing emotional trauma, distracted and unable to give me a straight answer.*"

"Is that how most women handle this kind of thing?"

"More often than you would guess," Karen said. "But you've been refreshingly surprisingly self-aware and emotionally honest. It gives me faith that you will see this through and come out stronger as a result."

"Thanks. That means a lot."

"Call back if you need me."

Karen's compliments were almost uncomfortable. Hannah knew why. The Bradley's didn't share family secrets. It had always been that way, even among the family members themselves. Once her mother's money rolled in, her spend-a-holic proclivities blossomed like spring flowers. More than once, she arrived at Hannah's front door with bags or boxes. Even furniture delivered by truck.

"If your dad asks, you bought this," she whispered.

Genuine truth was as scarce in the Bradley home as chastity in a whorehouse. To open up and share the entire ugly truth with a sensitive stranger felt frightening yet liberating.

Hannah arrived home and found Kyle in the kitchen.

He gathered in his arms. "How was it?"

"Interesting and emotional and scary."

"You want to talk about it?"

"Later."

"Dinner will be ready in a bit," he said. "Cheeseburgers, homemade French fries, and salad. Want a glass of wine?"

"How about a beer," she said.

He handed her a cold longneck.

"The kids joining us?"

"Nope. Just you and me. Evan is still on the wagon. He promised," Kyle said.

She dropped into a chair in the living room and slowly sipped her drink. Hannah tried to let it all go, even if just for a few minutes. Kyle called her to the table, so she finished her drink and put the empty bottle on the counter. He set the plates on the table.

"Want another?"

Hannah smiled in appreciation.

He returned with another cold beer. "Let's eat, then you can tell me about your day."

"Where are the kids?"

"Evan is at the movies, Gwen's at Kelly's."

The meal wrapped her in a flavorful embrace. The crispy fries set off the burger's hearty satisfaction. When she wiped her mouth, Hannah felt relieved.

Then she told the whole story. With a laugh, a few tears, and a heavy heart, she shared it all.

"Karen sounds like a Godsend," he said.

"She is. Now I need your arms around me."

After making slow love, Kyle cradled Hanna and planted delicate kisses on her freckled shoulder. Hannah closed her eyes and lost herself in that loving place. When she met Kyle, she fell for him instantly. He was everything her father was not. His willingness to share and please won her over immediately.

She thought of the nights in her childhood home when she heard her parents having sex. The brief and guttural exertion that wafted down the hall sounded like they were in pain. Hannah found it hard to imagine her mother capable of the intimacy necessary to bear five children. But that was a different time, and she imagined her father commanding her to service him. After Rebecca was born, her parent's room fell silent.

Maybe that was why her father cheated.

"What?" Kyle asked.

"Nothing," she said.

"You were whispering. You do that when you're working something out."

Hannah rolled over. "I know."

"Is it about today?"

Hannah nodded and kissed him. "Go to sleep."

CHAPTER THREE ~

That weekend Kyle insisted Hanna test drive new cars. With over 210,000 miles on her Kia Sorrento, he insisted she buy something new.

"Don't you want to be seen in something fancy?" he asked.

"Yes, but not like that family wagon. Something bigger and tougher."

"Name it," Kyle said. "We can afford it."

"And four-wheel drive," she said.

"Let's go shopping."

After three hours at the Chevrolet dealer, they drove home in a new Tahoe, with all the bells and whistles.

"How's it feel," Kyle asked.

Hannah smiled with pride. "Amazing."

"I thought so."

That night they dressed up and went to dinner, where they proudly handed the SUV over to the Valet. Hannah prayed the kid didn't scratch it. In the morning, they drove to the local mountains for the weekend to try out the four-wheel drive. Once home, Kyle spent an hour washing it.

"When do I get a new car?" Kyle teased.

"As soon as we get the cash," Hannah promised.

"At least you'll get to drive and pick up Rebecca's ashes in comfort," he remarked.

"That's true. I have a session with Karen afterward, so I'll be home kind of late."

"No worries, I'll keep the home fires burning."

"Just don't burn the house down," she joked.

* * * * *

Monday morning, Hannah's drive to the Mortuary was tedious in the bumper-to-bumper traffic, no matter how luxurious her ride. Every year the crowd of commuters grew, and 'rush hour' got longer. When she reached Los Angeles, Hannah tapped the phone interface button on his steering wheel and called Kyle.

"Hey, you there?" he asked.

"Almost. Traffic is horrible."

"I said you should have left earlier."

"Remind me never to move to L.A."

"Are you going to make it back for your session with Karen?"

"That depends on how long they keep me in this place," she said. "Hold on. I'm turning into the parking lot now."

"I'll let you go. Be careful."

"I will. Love you."

"Just think," Kyle said. "After today, you won't have to go up there anymore," Kyle said.

"Thank God for that."

Hannah parked and climbed from the SUV.

The sight of the Mortuary almost made her laugh.

Built to look like a Southern plantation, the funeral home dwarfed the small parking lot. Welcomed distraught patrons through ten-foot-high double doors.

Augustine's Mortuary arched the doors, painted in maroon script. Hannah shook her head and entered the lobby. Why did these places tried to emulate an 'old fashioned décor? As if it was more comforting to the grief-stricken.

A rotund man in a blue suit and horn-rim glasses met her at the door. "Mrs. MacAllister?"

"Yes."

"Welcome to Augustine's. I'm John Thompson. The office is right this way."

They passed a stairwell that dropped into what looked like a chapel. Stained glass windows caught the sun and splashed the floor with blending color. It reminded Hannah of spilled paint.

Thompson took a seat behind a massive wooden desk and gestured for Hannah to sit down. He folded his hands and gave her a practiced smile of sympathy.

"First of all, please accept my condolences for your loss. I understand your father also recently passed."

"He did," she said. "Then my sister killed herself on the day of his funeral."

Thompson looked shocked but maintained his decorum. "I am so sorry for your loss."

Hannah hid her impatience and said, "I appreciate your sentiment, but traffic is bad, and I have to be back in San Diego for an appointment. So, if I could sign for her remains and get on my way?"

Thompson smiled and said, "Of course."

His eyes betrayed his good humor.

He handed her a white paper bag that looked like the kind she got when she bought something at a boutique. Inside was a box the size of a pound of coffee, sealed with a gold foil tab. The whole package felt oddly wrong, but they had followed Rebecca's instructions. No urn. No fuss, and no muss. Her ashes to be scattered in the mountains.

Thompson said, "The death certificates will be mailed to you once the county releases them."

"And how long will that take?"

"We'll have them next week, and I'll mail them out that day." Then Thompson gave Hannah an almost embarrassed expression.

"Is there anything else?" Hannah asked.

"My staff and I were all fans of your sister's work. We wish to share how proud we are to be a part of her final preparations."

"Thank you," Hannah said.

As they shook hands, Thompson gave her a questioning expression.

Hannah thought, *This guy thinks I'm some cold bitch, unfazed by my famous sister's passing,*

"Thank you again," she said.

On her walk back to the Tahoe, she could not help but chuckle. She found it odd how people took celebrities as personal possessions. Ownership through worship. If they had known the real Rebecca, would they feel the same? Hannah could only shake her head.

She put Rebecca's ashes on the passenger seat and started the long trip home. By the time she fought her way back to the freeway, Hannah fought angry tears. She hoped to purge the sorrow before she sat down with Karen. That way, their session could focus on solutions, not a blubbering hour of simpering comfort. But the emotion did not pass, and the rest of her drive was an exercise in controlled fury.

*   *   *   *   *

Dr. Karen Gregory poured boiling water over a green tea bag, stirred in a pack of Stevia, and went back to her chair.

Her phone rang. Hannah.

"Hello."

"I had to go to Los Angeles, and traffic is bad."

"Do you want to reschedule?"

"Not if you can fit me in."

"I'm free for the rest of the day. So get here when you get here. How are you doing?"

Hannah's voice sounded strained. "I'm okay."

That meant she wasn't, Karen thought.

Hannah arrived fifteen minutes late and set her sister's ashes on the floor of the back seat. She nearly ran to Karen's office, then paused to calmed herself and casually opened the door.

"Sorry I'm late," she said.

"No problem at all," Karen said. "How are you doing?"

"Okay, I guess. I picked up my sister's ashes."

Karen gave her a sympathetic look. "How did that go?"

"Honestly? I gave the guy the cold shoulder. He wanted to be compassionate, but I cut him off."

"Because?"

"I was in a hurry."

"Hannah, you don't come across as the kind of woman to act like that. So, you gave the poor man the rough side of your hand because?"

Hannah sighed. "Because he knew Rebecca's work. He was a fan, and I wasn't interested in hearing some practiced speech about condolences and being sorry."

Karen leaned forward, "I have a question? Are you angry with your sister for what she did?"

Hannah rubbed her cheek and then exhaled softly. "I'm not mad at *her*."

"Go on."

Hannah rubbed her hands on her legs. "I'm mad at *him*."

"Your father." It was not a question.

Hannah nodded.

"We established that last time. Is there more?"

"I'm struggling with the imbalance we all endured."

"Because she was never hit?"

"Either was I," Hannah said. "But it's so much more than that."

Karen raised her eyebrows. "Go on."

"Let's just say she got so much more from him than we did. More in every way."

"Hannah," Karen said with a smile, "I know this is hard, but can we visit some specifics here?"

"There were times when I was worried if I had enough gas to get to school, and he was leaving twenty-dollar bills on her dresser every morning. She didn't have a car! She didn't have a license!"

"That's what I'm looking for."

Hannah's voice trembled. "Love, money, support, compassion, empathy, encouragement – you name it! So, is that why I have so much anger about this whole thing?"

"You tell me. What do you feel?" Karen urged.

Hannah paused a moment.

"If she never went without and was his favorite – why did she feel compelled to kill herself on the day of his funeral?" She asked. "Was it guilt? Shame? Sorrow?"

"Probably all of those," Karen said. "Besides anger, what are you feeling now?"

"Lost."

"Why?"

"Because I –" Hannah paused and looked stricken.

"Spit it out."

"Because he's gone, she's dead, and all that's left is this big house and a dozen accounts to settle so my brothers and I can start carving up the big pie my mother built."

"But that pie will give you the freedom to focus on you."

"Then, I'll be well off and lost."

"What would make you found?" Karen said.

Hannah shook her head, her face in her hands.

"I've known you for two hours, and I know that behind that strong exterior, there is a sensitive woman that wants an answer for a burning question she's never actually yelled out loud. So try and finally ask it."

"It'll sound trite and childish," Hannah said.

"Try me."

"Okay. Who am I?"

"You tell me."

Hannah seemed to collapse into herself. With her palms to her eyes and lower lip trembling, she drew a huge breath and let out a sad laugh. Karen reached across and put her hands on Hannah's shoulders.

"It's alright," she whispered.

Hannah regained her composure enough to find her voice. What came forth was a flood of events, emotions, and anxiety that painted the picture of her childhood. With a vacant father and a distracted mother, there existed unspoken desperation to hold the family together. As the oldest, she felt that she must make up for her parents while keeping her true feelings inside. Hannah blurted out the hostility and fear, finally losing her words in another round of tears.

"Hannah," Karen soothed, "that tells me what happened and why you're sad, but that doesn't tell me why you feel lost."

"I know," she huffed.

"That can wait, though. I have a question. What was the general tone in your home? Was there ever any happiness?"

"Of course," she said. "My mom left us alone, so we ran around like a mob. Dad didn't care what we did as long as we didn't embarrass him."

"What about the holidays?"

Hannah shrugged. "We had Christmas and Easter, being Catholics. Mostly obligatory stuff."

"And birthdays?"

"Oh," Hannah let out a sad laugh. "After the age of five, Mom just forgot about those."

"Meaning what?"

"Well, if you didn't remind her, it wasn't mentioned."

"I get the picture," she said. "We're out of time, but I want you to take five minutes and put you through a meditation. Just sit back, get quiet and breathe."

While Karen talked her through it, Hannah quieted her mind. After a minute of breathing and calm, she found his focus and pushed back the shadows that swallowed her. She opened her eyes to see Karen smiling at her.

"Feeling better?"

"Yes."

"When was the last time you cried like that?"

"Oh, I've been doing that a lot lately," Hannah said. "Mostly in the car. Before that, I'd say it was the day I threatened my father. I went to my room and wept into my pillow."

"Listen to me. You are not lost."

"Then, what is it?"

"That's what I want you to think about until we see each other again. Let's not wait a week. How about Friday?"

"Friday works," Hannah said.

"Good. Until then, I want you to breathe, cry when you feel like it, and allow yourself to grieve. If you refuse those true feelings, you'll –"

"End up like my sister?" Hannah said.

"Let's hope not."

Hannah felt nothing but gratitude when Karen hugged her at the door.

"You're doing great," Karen said.

Back at the car, Hannah brought Rebecca's ashes to the front passenger seat.

"Beck," she said as she pulled out of the parking lot. "You and I need to talk. Not now. I'm still too raw. But when we're both ready, we'll sit down and hash it out."

She imagined Becky standing and brushing her blonde hair away from her green eyes, smiling her Hollywood smile. That day, the last time she saw her, Beck waved and yelled something.

Hannah thought she didn't hear what she said, so she just waved back. On the drive home, she finally put it together. The last thing Beck did was blow a kiss, an act she first thought odd. Now Hannah realized what Beck yelled that day. *"In case I never see you again."*

Hannah wiped her eyes and drove home with a heavy heart.

*   *   *   *   *

Kyle opened the oven and checked the lasagna. Sauce bubbled, and the cheese topping looked like a pool of rich magma. Perfect. Hannah was due home, and after the day she had, a home-cooked favorite would help reduce the sting of her experience.

The sessions with Karen were a godsend, and he almost felt grateful for the 911 call that night. When the garage door rattled open, Kyle pulled the Caesar salad from the refrigerator, checked the garlic bread in the convection oven, and pulled the pan to sit for five minutes.

"Hi," Hannah called from the garage access door.

"I hope you're hungry."

"Starved," she said.

Hannah held a bag the likes she'd get from her local ULTA beauty shop.

Kyle raised his eyebrows. "That's her?"

"Yes. Hard to believe. Forty years, six-foot and 120 pounds of life and experience fit into a box the size of a pound of coffee."

Kyle took a furtive glance inside. Hannah was right, exactly the size of a pound of beans from an expensive coffee shop. He gently took the bag and set it carefully on the dining room table. Then he wrapped his arms around his wife.

"How'd it go with Karen?"

"Tough and enlightening."

"You can tell me about it later. Eat first."

"Where are the kids?"

"Evan's at Dan's, and Gwen is out with Seth. Sit yourself down, and I'll deliver hot, cheesy goodness."

Hannah poured a glass of red wine and waited at the table. Kyle made good on his promise. They ate, and he listened to her talk about her day. Hannah stole glances at the bag still sitting at the end of the table, as if Rebecca was invited to dinner.

"Hon?" she finally said.

"Yeah?"

"Did you leave her there on purpose?"

"Uh-huh," Kyle said and took a bite of pasta.

"Why?"

He ignored her question. "So, what did Karen say you needed to do?"

"Nothing specific yet, but I guess what she wants me to do is figure out who my family was."

"Meaning what?"

Hannah looked down and swallowed hard. "Who the Bradley's were. My father, mostly. Then she wants me to face reality, stop acting naïve, and discover who I am. Simple, right?" She finished her wine.

"Want another one?"

"No, but I do want you to hold me and tell me everything is going to be alright."

"I can do that."

After dinner, Hannah spent more time researching the history of Alabama, the formation of the cotton and slave culture, and the contributing factors of the tumultuous past. Again, Kyle came into the study and looked over her shoulder.

"You've been at this awhile," he said softly. "It's after 11:00, and I'm thinking about sleep."

"I know," she said and smiled at him. "But this has me by the shirt, and the deeper I go, the more I feel like I'm getting closer to something. I don't know what, exactly. But something."

"Don't stay up all night," he said and kissed the top of her head. "You have the meeting with the lawyer tomorrow."

"I know. Just a few more minutes."

ALABAMA – 1918 ~

World War I ended with sinister turbulence on the fields of France, 4,500 miles from Alabama. While Armisist was signed, Joshua Bradley stood in brooding silence on the steps of his shack. He'd gone to fight in the Great War with many of his Southern brothers. But after only one week in the trenches, Joshua took a ball to the thigh. There he languished in a field hospital, suffering from blood poisoning and fevers. Of the hundreds of his fellow soldiers that fell to mortar fire and lead, most died of infection.

More substantial than most, Joshua fought through the sickness. But his wound left him with a limp. When he returned home, the ship that brought him was laden mainly with the dead. With victory declared, his weak leg and stern disposition became his shameful memory of the battle he could not help win.

Joshua knew he had no choice but to do what his father, father's father, had done, farm cotton. He soon found a plot of land worth sharecropping and an owner willing to take a family.

"This ain't no picnic," the farmer spat. "You gonna' manage with that leg?"

"Yessir, I'll do jest fine."

"You read?"

"I do."

"Then look through this here contract and sign it if y'agree. I make all my tenants sign. If you welch, you get nothin'. Runoff in the middle a' the night, and I keep your name on a blacklist. Nobody'll touch ya' if'n you welch."

"I ain't never run out on my word," Joshua said proudly.

"Get to it then."

He read the contract before making his mark. It read:

To everyone applying to rent land upon shares, the following conditions must be read, and agreed to. To every 30 and 35 acres, I agree to furnish the team, plow, and farming implements, except cotton planters, and I do not agree to furnish a cart to every cropper. The croppers are to have half of the cotton, corn, and fodder (and peas and pumpkins and potatoes if any are planted) if the following conditions are complied with, but-if not-they are to have only two-fifths (2/5). Croppers are to have no part or interest in the cottonseed raised from the crop planted and worked by them...

It went on for pages regarding cotton yields, shares of sales, obeying rules. In simple terms, it meant him working for a rich man with more land than kindness. To him, Joshua was just a white nigger. Joshua skimmed the rest of the document.

It was signed: Charles Chilton, Landowner.

A lot of mish-mash horse pucky, Joshua thought. *Listin' ever' pumpkin, squash, and fence post.*

"You understand the term's this here contract?" Chilton asked.

Joshua nodded and scribbled his name.

They shook hands. Then Joshua collected his wife and children and moved them to the eighteen-acre plot with a ten-foot by 20-foot shack. There he put his muscular back and weak leg to work. Within weeks his wife was with child. Nine months later, she went into labor. He waited outside the shack while the midwife saw to the delivery.

The date was November 11th, 1919.

With the Huns defeated, the world returned to normal. In his second season of cotton planted, Joshua was making a life for his family. Four years and three children later, Dorothy died giving birth to their third. He was left with a newborn and no time or skills to tend to its needs.

"Lord help me," he whispered.

The news traveled fast, and it was his neighbors, not God, that offered help. A wet nurse came twice a day to feed the babe. But once she left, it was his duty to care for the child. Now alone with four children to raise, he worried about having time for his crop. That alone wore him out worse than the hardest day in the fields. The baby cried for milk.

"Where is that woman?" he asked of the empty, dusty road.

Joshua knew there was only one solution to his dilemma; he needed a woman in the house. With Dorothy in her grave only two months, he worried some might look at him in shock and disgrace. But he had no choice.

"Ain't a man's job to care for a babe," he said out loud. "Even the Bible says so."

The child wailed louder, and he resigned himself to the task of finding a wife. When so many men came home to the graveyard, the county became crowded with widows, all looking for a strong man to offer them solace. Even in church, many of them gave him eyes, nearly begging him to take comfort in their mournful loneliness. Joshua decided this Sunday he would return the smiles and pick the one he fancied.

He spied the wet nurse coming up the road. She lumbered breathlessly to his font path. Her round, pink face beaded with sweat, and her copious bosom heaved under her exertion.

"I's sorry, Mista' Bradley. Runnin' late t'day. My las fam'bly had me wait."

"He's hungry and hollerin' to raise the dead."

"Glory, but don't he fuss. I'll get right to 'em."

"Thankee," he said.

Soon the crying was replaced by the woman's soft lullaby. His other children came up the road, and he watched them with a hard eye. Matthew, his eldest, walked ahead of the other two. His younger son, Harley, held his sister's hand. The girl shuffled to keep up with her brother.

"Daddy," Matthew greeted his father. "How'r you?"

"Fine boy, how was school?"

"Very well," the boy said and smiled.

"Got homework?"

"Done a'ready."

Joshua suspected the homework went ignored, and his grades suffering. When graduation came around, he'd watch his classmates take a diploma. Not that Matthew wasn't smart. He was too smart for his own good. Joshua knew that kind of trouble. His brother was smart as a whip and doing time in Andalusia, the local prison farm.

"You best be sure you're takin' your studies serious."

"I'm the smartest one in m'class."

"I's sure of that."

"You need any help, daddy?"

"Not unless you can beg the cotton t'grow."

"I jest might," Matthew said. "I's got some ideas about that very thing."

Harley dragged his sister to the house.

"I'm hungry," she whined.

"There's food inside," Joshua said. "Mind the nurse. She's feedin' your brother."

Just then, the sheriff's wagon turned up the hill and bounced along the ruts. When the dust settled, the deputy shifted his bulk from the driver's seat, carefully placed his hat on his head, and climbed out of the car.

"Jonah," Joshua said with a nod.

"Yo' eldest around?"

"He was right here."

But when they turned, Matthew ran across the field as if chased by the Devil himself.

"Damn that boy," Joshua said. "What'd he do now?"

"Seth at the grocers says he was stealin' melons off the stoop, and Carl at the hardware says he's got some merchandise missin', and yo' boy was spied in the vicinity."

"When was this?"

"This mornin'. That means the truant officer lookin' for him too."

"Dontcha' worry," Joshua growled. "Next time you see that boy, he'll be sittin' on a pillow in his chair in school, his butt'll be tanned, but good."

"Hope so. If'n it ain't, I'll hafta' come back and take the boy into custody."

"It'll be. You can bet'cher life."

"I'll hold'ja to that. G'day."

The sheriff pulled away in a cloud of dust.

CHAPTER FOUR ~

Late afternoon sunlight cut through the blinds and painted the top of the conference room table like prison bars. Hannah had an instant dislike for this man. Maybe it was his expensive suit, the spray tan, and dyed hair. Whatever the reason, she tried to focus on the event and not the person. It was the reading of her sister's will, after all.

Hannah felt the drawn out drama as he made a show of glancing through the few pages of documents, then dramatically held up a sealed envelope decorated with pale roses. To her, it looked like stationery from a specialty paper store. Hannah waited while Andrew swallowed nervously.

"I'll be recording this meeting with your permission," the lawyer said. "Anything said or disclosed here will be private and protected by the client/attorney privilege. Any questions?"

"No," Hannah said. Andrew shook his head.

"Excellent," The lawyer said and pressed the start button on a digital recorder. "For the record, I am Liam James Hooker, Rebecca Elisabeth Bradley's attorney. I received a package from Rebecca by way of UPS that contained a letter for my eyes only, assorted paperwork for expediting her wishes, and this envelope to be opened in your presence. Before we begin, are there any questions?"

"When did you receive all this?" Hannah asked.

"The day after her overdose."

"Jesus," Andrew whispered. "She planned all this."

Hooker continued, "According to Rebecca's wishes, the contents must be read to both of you."

"Always the drama queen," Hannah said.

Hooker used a letter opener to slice the envelope, releasing the scent of dusty rose pedals.

"I gave her that perfume for her birthday," Andrew said.

Hooker withdrew the folded contents. "Before I read this, I need you both to verbalize your response for the record."

Both said yes.

"Here we go. It begins with a handwritten note. *Dear Hannah and Andrew, please forgive me. I know that nothing I could say would make you understand why I chose to do what I've done. There's a part of me that doesn't think I can go through with it. But if I did, then you are listening to this note. Please know I loved you both.*"

Andrew put his hands over his face while Hannah felt a nagging anger. She'd have plenty to discuss with Karen later.

"I'll give you a minute," Hooker said.

Andrew pulled a handkerchief from his pocket and wiped his eyes. "I'm okay."

"She signed it simply, *Rebecca.*"

"Go on," Hannah urged.

Andrew looked nervous as Hooker put the page face down on the blotter and began to read: "I, Rebecca Elizabeth Bradley, being of not so sound mind and not so sound body, do at this moment bequeath the following items."

She listed a 2011 Mercedes, the sum of eighty-four thousand and some odd dollars in her bank account, all her furniture and otherworldly belongings, all to go to Andrew. She declared her undying appreciation for his loyalty and love. Those words brought color to Andrew's cheeks.

"Finally," Hooker read, "I leave one antique banjo, given to me by my father, to Hannah Lee MacAllister. Of all the Bradley children, she would be the only one that could appreciate it. I once again hope that you understand I had no other choice but to take this selfish act. I love you both."

"Jesus," Hannah said.

"It is signed, Rebecca Elizabeth Bradley."

Andrew wept, and Hannah put her hand on his shoulder.

Hooker continued. "Finally, Rebecca wished her ashes scattered at sea, and she requested you, Hannah, be responsible for this."

Hannah sat back and asked, "Is the Banjo here?"

"No. I'll mail it to your home address."

Hannah nodded.

"If there is no challenge to the division of this property and money, I have some papers for you to sign," Hooker said. "I will be in touch regarding disbursement. As I said, I'll have the banjo shipped to you. Andrew, the lease on the condo is paid until January, so you may stay until then as a resident of the property. If you wish, you may speak with the landlord about transferring the lease."

"I wouldn't want to live there without Rebecca," he said.

"Then you may vacate any time before the lease is up. When you feel up to it, I need your signatures so I can get started."

Andrew took a deep breath.

Hannah swallowed her emotion.

They signed, and Hooker offered practiced condolences while he walked them to the door. In the hall, Hannah shook her head and let out a sad laugh. "Jesus, I could use a drink."

"Me too," Andrew said. "But I'm sober. I'll join you for some coffee."

Hannah patted his shoulder, and then they walked to the elevator. On the street, they found a small restaurant and stepped out of the L.A. bustle. Hannah caught the waitress's eye and pointed to a booth by the door. They slipped into the deep bench seats. Pure Hollywood, the place offered a mixture of modern Asian and West Coast funk. Bold graphics of bamboo splashed across a back wall. The menu, classic California cuisine.

"We ate here once," Andrew said absently. "Good food."

The waitress smiled at them. "Hello, early lunch?"

"Just coffee," Andrew ordered.

"What's on tap?" Hannah asked.

"The usual, and I have lots of local craft beers."

"Do you have Ridged?"

"Yes, we have the CalCoast Ale," she said.

"I'll take that."

She went to fetch the drinks.

"You know?" Andrew said with a sad laugh. "I've been sober thirteen years, so I missed out on all this new craft beer buzz. Funny I'd think about that now."

"How long were you and Rebecca together," Hannah asked.

Andrew looked thoughtful. "It would have been four years next month."

"Did you guys talk about getting married?"

"I asked. Rebecca said she was a two-time loser and didn't want to go through that again. When I promised I wasn't going anywhere, she said she might."

"That sounds like her."

The drinks arrived. Hannah took a sip.

"How is it?" Andrew asked.

"Good," Hannah said. "Can you help me understand the banjo? I noticed it was gone when we did the inventory."

"Oh, yeah, that was odd," he said.

"Not that it was a big deal. My mother was an estate sale junky."

He shrugged. "She brought it home after she went to see your dad when she heard he was dying. She put it by the fireplace and never touched it. One day I was plucking away on the couch, and she screamed at me."

"Did she say anything that would have given you a reason to think she'd kill herself?"

He folded his hands on the table. "About a week before she did it, she came home from an audition and didn't get the part. Out of the blue, she accused me of never loving her."

"That must have been a shock," Hannah said.

"Then she told me the only man that ever truly loved her was her father."

Hannah sat back. "How'd she define that?"

"You knew she was bipolar, right?" Andrew asked.

"I suspected, but I didn't know she was diagnosed."

Andrew looked down at his cup. "When we went on our first date, she told me she was bipolar and a first-class bitch. Selfish and emotionally unavailable., she warned. She told me that if I wanted to run screaming, now would be the time."

"And you didn't?"

"I said, *Hey, this is LA, who isn't?*"

"Good answer."

"She asked me to move in a week later."

Hannah looked closely at Andrew. Handsome and fit, tall enough to make Beck feel normal. At first, she thought Andrew fit the mold of the typical LA struggling actor that hooked his wagon to a sugar momma and lived the arm candy, boyfriend life. Now she felt terrible and utterly wrong about this guy.

"Four years?"

"Yes," Andrew nearly whispered. "She said our relationship lasted longer than her two marriages combined."

"She must have loved you."

"We were compatible."

"It must have been more than that," Hanna offered.

"I understood her," he said. "You know, I let my modeling and acting career go for her?"

"That sounds like Beck."

"She hated to be called that. I did once, and she threw a wine glass at me. *It's Rebecca!,* she screamed. She said if I ever called her 'Beck' again, she'd throw me out with nothing but the shirt on my back."

"She was always Beck when we were kids."

"She said that's why she knew you guys hated her."

Hannah looked shocked. "Come again?"

"She told me that when she was in the sixth grade, she played Beck Thatcher in a stage production of Tom Sawyer."

"I remember that."

"She said that after the play, she asked her parents how they liked it. Your mom said the play wasn't realistic, and your dad said nothing."

"Sounds like Mom," she said. "Always the pragmatist."

Andrew continued, "Later she asked your father again and he said he didn't like stories about the South. They were – let me get this right – *disrespectful and perpetuated a stereotype of all Southerners as ignorant and racist."*

"Jesus," Hannah said.

Andrew nodded. "Did you see *Midnight Sun?*"

"Yes, my Husband and I loved it."

"Rebecca was offered the role of Sissy in that movie. She turned it down. When who they cast won the Oscar for Best Supporting Actress, I asked her if she regretted not taking it. She said no. Know why?"

Hannah nearly held her breath. "What'd she say?"

"Because the character spoke with a Southern accent, and she would never do that to her father."

Hannah shook her head. "So, she thought we called her Beck because we wanted her to, what? Feel the pain of her lack of my father's approval?"

"I don't know. I never pursued the issue any further."

"I had no idea," Hannah said.

"Did having this conversation help explain any of this?"

Hannah shrugged.

The waitress walked up. "Anything else?"

"No, thanks." Hannah handed her a debit card.

They walked back into the sunny Los Angeles afternoon and stood in silence. Hannah broke the quiet. "Andrew, I want to apologize for having been distant while you guys were together."

"That's okay."

"No, it's not. Her two husbands were assholes, and I assumed you were the same. Now I know you genuinely cared for her. The fact she left you everything shows that."

"I hope she loved me, but I also knew her heart had an iron cage around it."

Hannah shook his hand. "I better go. Call me if you need to talk."

"Thanks," Andrew said. "Hey, I do have one question."

"Okay."

"What do you know about Little Bear Creek?"

Hannah furrowed her brow. "Never heard of it. Why?"

"She mentioned it when she was ranting about her terrible life. She said everything would have so much better if it hadn't been for Little Bear Creek."

"No clue," Hannah said.

The walk back to her car felt dark on such a bright afternoon. Traffic seemed to go silent, and one thought ran through Hannah's mind. Rebecca lived her life in a self-created cage and could only escape it through high living and make-believe. No wonder she became an actress. Out there, she could be whomever she wanted, while in the confines of her own home, she was a small girl begging for her father's approval.

And she called that love.

*   *   *   *   *

The beautiful weather drew Karen Gregory to open the office windows. Not too hot, just enough breeze and the smell of honeysuckle wafting up from the planters. How could anybody be in crisis, desperation, or hopelessness on a day like this? But, she knew people. No matter the weather, emotional storms were inevitable. She checked the clock. Hannah would soon be coming from the reading of her sister's will.

She arrived at precisely three o'clock.

"Good afternoon," Karen said. "Tea?"

"No, thanks. I am so glad to be out of that traffic."

"I can imagine. Tell me, how'd it go?"

"Honestly?" Hannah said. "It was odd, a little bit crazy, and very bizarre. Exactly what I expected from Beck."

"My husband and I saw her in the movie *Headlands*," Karen said. "Am I to guess that she played that part so well because she played herself?"

"When Kyle and I watched it, he leaned over to me and whispered, *didn't we just see this at her birthday party last month?*"

Karen chuckled. "So, what did you find out?"

Hannah opened her mouth, and the details flowed like a broken dam. She described the drama of the reading, the mystery of the banjo, and her time with Andrew.

"We shared a drink, and he gave me some insight into their lives together," she said. "Interesting stuff, to say the least."

"How'd he hold up?"

Hannah shrugged. "Okay, I guess."

"Please. We have to be open and honest here," Karen said.

Hannah leaned forward and put her face in her hands. "He was a basket case. They had an interesting relationship. He embraced the 'boy toy' role and endured emotional servitude. He shared his pain about wanting the kind of relationship they could never have. From the way he described it, he was almost subservient."

"What will he do now that she's gone?"

"Well," Hannah said. "He'll be okay financially for a while. He inherited everything."

Karen looked at Hannah over her glasses. "But he won't have her. All the possessions in the world can't fill the void if he had her that high on a pedestal."

"He'll probably find somebody else just as unreachable."

"That was your impression?" Karen said.

Hannah nodded. "He's handsome, an actor, and, despite his outward appearance, he nearly fell apart at the hospital. I had to drag him away so the doctors could do their work. It felt like a scene in a movie. I think he lived for the drama and trauma. Otherwise, why would he have stayed with somebody that accused him of not loving her?"

"Tell me about the banjo."

"It hung on my Parent's living room wall for twenty years. Then, when we visited, and my kids were little, they wanted to play with it, but my dad said no."

"Why was it so important?"

Hannah raised her hands. "Your guess is good as mine. But, of course, I always guessed it was another odd decorator thing my mom picked up in her thrift store travels."

"Thrift stores?" Karen asked. "With all her money?"

"She may have made a fortune, but she was still a sucker for estate sales and antique stores," Hannah said. "To call her decorating eclectic is being generous. It was more a mish-mash of trash and treasure with no order or point."

"Your sister made no mention of why she took it?"

"Andrew said she just showed up with it."

Karen asked. "How was your relationship with your dad once he got sick?"

"Better, I think," Hannah said in a questioning voice. "I felt sorry for him, I guess. His mind was fading, and he was so frail. I had the time, so I dropped by twice a week and read to him."

Karen pushed. "Did you talk?"

"Not really. His ability to communicate was deteriorating. So mostly, I just sat with him."

"And did you feel like you were helping him?"

"Honestly?" Hannah sighed. "I did it mostly out of obligation or guilt."

"Guilty of what?"

Hannah sat quietly, then said, "Because I had learned to hate him. But when he began having spells five years ago, I felt I better get to know him by being there for him."

"Wasn't that your mom's job?"

"Oh," Hannah laughed sadly. "Mom pretended nothing was wrong. *He's fine,* she would say. More than once, I found him lying on the grass outside the house, sunburnt and dehydrated."

"Did you report that to the authorities?"

"We did, but when the social worker showed up, Mom convinced her it was all a misunderstanding."

Karen cocked her head. "How did she accomplish that?"

"She was quite the saleswoman. That's why she was so good at her job. Then, a year later, she died in her sleep. Dad found her in the morning and called me."

"How did he handle that?"

"He showed no loss or sadness, so I had him evaluated. Early dementia, the doctor said."

"Was Rebecca part of that decision?"

"Uh, no," Hannah said. "My brothers and I handled that. Beck was too busy with her career. She only made appearances when she wanted to brag about her latest role."

"Then what?" Karen asked.

"They declared him incompetent, and I was named executor."

"That must have been a daunting task."

A brief silence hung between them for moment.

"It was," Hannah said. "My mother had her entire business and personal life in a convoluted mass of accounts and stashes of cash, land holdings, and stored antiques. I handled a consolidation the likes of William Randolph Hearst. The estate paid me to manage it, so it was never a financial burden, just emotional."

"And what help did you get from your brothers?"

"Not much, but that was my doing. Two have families, and they work real jobs, so to be a part of it would have been a logistical nightmare. My brothers were genuinely relieved I stepped up."

"But you have a family," Karen said. "Why was that not a burden for you?"

Hannah shrugged. "Being self-employed gave me a flexible schedule. It wasn't a full-time commitment so I could juggle the responsibility."

Karen tapped the pen of her pad. "Was that your M.O? Stepping up and taking charge?"

"Being the oldest in a dysfunctional family, it just became my job."

"So, your brothers are not like you?"

"Good question," Hannah said. "They live responsible lives and have kids and mortgages."

"But, you're the caregiver," Karen said directly.

Hannah sat for a minute and then nodded. "Yeah."

"What about your father?"

"I know he was the alpha male in his family," Hannah said. "He was the only one that wasn't a screw-up. And there were eight of them."

"Were your brothers ever screw-ups?"

"No, well – maybe when we were kids."

"But you were the good girl," Karen finished for her.

"I guess."

"Hannah? You said the day you blew up that you felt remorse because you were acting like your father. You said the last thing you ever wanted to do was be like him."

"I didn't. I don't."

"Hold onto your butt. I have some bad news for you."

Hannah gave her a severe stare. "This is going to hurt."

"You're a lot more like your father than you care to admit."

After a full five minutes, Hannah said, "Shit."

"Hard to swallow, isn't it?"

"I've spent my whole life doing everything I could to show the world I was not like that."

"And he probably had that same plan. But somehow, from what you've told me, he was exactly like your grandfather. Just with a degree and a belt, instead of a hickory switch."

"I was afraid of that."

"You're not exactly like him," Karen assured her. "But you can't spend your life under the influence of a man and not carry some of those inherent characteristics with you. You've broken the chain where it counts most, but there's a core issue here you need to understand."

"Okay," Hannah said.

"Family violence and abuse are like a virus that infects everyone. No matter how much the abused and beaten swear they will never be that way, it eventually manifests somehow. Some people become doormats, and others become heroes. You, Hannah, became the hero.'

"You're right."

Hannah frowned at this realization.

"But the hero personality, driven by a need to protect, can easily become corrupted into a bad thing. It can mutate into a controlling and angry personality."

"Like my father," Hannah said.

Karen nodded. "Just like him. In the end, Hannah, if we don't process the trauma in our lives, we are destined to repeat the behavior or become a paralyzed victim. Right now, you are drifting into a grey area where either side could seduce you."

"Sounds bleak," Hannah said.

"Not necessarily. Now that you understand, you can make changes. With understanding comes the possibility of forgiveness. I think it is likely the only way you'll have a chance to lay your demons to rest."

"And how do I do that?"

Karen smiled. "People don't develop behaviors in a vacuum. Your parents and grandparents were who they were due to what they went through. So, you have to get to know them."

"I was afraid you'd say that."

"Hey, sometimes healing is painful. So I suggest you research the family history and discover the truth about your father's roots."

"Regarding that," Hannah said. "Andrew shared that once when she was manic, Beck said, *everything would have been so much better if it hadn't been for Little Bear Creek.*"

"There you go. Start with that," Karen said. "We're out of time. What's next for you?"

"I have to finalize the estate and do all the fun things that an executor does to liquefy my parent's holdings. Then I get to pass out the spoils to the beneficiaries."

"In your downtime," Karen said, "do some digging. Then, call me if you need to."

Hannah stood. "Jesus, this self-examination shit is a bitch."

Karen offered an encouraging smile. "Yes, it is. But done correctly, the pain is always worth the gain. So I suggest you start by solving the mystery of the banjo. My guess is that will lead you to Little Bear Creek."

ALABAMA 1940 ~

Elizabeth Bradley bore down and squeezed her eyes tight. A high whine escaped her clenched teeth while the midwife held her hand. Small and black as pitch, the midwife was gnaw-boned with thin, scarred cheeks. Not from an accident or attack but from the people she once lived with in Africa. Her childbearing years long passed, she now lived to see women through their miracle of birth. Mattie's own children were sold away from her years ago. Her thin, brown fingers probed until she could feel the baby's head.

"Almos' thea' sweetie. Jest a bit mo', den we be done."

"Anotha' baby," Harley snorted. "I swears, I thought y'was too old fer this."

"Hush!" Mattie scolded. "Be respectful."

"Respectful?" Harley laughed. "I'll be Goddamn broke f'anotha' mouth t'feed."

"Hush, I said."

"Don' hush me ya' ole' woman! You look t'be a hundred years old, ya' nasty hag?"

"Gitcher drunk ass outta' hea," she rasped.

"Happy t'ablidge ya'."

Then Harley staggered out of the lean-to and into the dark.

"Why these damn kids alwas' git born in t'middle a t'night?" he hollered at the moon. "Six wasn't 'nuff? Damn, seven kids?"

"Neva' mind him," the midwife whispered. "Dis be God's work."

"But I'm feelin' like the devil, Mattie," Elizabeth whined.

The wind came up as if searching for the drama unfolding in the small shack. Six children, ranging from eighteen months to eight, huddled on the porch. The youngest cried for their mother.

"Y'momma's busy," Harley laughed. "Damn busy. How we gonna'' fit all these kids in this small house? No mo' room here by the creek. No Goddamn room."

Harley wandered away into the night, where the wind swallowed his voice. Then it snuck into the shack and flickered the flame in the oil lamps. Elizabeth drew a tired breath and tried to rest before the next contraction. When it came, it was like rolling thunder, starting in the distance and then building to a bone-rattling explosion that shook her and the house to the foundation.

"Dis gonna'' be a big child," Mattie said.

"I neva' felt one like this," Elizabeth heaved.

Elizabeth leaned into her pain and pushed, then screamed to the heavens. In a mirror of her pain, the clouded sky answered with a crack of lightning. Thunder rolled just as her body opened as the new life tore out of her. She felt empty in every way and fell back, lost in sobs.

"Lordy," the midwife said, "this be the biggest baby I eva' saw. A boy, a fine big boy."

"Anotha' boy."

Elizabeth opened her arms, and Mattie put the gurgling baby on her stomach.

"He ain't cryin'," Mattie said softly. "Thas' odd he ain't cryin'."

She watched the mother suckle the babe and felt a loss somewhere between her withered womb and wrinkled breasts. Every time she held a newborn, she quietly wept for her lost children.

"Good thaing y'got lotsa' milk. Dis one gonna" need it all."

Elizabeth suddenly jerked, leaned forward, and whined again in pain. With her baby at her breast, she clutched her abdomen, and her body convulsed. "This neva' happened before."

"Lay back, child. It jest be the afterbirth comin'."

Then, in a lack of fanfare and quiet repose, a baby girl, only half the size of her brother, came forth of her own volition.

"Glory be," the midwife said quietly. "Anotha' babe. She ain't no bigga' then a pup."

"It's a girl?"

"Littlest baby I eva' done seen. Lemme' see if she be breathin'."

"Is she alive?" Elizabeth asked in desperation.

Mattie carefully picked up the quiet newborn and held her in cupped hands. Another thunderclap rolled over the house, and the six children on the porch began fussing with fear. The night grew darker, and the air became wilder. Then it began to rain.

"Momma," Robert cried. "We're all gettin' wet."

"Is she alive?" Elizabeth demanded in maternal fear.

Her answer came in the sound of a hearty intake and then a screeching cry as the baby announced herself and made the world listen.

"She jest fine. Le's put her next t' her brotha'."

"Momma?" Robert called from outside.

"Y'hush now," the midwife yelled back. "Yo' momma' need t'rest. Y'can come in s'long as ya' be quiet as mice. Can ya' do dat?"

The children promised.

"Then, c'mon in. Quiet now."

They scuttled in and formed a circle around their mother and watched the two babies' now suckling at her breasts.

"Come, children," Mattie whispered. "Git in yo' beds. We'all needs our rest."

Each found their place and curled up under scratchy blankets. The rain pounded the small shack, and the roof dripped. The midwife settled back in a rickety chair and kept a close eye on the babies. When they were fed and sleeping, she carefully cut the umbilical cords, gathered the soiled blanket from under Elizabeth, and wrapped the afterbirths in a bundle. She would bury them in the morning.

Both babies breathed against their mother's body, and Mattie smiled at the miracle. One big and one so small. She prayed the little girl would live. She knew the big boy would thrive. But that was a worry for the morning. She settled back, wrapped her arms around her bony shoulders, and smiled at the family. Another squall beat the shack and the night grew older.

"Bless me," she said softly.

Mattie reflected on her own past, what she knew of it. There were no records of her birth, and she'd only known the cotton fields and the white man's tongue. She knew her own time on this earth would be short. But these children were born to a storm, especially this girl nobody knew would come, had a life facing them. She prayed they knew happiness. Mattie closed her eyes and then shook off her exhaustion.

"Don' fall asleep," she said out loud. "The debil's in the air dis night. I's keepin' an eye on thangs hea'. Lord, you look in on us from time t'time, but I doin' yo' bid'ness t'night."

*   *   *   *   *

Sometime between moonset and dawn, the clouds blew over, and morning broke clear and muggy. Harley stumbled home with a rag doll in one hand and a nearly empty bottle of whiskey in the other. His head pounded, and his boots slogged through the muddy ruts on the road. Where the doll came from, he had no idea. He remembered very little from the night before, except that his wife was giving birth. When she told him she was pregnant again, Harley got angry. He figured Elizabeth was too old to take his seed one more time.

Damn God!

His father once said the Almighty was an angry savage that bestowed judgment on man for being exactly what God meant him to be. Did it not say he made man in his image? Then God was a spiteful, petty, hurtful, and demanding bastard who wanted his way and was willing to do anything to get it. Probably a whiskey drinker, to boot.

Harley stepped into a puddle.

"Dammit," he growled.

He shook off his boot, lost his balance, and fell into the muck.

"A'righty," Harley said to the sky. "Now y' got me on m'knees."

When he was on his feet, he discovered the bottle broken and the doll covered with mud. Oh well, he'd wash it clean when he got home. He wondered what she had and hoped for a boy. More help in the fields.

When he reached the house, the midwife stood on the stoop wearing an expression of condemnation. She held a blanket tied in a tangled knot.

He gave her a wide smile. "What's it, then?"

"Yo' a good fer nuthin' drunkard, Harley Bradley."

"An' you' a skinny, old, nappy-headed nigger that ain't gotta' no right t'judge me on my own porch. What she have?"

"You one short, you nasty-ass no good," she retorted.

"Meanin' what?"

"She had two, tha's what I means."

Harley stopped in his tracks. "You lyin'."

"Go sees fer yo'sef. Boy and a girl. Don't know if the girl gonna' make it. She awful small. If that big boy don' take all de' milk, maybe she make it. She gonna' be small her whole life. Seen it befo'. Now git in'ner and see yo' new ones. An' Harley?"

"What?"

"You bes' be gettin' yer life straight or God his'sef gonna' come down and make you sorry. As sho' as I's standin' heah, you gots the debil in ya.' Dat gonna' get you in mo' trouble den you can live wif."

"I'll keep that'n mind," he sneered. "Now git yer boney ass offa' my porch, an' take that mess with you."

"Dat mess be the soul of yo' chillin'. I'll make sho' the debil don't know where they buried. Dem chillin' needs God and my blessin' to keep dem from Satan and da' likes a' you. Good luck, Harley Bradley. You's gonna' need it."

Harley sneered and then spat. "Lot you knows about it. Get yo' skinny butt off my porch."

*   *   *   *   *

Mattie cradled the precious bundle down into the hollow. Deep between the earth walls and at the bottom of the gorge, a creek pooled among the ferns. The sacred place where she always buried the evidence of birth. They called it *Little Bear*, not because of cubs. No, *Little Bear* shared the life given by the river's bounty. The very reason the valley grew such fine cotton.

In her world, the empty womb sack held the last vestige of the newborn's spirit. Unless she buried the flesh and said a prayer, the soul would not rise back to God. Mattie believed Harley Bradley's sack must have been left to the hands of the Devil. That was why he drank and cussed and hated. Mattie felt terrible for her harsh words, but he just made her so mad.

When she reached the basin, Mattie said a prayer, dropped to her knees and dug a hole big enough to cradle the blanket in God's earth. After filling the hole and stomping the ground flat, she found the heaviest rock she could carry and placed it over the grave.

"Lord," she whispered. "I prays dis babe live an' be yo' servant. Watch ov'a her and sees she git the chance at life she deserve. I pray in yo' name. Amen."

She once tried to remember the number of souls she protected there. Each one a gift to God, and a price paid for losing her own children. She washed her hands in the creek, dried them on her thin dress, and began the arduous trek out of the ravine.

"God is good," she said.

While Mattie stared at the water, Harley Bradley looked at the big boy and the tiny girl.

"Two more mouths t'feed," he whispered.

His other daughter suddenly pulled the wet and muddy ragdoll from his hand.

"Please, God," he said with a laugh. "No mo' kids. I'm beggin' ya' please."

The two babies began to cry, and other children joined in.

"Weepin' Jesus on th'cross."

His head throbbed with the need for alcohol. Being Sunday, there was no work to be done. Harley went looking for another bottle of whiskey.

CHAPTER FIVE ~

Hannah received six copies of her father's death certificates in the mail, but most were unnecessary. Once her father was declared incompetent, the family trust reverted to her control. She and Kyle spent the morning like any other. They walked into town, stopped and got frozen yogurt, and enjoyed themselves in the shade of the trees in the town center. Young mothers pushed babies in strollers, and the old couples walked through the park. Kyle rubbed Hannah's neck, and she gave him a thankful smile.

"So, today?" Kyle asked.

"Yup."

"Do you know how much?"

"I have a pretty good idea."

"Are you going to tell me?"

She feigned insult. "No. You'll have to wait and see."

They played this game for three days.

"Okay," he said with false indignation. "But it's not enough you're in the doghouse."

"That's the wife's line. Besides, we don't have a dog."

There was no malice. Both knew their lives were about to change. They walked home hand in hand. Kyle led her to the bedroom, where they made easy love. Then Hannah looked at her watch and groaned.

"I better get going."

"You're meeting your brothers?"

"I am."

"Then, I'll probably have to drive you home after that celebration."

She dressed and kissed him goodbye. "I'll call if I need that. I promise I won't drive drunk."

"I love you," Kyle said.

"Me too."

Hannah stopped at the bank and picked up four cashier's checks. She left a small balance for any unexpected cursory expenses. Then Hannah called her brothers and told them to meet her at the restaurant. She could hear the excitement in their voices. Not that she blamed them. Life was about to change. The balance was more than enough after settling any remaining debts, closing accounts, and paying off the lawyer. Hannah arrived first to secure a quiet table.

a relic of a lost era, Carlo's Steakhouse took up a corner lot outside the business district. Squat and heavy, it looked like a man dressed in an old-fashioned suit among the stark and antiseptic buildings surrounding it. The restaurant did a great business serving generous cuts of perfectly aged meats to couples looking for no screaming kids. A basket of hearty multi-grain bread was thrown in for some variety. If you wanted greens, there was the signature Chef's Salad on the menu.

Bittersweet memories.

SECRET of LITTLE BEAR CREEK • THOMAS K. MATTHEWS

When Hannah stepped through the doors, she had sudden pangs of memory. Her father was not much for sentiment, but he had one tradition. For each child's birthday, starting at ten, he brought them to Carlo's for dinner. No siblings, Mom, or friends – just the birthday child and Dad. You ordered whatever you wanted. The wait staff sang Happy Birthday. After the meal, an impossibly tall ice cream sundae came to the table. Dad shared a bite or two, but the rest was all yours.

"Well," Hannah said to herself, "it all ends today."

Eduardo, the headwaiter, came to meet her. No hostess. Carlo insisted each waiter seat their section as a display of personal service.

"Welcome, Mrs. MacAllister. Please accept my condolences on the passing of your father. He was a good customer for many years. And I am so sorry to hear about your sister. She was so beautiful and a talented actress."

"Thank you."

"Just you today?"

"No, my brothers are meeting me. Can we have the corner booth?"

"Of course. My section. Come, I'll send the boys over when they get here."

"Thank you."

The seats surrounding the triangular table felt deep enough to swallow you. Behind Hannah, very realistic plastic ferns bordered the wall where paintings of hunters with their dogs hung in sad tradition.

Carlos returned. "Anything to drink while you wait?"

"A bottle of Heineken," she said.

"Coming right up."

Hannah waited in reflective silence.

The beer came on a small silver tray, and Eduardo carefully poured it into a tall, chilled glass.

"Edwardo, how long have you worked here?" Hannah asked.

"Since 1978," he said proudly.

"I remember every birthday," Hannah shared.

"Me too." He looked up when the front door opened. "Your brothers."

Then he hurried away.

"Hey, look who's here sitting in the corner," Clem yelled.

"Hey, guys."

Otis, Leigh, and Clem dropped into the booth and gave Hannah broad smiles.

"That your Tahoe outside?" Clem asked.

"My present from Kyle."

"With gas as it is, you must be nuts."

"I can afford the gas now."

"Whatcha' drinkin?" Otis asked.

"Heineken."

"Eduardo, three more just like that," Otis called. "And a shot of Chivas."

"Right away, sir," he said back.

"Man, I love this place," Clem said. "All we're missing is Dad and a big-ass sundae."

Leigh said. "Think the old man is wondering what the hell we're doing here?"

"Oh, he knows," Otis said. "How'd we do, Hannah?"

She smiled and pulled four envelopes from her jacket purse. "Not too bad. Want these now, or do you want to wait until after the steak and the booze?"

Leigh smiled. "I'd like mine now, and then we can fight over who'll pay the bill."

"The bill's taken care of," Hannah said and handed each brother an envelope. Otis tore his open and whistled. Leigh shook his head. Clem slapped the table.

Each cashier's check was for the same amount – four hundred and eighty-seven thousand dollars and thirty-four cents.

"That's just the cash," Hannah said. "The house and land will bring us about the same amount again when they sell. And this Sunday is the great furniture and decorator grab."

Otis said, "This is definitely a cause for celebration."

Eduardo returned with the drinks and asked what he could get for them. They all ordered the house prime Porterhouse, baked potato, and vegetables.

"Very good." Eduardo rushed off to tell the chef. But, unfortunately, he left behind rolls and whipped butter.

"I always wanted to order one of these, but dad always said I'd never finish it," Clem said.

"That's funny," Leigh retorted. "Dad told me once that he felt the only one able to finish it would be Hannah. The fact you stand a head taller than all of us is probably why."

Hannah raised her glass. "Before we begin, I want to drink a toast to Beck. Her unhappy life ended with a tragic twist. I hope she has found peace."

"To Beck," they echoed.

"How'd all that go?"

"Later," Hannah said.

"Speaking of Beck, how's the counseling going?" Otis asked.

"Oh, thanks for the buzzkill," she said.

"No, really, Hannah, how's that going?" Leigh pressed.

"Why?"

Leigh swallowed his voice, afraid to be honest.

"Tell me," she pressed.

"You went a little nutty that day. Not to mention how you've been carrying the brunt of all this shit and dealing with Beck's drama. I want to know my big sister is okay."

Hannah finished her Chivas, dabbed her lips with a napkin, and closed her eyes. "The best way to put it? Dr. Gregory has me looking under a lot of rocks. Some of the shit I'm finding is pretty rough, and some of it is very liberating."

"About Dad?" Otis asked.

"About all of it," she said. "She asks me some serious questions I didn't have an answer for. She suggested I needed to find those answers."

Hannah took in her brother's faces. The celebration and avarice of their first meeting felt replaced with a shadow of, what? Fear? All of them wore the same expression.

"I can tell you this," Hannah said. "Kyle is thrilled."

"Uh," Otis said, "Alice asked if I'd see somebody too."

"Me too," Leigh added. "Claire suggested it."

"What about you, Clem?" Hannah asked.

"Well, I'm not married, and Lisa doesn't seem to mind that I'm an emotionally constipated, frightened of commitment bastard that screams in his sleep. But, yeah, I was curious too."

"It's the best thing I ever did. For my family and me."

"What's she want you to do to get those answers," Otis asked.

"Karen wants me to dig into Dad's past."

"God, he'd have hated that," Clem said.

Eduardo returned to the table. "Another round?"

"Oh, God, yes!" Clem answered.

The meal arrived. Inch-thick steaks done to perfection. Though the baked potato was undercooked, nobody cared. Hot bread sopped up the last of the savory drippings. The second round of drinks capped off the meal. They were all tipsy, very full, and once again full of levity.

"Coffee?" Eduardo asked.

"And four birthday sundaes," Hannah said.

Leigh groaned. "Really? After all that?"

"Have to," Otis said. "Tradition."

"Okay, bring 'em on."

Eduardo collected the empty plates, then returned with four stacked cups and a stainless-steel pot of rich, strong coffee. He poured and nearly bowed when he left.

"Did dad ever tell anybody how he found this place?" Leigh asked.

"He probably met his mistresses here," Otis said.

Hannah raised her eyebrows. "It's certainly the kind of place that would pride itself on keeping a man's secrets."

The sundaes came. The tall glasses heaped with ice cream and toppings looked as daunting as they did when they were kids. Hannah raised her spoon. "To dad!"

Then they all took a bite.

"There. Now I can let the rest melt," Otis said.

Eduardo appeared. "Anything else for you?"

"No, we're doing fine. Thanks."

"Please accept my condolences on the passing of your father," Edwardo said. "He was a good customer, a great man, and a loyal friend."

"Did you know our father outside the restaurant?" Otis asked.

Eduardo only smiled and left them to their coffee.

"Guess that's a secret, too," Otis said.

They all smiled.

They talked until the warmth of the alcohol left their minds. Hannah's cell hummed.

"That's Kyle. He's probably wondering if I'm too shitfaced to drive."

"Yeah," Otis said, "I better go."

They left a hefty tip and walked in a somber group out the door. Eduardo watched them go and Hannah wondered if he thought he'd ever see any of them again. He was right. This was her father's place, and they had no business returning Hannah waved, and Eduardo nodded. In the parking lot, they stood in a circle.

"Okay then," Hannah said. "See you guys Sunday for the rummage and trade fest."

They hugged and went to their respective cars.

"I'm going to buy a Corvette," Leigh yelled.

Hannah called Kyle and assured him she was full, sober, and on her way home. But before she put the Tahoe in gear, she pulled out the check and stared once more at the numbers.

That was that. A lifetime of angst, bullshit, sadness, and tumult. Ended with a piece of paper worth enough to change a life. Was it enough? Was that the price of reparations for the emotional trial they all endured?

"Dad," she said to the check. "Thanks for paying for my therapy."

Her phone buzzed—a text from Otis. *Can I get Karen's number?*

At that moment, Hannah knew no amount of money was enough for what they lived through. Her drive home allowed too much time to think, and the revelry of the meeting fizzled like a dud firecracker. More than that, it seemed to add a heavy emotional weight to the cashier's check in her pocket.

"God help us all," she said out loud.

The drive home was sullen.

*   *   *   *   *

Kyle busied himself with the mundane action of ordinary chores. He moved the laundry from the washer to the dryer, carefully watered the houseplants, and took out the trash. But, while he moved from place to place, his mind felt anything but ordinary. When Hannah came home, she would bring a sum of money that would relieve many burdens. More than that - he hoped Hannah would walk through the door free from the stress and the anxiety of managing her dead parent's affairs.

He felt a pang of guilt for putting her parents in such a restricting box, but once they married, Hannah's folks never called to speak to him, never asked about their children or remembered their wedding anniversary.

Her parents lived a sequestered life where day-to-day and month-to-month became a blur. Many times, the only time they spent time with them was Christmas and her mother's birthday. Now the transient thread to his wife's past was severed. However, her brothers would always be there, and that connection would endure.

Kyle thanked God that his loving family would continue as the emotional backbone for them. When they married, Hannah felt welcomed into his family with hugs and celebration. Just when he sat down to watch a football game, he heard the garage door open. Hannah came in, and he met her in the kitchen.

"Hi," he said. "How'd it go?"

"Oh, the guys were happy, and we overate."

"Sounds like fun. You look tired."

"I–" Hannah said, then her lower lip trembled.

Kyle put his arms around her and let her cry. Hannah trembled, so he picked her up and carried her to the couch. Kyle rocked her while her heart emptied the angry sadness. He suspected his wife's tears were for the haunting questions she always wanted to ask and would go forever unanswered.

Hannah gave Kyle an apologetic smile. "Sorry about that."

"No problem. Feel better?" he asked.

Hannah nodded. "Yeah."

"Can I see it?"

She reached into her purse and handed him the envelope. When Kyle looked at the cashier's check, his eyes widened slightly, and then he smiled.

"Wanna go shopping?" Hannah asked.

All he could do was smile.

* * * * *

The following week dragged by. Hannah kept herself distracted by writing her last article. Then they met with their accountant.

"There they are," Jack said when they entered the office. "Tell me."

Hannah gave him the number.

"This sets you guys pretty well."

"But not for life," Hannah said.

"That depends," Jack said. "With no taxes due, and when the house sells, you could be pretty set if you put yourself on a conservative budget. I recommend Kyle keep working, of course."

"Of course," Kyle said. "First, Hannah is going to take some well-deserved time off and write the great American novel."

Hannah smirked, then shrugged.

"I don't blame you," Jack said. "Take a well-deserved vacation."

"We talked about a month in Europe."

"Sounds like fun," Jack said. "Write the book there and write the whole thing off."

Hannah laughed softly. She always considered herself the underachieving one. Her brothers, even Otis, seemed to manage building businesses that guaranteed solvency, while Hannah often felt herself falling short. Such was the life of a freelance writer. When the recession hit, she went to her mother for support. She expected every dime paid back one day.

"We need to keep things straight for the sake of the estate," she said. "I keep a list. I don't expect you to pay me back until it isn't a burden."

Hannah could only laugh. Being under her mother's thumb was no picnic. Her brothers shared the sentiment. Ironically, as the executor, she discovered nothing mentioned regarding owed money. She could only laugh. It was so typical of her mother.

"Hannah?" Jack asked. She snapped back from her reflexive state. "Do you have any other questions?"

"No," she said. "Thanks for the advice."

When they got home, Kyle gave her a curious look. "How are you feeling?"

"Like a huge rock has been lifted off my shoulders."

"Let's go celebrate," Kyle said. "Remember, I will be gone this weekend to see my dad."

"I almost forgot about that," she said.

"What are you going to do with yourself?"

"I think I'll write."

"No prize for guessing your topic."

Saturday morning, Hannah kissed Kyle goodbye and wandered the house. Her earlier elation shifted to an odd restlessness. With money in the bank and no estate to manage, she didn't know what to do with herself. Hannah finally sat in front of her Mac, tentatively clicked her text icon. She stared at the flashing cursor on a black screen.

"Okay," she said out loud.

She typed 'ALABAMA'S BOY' in 24-point Times.

The return key took her to the first sentence. 'What is the secret of Little Bear Creek?'

She took a breath, let it out, and typed:

CHAPTER ONE:

Five spaces down, she wrote one ominous question: *Can a man escape his past? Not just his history but also his father's and all the fathers before him?*

At that moment, Hannah realized that to embark on this undertaking would be a perfect way of understanding, not just her father, but the whole Bradley story.

Hannah saved her file and clicked the search icon. She typed in *Little Bear Creek, Alabama*. She found a lake where happy people kayaked down a deep gorge called *Bear Creek*.

No, it couldn't be that easy.

When her father began to deteriorate, she toyed with the idea of chronicling her father's past, told as fiction. But the fear and potential emotional fallout seemed too daunting. The idea lay dormant for nearly two years.

Her cell rang. Kyle's smiling face filled the screen.

"Hey there."

"Hi." He sounded happy. "What are you doing?"

"Trying to write," she said. "What about you?"

"To be honest, I'm a little tipsy."

Hannah laughed. "And how did that come to be?"

"Dad and I went to this little bistro for lunch."

"I hope you didn't drive," Hannah said with a laugh.

"No, we walked. I was thinking about you all alone. I miss you."

"Me too."

"Are you sad?" Kyle asked.

"No, just lonely."

"Are you seeing Karen today?"

"I am. What's next now that you and Dad are oiled up?"

Kyle lowered his voice. "Mom's coming to visit. She had to come into the city for business, and so she's going to have dinner with us."

"Why are you whispering?"

"Dad is on the phone with her now."

"Is he being nice? Since their divorce, he seems to get mad at her if he's been at the wine."

"I think they've worked that out."

"I should hope so," Hannah said, "It's been ten years."

"Well, I just wanted to call and say I love you. I'll call you tonight."

"Okay," Hannah said with a smile in her voice. "I love you, too."

"Gotta' go." Kyle hung up.

A knock and ring of the doorbell startled her. Through the peephole, he saw a uniformed man holding a large box. She opened the door.

"Hannah MacAllister?"

"Yes."

"Sign here."

She gave the sheet a quick scrawl and accepted the box. From inside, there was a metallic strum, and she smiled—the banjo.

Hannah closed the door and said, "My inheritance is here."

She retrieved a knife from the kitchen and carefully cut the bands of shipping tape. When she opened the lid, the tarnished brass glinted in the afternoon light. The leather cord the instrument hung from looked old and fragile. She carried the banjo to the living room, sat on the couch, and strummed the strings. The twanging warble made it clear the instrument was never tuned in the time it adorned her parent's wall.

She had to admit it was a beautiful piece. Though the brass body needed a polish, the intricacy of the construction was impressive. Besides some discoloration on the face, the wooded neck and details were in remarkably good shape. Probably why her mother bought it at whatever flea market, thrift shop, or antique store that she found it. At the base of the strings, along the face curve, the name 'Gibson' caught her eye.

Hannah dragged his fingers across the strings again and what assaulted his ears was not just noise but a reminder of the past her father so desperately tried to ignore. She imagined the scene Beck must have performed when she took the thing off the wall.

"I'm taking this home," she must have declared. *"I want this as a reminder of my dying father!"*

Hannah could almost hear the director call, *"Action!"*

"The great family heirloom," Hannah joked to herself. "I know exactly where I'm going to put this."

She went to the hall closet and placed the banjo between assorted forgotten brooms.

"Until the next garage sale," she said as if in a play. "Now I want a beer. Or two! Oops, no, I have a session with my shrink."

She took a quick shower, dressed casually, and arrived early. Small sounds wafted through each office door. Karen was with another client, so Hannah worked on her outline for the book.

Her internal narrator said, *can a woman escape her past? Not just her history, but her father's and all the fathers before him?*

The door opened and a woman passed by, dabbing her eyes with a tissue. Hannah gave her a warm smile. Karen called her in.

"Hello Hannah, sorry to keep you waiting. So, how're you doing?"

"Okay, I think."

"You think?"

Hannah gave her the rundown of the last week's events, then finished with the banjo's arrival.

"Have you looked into what that's about?"

"No. I'm not sure how important it is."

"Even though your sister wanted you to have it?"

"Pure Beck drama," Hannah said.

"We can come back to that. How're things at home?"

"Good. Less stress. Kyle is visiting his parents,"

"How're are you doing alone?"

"I've some time to look at myself," Hannah said. "By the way, did any of my brothers call you?"

"Yes," Karen said with a smile.

"I know, confidentiality."

"Have you put some thought into you learning something about your father's past?"

"I did. But–"

Karen put up her hand.

"I'm going to interrupt. I suspect you're about to give me some rationalized and placating concoction of reasons why you should leave it alone and move on with your life. Especially now that you have the money."

Hannah felt challenged. "I don't know about that."

"Hannah, look at your body language."

She found her hands folded so tightly her fingers turned white. Hannah's shoulders had come so high she nearly hid her neck.

"You look like a tortoise trying to go into its shell."

"Shit," Hannah said and went limp.

"Now listen to me," Karen said. "Denial is not a river in Egypt and pretending everything is okay plants a seed of sorrow that will eventually grow into a great oak of ache."

Hannah chuckled. "Did you just say those things to make me laugh, or were you serious?"

"What do you think?"

"Both, maybe."

"I said them because they're both corny as hell and would get your attention."

"Okay."

"What I see is a classic case of neglect and abuse with no resolution," Karen said. "Your sister took the easy way out when her misdirected need for your father's approval died with him. The fact your brother reached out means the money gives no solace. And the emotional stress you've been under has that angry child in you demanding an explanation. Understand?"

Hannah nodded.

"Say it."

"I understand."

"I suggest you find the truth. Then, learn what you can to get some closure."

Hannah gave her a fitful slare. "And how would I go about doing that? There's no record, and nobody left to tell the story?"

"C'mon, Hannah. You write for a living, you do research, and you certainly know how to use a computer and the Internet. It's all the rage."

Hannah sat back. "I know you're right."

"And?" Karen urged.

"I think I'm afraid of what I'll find. The banjo felt creepy, and I remembered the scene from Deliverance with the kid on the rock with white eyes. I think I'm afraid to face what we were and where we came from."

"But that is where salvation is hidden: In the past. Now you have the security and the time. I bet you could have this figured out in a week."

"Okay, I can look into the hospital records for the town my dad was born," Hannah said.

"Now you're talking. What else?"

Hannah suddenly felt a chill. "Genealogy research and family tree digging."

"That sounds like it could be fun," Karen offered.

"Maybe, or scary as hell."

"But Hannah, be careful not to take something like this too lightly. You could find some things that may be emotionally triggering. Make sure you have your eyes wide open and your expectations in check."

"Good advice," Hannah said.

"I think that's enough for today. See you next week. Call if you need me."

On the drive home, Hannah allowed her mind to drift into fantasies of her Southern roots. She knew the two-line manuscript she'd opened earlier was the guiding question to drive this lunatic mission. She imagined Kyle's reaction. But then, a trip down made sense. Boots on the ground and nose to the grindstone, the two of them could track down the past. But not all work. They could also turn it into a vacation. She arrived home and called him. No answer, so she left her love and told him to call before he went to bed.

For dinner, she fried two eggs and put them open-faced on toast. But when she sat down to eat, Hannah stopped and stared at her plate. A wave of gooseflesh washed through her. Hannah realized she ate eggs this way because her father did. And he ate *his* eggs that way because that was how *her* grandmother must have made them for the family.

Traditions? Habits? Lineages passed down through, not just food, but behaviors.

Hannah shivered. Dr. Gregory was right; she'd lived under her father's influence her entire life, and so much of him was a result of a learned pattern. She remembered the family's fear when her father lost his temper. How he used a quick and fluid motion when he removed his belt for a beating, how he looped the thin leather around his thumb and gripped the buckle tightly in his fist. When he snapped the belt, it sounded like a rifle shot. That crack the prelude to pain and agony.

But never on her or Rebecca, just the boys.

To hear the screams and cries from another room constantly tortured her. Those terrible memories fed her guilt from being spared because of gender.

When Even turned three, Hannah dropped to one knee and gripped a belt like her father.

"Hey Evy, want to see something cool?"

He smiled and nodded. When Hannah popped the belt with a jerk of her hand, Even's eyes widened. He laughed and clapped his hands. "Again."

When they both grew tired of the game, Hannah sat with the knowledge her son would never know that fear. The device of torture was now nothing but a game. She nearly wept in relief. At that moment, the fried eggs suddenly looked as unappetizing as rotted meat. Hannah put them down the garbage disposal and then drove to a local burger joint. She consoled herself with a double bacon cheeseburger and onion rings. After dinner, she called Kyle and left a message. Back home, she sat at her computer and booted up the browser.

"Here we go," she said and typed in 'Alabama.'

She searched out the family name and researched the town where her father last lived before moving North. An hour later, she had printed several pages of reference.

Kyle called her back.

"Hey there," she said.

"Hey, back. I got your message. You sounded sad. Everything okay?"

"Yeah. I've been hunting Alabama ghosts online."

"Meaning what?"

"Homework for my therapist."

"How does that feel?"

"A little scary," she said thoughtfully. "But, she says I have to learn the truth."

"Meaning?"

Hannah let that sink in. "Karen wants me to track down the family and get some answers."

"I see," he said in an odd tone. "Are you okay with that?"

"I have to be," she said. "I thought we could make it more than that. We can turn it into a trip, see the South, eat some authentic food, and look around."

"I see," he said. "I–"

Hannah interrupted. "Karen said that if I don't process the trauma, I'll either eventually become like my father or become a paralyzed victim to my past. She thinks it's the only way I'll put the past behind me."

Kyle was silent.

"Are you there?"

"Yes," he sounded hesitant. "Did she suggest you going down south?"

"She said I needed to face my father's history so I can understand where the sickness came from."

Kyle said, "I think you should talk with her and make sure that's what she meant."

Hannah sat silently. Kyle's common sense extinguished her excitement.

"Listen," he said. "Please don't think that–"

"No," she interrupted. "You're right. I'll talk with her and get some clarity."

"Honey," he said. "I think we should do that together."

"I'll ask her about that," Hannah said. "How did things go with your parents?"

"Surprisingly well. We got through dinner."

"I miss you," she said.

"And I miss you. I'll be home tomorrow night, and we can talk more about this."

"Okay," she said. "I love you."

"Me too," he said, and they hung up.

Hannah showered, dressed for bed, and lay in the dark. Sleep did not come for hours, and when she awoke, her pillow was wet with tears. Then, somewhere in the recesses of her mind, she heard a banjo twang, the sound of flowing water and wind in the trees.

At that moment, she knew she would, most likely, be going to Alabama.

That made her shiver.

CHAPTER SIX ~

Hannah and Kyle sat in separate chairs, facing Karen Gregory. Kyle wore an expression of expectation. Hannah looked uncomfortable.

"Glad to have both of you here," she said. "Thank you for coming in. There's been a lot going on with you guys."

Kyle nodded, and Hannah gave her an awkward smile.

"From what I understand, there are some issues regarding Hannah's finding the family's roots."

Kyle said, "We been discussing the idea of her plan to go to Alabama. We're in conflict about whether she should go alone, or I should be there. We want your opinion."

Karen looked from one to the other. "What seems to be the issue?"

Hannah said, "I suggested we go together and make a trip out of it. But Kyle's not convinced."

"Share that with me," she said.

"Business and pleasure don't mix," he said.

Karen took them in. They had a bond not often seen in couples these days. Despite Hannah's strength, Kyle maintained supportive protectiveness. She understood their conflict.

"Kyle," she said. "How would you feel about Hannah doing this alone?"

"I think it could help her reconcile her issues with the family. I worried my being here would be helpful or a distraction."

"What about you, Hannah?"

"I'm torn as well."

"Tell me why?"

"I'd love to see the South together, but a sightseeing trip might defeat the purpose of a fact-finding expedition. That's what Kyle called it."

Karen put down her pen and looked directly at Hannah. "There's an old saying, don't mix business with pleasure. And I know you well enough that if Kyle joined you, the distraction of his being there could make it mostly pleasure."

"I understand," Hannah said. "I–"

"Let me finish," Karen interrupted. "You either go down there searching for closure, or it's a vacation. It can't be both ways. What you need to do is something that requires all of your focus and attention."

"I get that," Hannah said.

"Are you ready for something like this?" Karen asked.

Hannah looked at Kyle, and he took her hand. "I've done some research and have a lead or two. First, I'd have to plan an itinerary. Then I'd follow my clues."

Karen nodded and said, "I think this should be sooner than later."

"You do?"

SECRET of LITTLE BEAR CREEK • THOMAS K. MATTHEWS

"I do, too," Kyle said. Hannah gave him a surprised look. "I have to say something and, please, don't take this the wrong way."

Hannah held her breath. "Okay."

"I lied to you. I didn't go up to Dad's because he invited me. I went up there because it was becoming too serious and stressful around the house. I needed a break."

"Wow," Hannah said.

"Listen to him," Karen said. "This is important."

He continued. "I love you, and I want the rest of our lives to be incredible. But that can only happen if you purge the demons of your family. I was genuinely afraid of what you became that night. As much afraid for you as I was for the rest of us."

Hannah held his gaze. "I understand."

"It doesn't mean that–" Kyle started.

"No," she interrupted. "That's why we're here. I don't want it to come back, either."

"Hannah," Karen said softly. "I sense a hidden reaction to Kyle's concern. Defensiveness? Hurt?"

"No," Hannah said. "More like hopelessness."

"Hopeless of what?"

Hannah looked at her husband and then back to Karen. "That the Bradley past curses me. That too much-hidden fear and sadness has built up a wall in me that will never really allow me to know myself."

Kyle took her hand. "All the more reason to take this trip."

Karen took off her glasses. "I have to agree with Kyle. But only if you feel up to it. If you go ghost hunting with your expectations in the wrong place, moments of awareness could end up feeling like nightmares."

"What would you suggest," Hannah asked.

"Some more time with me," Karen said. "However, we'll focus on expectations, boundaries, and realities. You best approach this like an archeologist sifting through sand for clues to the past. Going in raw would be throwing yourself into the fear and doubt that your father's past reinforced through silence and rage."

"I get it," she said.

"We'll work on that," Karen said. "If we don't find that balance, I'll suggest you not do this."

Kyle squeezed Hannah's hand.

"Do you have something to share?" Karen asked.

Kyle smiled. "I know my wife."

"Okay."

"What you just suggested offered a challenge. The one thing I know for sure, Hannah never backs down from a challenge."

"I think I have a positive compromise to this situation," Karen said. "Kyle, you should join Hannah for the trip down. Moral support, in a way. Settle in, stay a couple of days until Hannah feels comfortable. Then Hannah will continue alone."

"I can do that," Kyle said. Hannah took his hand.

Their session ended with handshakes and encouragement. Once outside, Kyle let out and an exaggerated sigh and hugged Hannah. She lost herself in his arms, knowing safety lived there.

"Let's get some lunch," he said.

"Fish and chips," Hannah said. "I doubt I can get decent fish and chips in Alabama."

"You'll know everything about Alabama by the time you leave."

When they got home, Hannah called the kids together.

"We have something to talk about. Your Dad and I have seen my therapist, and we've decided I am going to take a trip down south to find my family's legacy."

"That sounds intense," Evan said.

"Probably will be," Hannah said. "I'll be doing research and planning my itinerary over the next two weeks, then flying down south."

"Mom," Gwen said. "Are you sure you want to go alone?"

Hannah smiled at her. "Dad will be with me for two days, then come home. Trust me. I'll be fine."

The kids nodded; their faces masked worry.

After dinner, Hannah sat down at the computer while Kyle looked over her shoulder. More research on modern Alabama showed bustling cities and green landscapes. Lakes and streams filled the pages, while a vintage postcard graphic invited visitors to the "Friendly State."

"Looks okay," Kyle said.

She dropped the menu to her bookmarks and clicked a saved file. An ancient image of a ragged family in front of a leaning shack filled the screen. Scratched into the old photo was an inscription. *White sharecroppers – Alabama.*

"There it is," she said. "My Father's past. The date says 1918. Times have certainly changed."

"Let's hope so. Want a beer?" he asked.

Hannah nodded. While Kyle went to the kitchen, she closed her eyes. Was that the Alabama her father escaped from? If so, it helped her understand so more much about him.

Kyle returned and handed her the beer.

"I've had enough," she said. "I need a distraction and foot rub."

"I can offer both," he promised.

They turned on a familiar and easy romantic comedy, and Kyle slowly massaged the tension from Hannah's legs. She lost herself in the mindless familiarity. When her cell rang, she furrowed her brow at the 907-area code.

"Robocall," she said. "Probably another gold digger looking for me to invest my inheritance. They've come out of the woodwork."

Hannah let it go to voicemail. Her phone alerted her of a new text message.

I hope I have the right number. This is Matt Bradley. If I'm wrong, I'm sorry.

"Holy shit," Hannah said softly.

"What's up?"

"My father's brother just reached out."

Kyle stopped rubbing and gave her a surprised expression. "Which one?"

"My uncle Matt. He left a voice message." She tapped the icon.

"Uh, hello," a gruff voice said. *"This is Matt Bradley, Robert Bradley's youngest brother. I'm calling from Seattle. I hope I have the right number. If I don't, sorry to have bothered you."*

"Jesus," Hannah said.

"His voice sounded so much like your father," Kyle said. "Are you going to call him back?"

Hannah sat up and dialed.

"Hello?"

"Hi, Matt. Yes, you called the right number. I'm Hannah, Robert's oldest daughter."

"Thanks for calling back. I just got word about his death from one of his old teaching colleagues," he said. "I found his obituary online. It said his children survived him, and your name was listed. So, I searched and found his obituary. I called the first matching name I found on Google."

"I understand."

"I got lucky. So, you're the oldest?" His voice had a shadow of a Southern accent.

"Yes."

"The last time I saw him was at his retirement party. That was almost, what, fifteen years ago? I think I may have met you."

"I don't think so," Hannah said. "I'd have remembered meeting one of my uncles."

"You're tall, blonde hair? You gave the eulogy."

"Yes, that was me."

"We met at the bar. I commented about it being a great party, and you listened to me blather and then excused yourself. I was pretty drunk."

"Yes, I remember."

At least six foot two and probably four hundred pounds, his hand like a baseball mitt. Matt wore a crew cut and a red face. His suit fit like a gladiator wore armor. At the time, Hannah assumed he was a football coach for the university.

"I guess I forgot to tell you I was your uncle," he said. "I traveled for work and was in town, so I came by. Back then, I never passed up the chance at free booze. My life was a mess then. I don't drink anymore."

"I'm glad you called," she said. "I was just about to try and track somebody down from the family. I'm writing a book about dad's life and realized I didn't know much about it."

"A book," he said. "That would be a wild one. Your dad never said a word?"

"Not a thing."

"When your dad left Michigan, he cut all strings. We heard nothing from him until my father, your Grandad, died."

Hannah said, "I remember. He and Mom went looking for everybody."

"They didn't find me. I was three sheets to the wind and running around the world on business. Commercial electrical sales. I spent about two hundred days a year on the road."

There was a reflective pause. "So, you're writing a book about him? That'll be something of a story."

"Maybe you could answer some questions for me," she said.

"I'll try," Matt said.

"I'm looking for information about his life in Alabama."

"That's where I can't help you," Matt said thoughtfully. "I was too young to remember. But from what I've heard, it was rough. So, your dad never talked about it?"

"Never," Hannah said.

"I was only four when we moved to Detroit. I have some snippets, but they're vague. My life was in Michigan."

Hannah said, "That will help. I'm writing about that too."

Kyle's phone buzzed, Ryan texting he'd be home late.

"Matt, just a second," she said. "Honey, who was that?"

"Evan checking in."

Matt said apologetically, "I didn't think you might be busy with your own life. If you need to go?"

"No, it's fine," Hannah said. "This is a perfect time. We've got almost fifty years to catch up on."

"My wife says I don't know when to stop blabbing," Matt joked. "I guess that's why I made a good salesman. I have a recollection of my folks saying we were moving. Dad told my mom to pack. So, I ran fast as I could because he wielded a switch like a demon."

Hannah remembered the belt. The fruit doesn't fall far from the tree. "Where did you live?"

"Jackson, outside of Birmingham," he said. "I do remember everybody talking at once. I put my hands over my ears and burst out crying. I may have been big, but I was sensitive as a baby kitten."

Hannah felt another chill. Her brother Clem was the same way. Easy to cry, easy to scare.

Matt went on, "We packed everything and went straight to the train station. I can't believe I remember that much."

"Thanks for all of that. It helps a lot."

"Any time. I mean that. At my age, anything helps fill my day. I have diabetes, and I'm on dialysis two times a week. I sit for four hours while they scrub my blood."

"I'm sorry to hear that," Hannah offered.

"Well, I'm almost eighty, and I've been dumping booze and bad food into me since I can remember. So, I have nobody to blame but myself."

"Thanks for all this. One last question."

"Shoot," Matt said.

"I'm going down South to research the family. Got any idea where I should start?"

"Muscle Shoals," Matt said. "That's muscle like in your arm, not the shellfish."

"Never heard of it."

"Look it up. Your Uncle Clem ended up there. Helluva' musician. He was a drunk, like me, but also rootless. Traveled around a lot and finally met a good woman and cleaned up his act. I'd start there because it's at the top of the state and

Jackson's at the bottom. You can work your way down. Good luck and be careful down there. It ain't always a good idea to dig up old bones."

Hannah shivered. "I'll keep an eye out."

"Bye now," Matt said. "And Hannah? I mean it about calling anytime. I can't wait to hear how this plays out for you."

"I will, I promise."

Kyle said, "That was unexpectedly helpful. If I saw that in a movie, I wouldn't have believed it. I don't mean to keep coming back to this, but are you sure you're up to this?"

"I have to be," she said. Hannah felt that her life might just depend on it.

ALABAMA – 1941 ~

The October sky was clear as a deep, still lake, though the temperature hovered around eighty degrees. Despite a soft breeze, the humidity wrapped the air in a wet blanket. Anybody toiling outside became painted with a coat of sweat. With the cotton harvest over and the gins working at full capacity, the sharecroppers took a well-deserved rest, praying for enough yield to keep their balance in the black. Unfortunately, to find yourself in the red often became an impossible obstacle to overcome. It could force the sharecropper to feel trapped or even go hungry.

Tenant farmers often found themselves bound to menial labor to pay back the cost. Then, when that shackle of servitude became too much to bear, families sneaked off in the middle of the night. More often than not, the landowner could have cared less. Desperate and willing families were a dime a dozen. If not, the owner planted the vacant property himself. Either way, he won.

For three years, Harley Lee Bradley broke blessedly even but never put a dime aside for himself. Instead, he made a few extra dollars playing the banjo in a local honky-tonk. But, even second-hand clothes for eight children cost. As a result, they never owned shoes. All eight kids worked and played barefoot. Even went to school shoeless.

Harley never missed a day in the fields, no matter how late he stayed out or how much he drank. Extra money to provide for the family. But, every time it looked like a dollar could be saved, that bastard of an old truck needed a new transmission belt, or the yield fell short.

Today they moved to a new farm. Not because the former landowner was a cheat or a swindler. Mr. Lenny was a fair man. No, the Bradleys had to move because Lenny discovered Harley was making whiskey. Being a God-fearing Christian man, he had no choice but to ask them to go. To have the demon drink made on his property was a sin beyond forgiving.

"But it only be for me," Harley explained. "I ain't sellin' it."

Lenny looked Harley in the eye. "I'm sorry, but the Bible says, *Envyings, murders, drunkenness, revellings, and such like: of the which I tell you before, as I have also told you in time past, that they which do such things shall not inherit the kingdom of God.*"

"But I ain't drunken. It jest a bit of drink t' relax."

But Lenny would have none of it, demanding they leave by the end of the month. Being a man of action and point, Harley had the family packed and a new contract signed by the end of the week. He asked Mr. Cunningham, right up front, if it was okay to take a drink now and again.

"Okay by me. I might even join you from time to time."

"There be a honky-tonk nearby?"

"Closest is Grady's, about two miles South."

Harley smiled wide. "Tha's good. I plays a mean banjo. Make a little extra cash playin' at night."

Cunningham said, "I play a bit of piano myself. Maybe we can play together sometime."

"That'd be fine. That'd be just fine."

A spit and a handshake sealed the deal.

The drive to the Cunningham farm, six miles up a rough, took half a day. The old truck bounced precariously on worn springs. The older children held on in the back of the truck while the younger ones clutched at their siblings.

"Harley, watch the ruts," his wife scolded. "We's gettin' knocked silly back here."

"I ain't hittin' 'em on purpose," he yelled back.

Behind them, the old cotton wagon lurched in tow, laden with clanking tools. Dust from the sun-beaten lane covered the family. Not one child cried or complained. Their daddy wielded a switch with relentless tenacity.

Robert pointed. "That must be it."

All of them strained to see when the farm came into view.

Elizabeth said, "Looks nice."

Harley slowed at the drive, downshifted, and slowly dragged the cotton wagon over the rough entry, then stopped in the shade of a tall Dogwood.

He climbed out of the truck. "There she be."

"The house look bigger'n than the ol' one," Elizabeth said.

"Cunningham says it got three rooms. I'll go 'nounce us."

While Harley climbed the short, steep hill up to the owner's house, Elizabeth called for the children to hop down. "Come get in a' line. I wanna' make a good impression with th' new boss."

They all nodded.

Robert stayed quiet, though he despised the theatrics.

The brood knew the drill, and each lined up, shoulder to shoulder in the order of age. Harley appeared on the edge of the embankment with the landowner in tow.

"Momma," Robert whispered. "He's –"

"Hush now," she nearly bit. "Be Christian and proper."

"Yes'm." Robert took furtive glances as the farmer approached.

"Mr. Cunningham, this here's my family. My wife, Elizabeth. These be my kids." Harley walked down the line and tapped each on the head. "Robert, Ruby, Otis, Clem, Rebecca, Luke, Matthew, and Sarah."

"Hello," the farmer said. His smile was wide and friendly. "It's nice to meet y'all."

He shook each boy's hand and patted the girl's heads. His grip felt strong, and his shoulders rolled with muscle beneath his shirt. At least a head taller than Harley, his face scarred from his left eye to his jawline. As if a great bird had buried its talon in his face and ripped it free.

"Nice'ta meet you as well," Elizabeth said.

"Well then, I'll let you folks get settled. My wife will have supper at seven, and you're all welcome to join us."

"Thank you, sir," Elizabeth said.

She was shocked. No farmer had ever extended such an invitation before.

"See you then," Cunningham said and climbed the hill.

"Well, ma," Harley said, "I'm gonna' go look over the field, you go see your new house. Robert n' Matt, come with me. Resta' you, stay with your Ma."

With her six children in a row, Elizabeth picked up her skirt and walked the dirt path to the house. Behind the house and up the hill, the cotton barn stood against the sky.

"That's a good barn," Clem whispered.

"Look new," Luke said.

Matthew, only three but already near as tall as his brother, held his sister's hand and smiled with excitement. Sarah, the youngest, stood open-mouthed. None of the Bradley clan had ever seen a farm like this. They stopped in the shade of a grove of Dogwoods growing in the gorge. The gurgling water and shaded lot felt like heaven compared to the tin-roofed lean-to they'd just left behind.

Ruby, age ten, held her mother's hand and stared at the house. Five steps led them to the front porch; the windows had curtains. A basket of fresh corn waited beside the door, and a hand pump for clean well water sat in patient silence over a wide tin basin. The stout, stone chimney stood, blackened and sharp against the blue sky, and a wood shake roof promised protection from the weather. Pitch-sealed windows promised no drafts and quiet nights.

"Momma?" Rebecca tugged at her mother's skirt. "This be jest fo' us?"

"Yes, baby."

The children crowded around their mother and looked out over the stream bed to the field on the other side. Already plowed and ready for planting. Harley and the boys walked the boundaries. Elizabeth knew her husband was pleased.

"Can we go in?" Luke asked.

Elizabeth said. "Wait here 'til I look it over."

Robert took a defensive position in front of his siblings as if something might come out of the sturdy door. Elizabeth lifted the latch and pushed the door inward. When her eyes adjusted, she nearly cried. Three times the size of their last home, the floors were swept, and the kitchen offered a real stove. Pots and pans hung from hooks. A heavy table, big enough for them all, waited in the kitchen. Bunkbeds line one wall, and two iron beds made up on the opposite side.

"My, my," she said in a hushed voice. There was room enough for all.

Above her head, what looked like a tarnished copper kettle hung from the ceiling from a knotted rope. A coil of wire ran down to a glass bowl. She looked around for an oil jug and a ladder to reach such a high lantern, but none was found. She soon discovered a black box mounted by the door. An odd, raised lever jutted from the center, and a wire ran up the wall, across the ceiling, and into the kettle. Like a woman reaching for a snake, she carefully grasped the lever and pulled it down. The glass hummed, and the kettle filled with light.

"Lawd A'mighty," she said.

"What Momma?" Matthew asked.

"C'mon and see," she said.

They all stood in awe. Not that the Bradley children had never seen electric light before, but this was the first time they had seen one in their own home.

"It's beautiful," Ruby said.

"Sho 'nuff is, baby. It most surely is."

Harley looked up when he heard the laughter from the house. He slapped his leg and gave both his boys a rub on the shoulder. Luke and Robert exchanged a curious look and thought their father had lost his mind.

"Know what that is, boys?" he asked. "That's your momma' seein' that's she's got 'lectric lights for the first time."

"Electric lights?" Robert gawked.

Harley smiled wide.

"That's right. No mo' doin' schoolwork by lantern. Shee-it no, we gots runnin' water and 'lectric lights, and a new outhouse jest dug. Ain't that the damn'dest, boys?"

Both nodded. Across the creek, their mother waved to them from the porch. Harley cupped his hands around his mouth and shouted, "You likes it, Liz?"

"I love it," she shouted and went back into the house.

"Well, boys, be best be gettin' that truck unloaded. Let's get settled in and washed up and get up to supper with the new boss."

"Daddy?" Robert asked.

"What, boy?"

"We goin' to get t'stay this time?"

Harley's face darkened, and his hand swift.

Robert stumbled back, lost his footing, and fell to the ground. His father dropped to one knee and grabbed Robert's face with his callused hand.

"If'n you ever sass me like that agin', I swears I'll kick you from one side of this field to t'other. You get me, boy?"

"Yes, daddy."

"Then don' let that happin' agin'. Luke, get yer brother on'is feet." Harley stomped off, shaking his head.

Luke helped Robert up. "Why'd you do that?"

Robert watched his father storm off. "You know why."

"You crazy, Robby, you know that?"

"Nope. Now he's got it outta' his system, and tonight he won't find no reason to get mad and hit nobody else. That's why I done it."

"Still," Luke said, "why you take it like that? Let him hit somebody else for a change."

"Like Becca or Sarah? Na'ah, I'd rather get a fat lip or black eye than let that old bastard find a reason to hit them. Or you."

"You boys comin'?" their father yelled from the edge of the field. "Stop gabbin' like some ole biddies at the fence, and let's get unpackin'."

"See," Robert said. "He's already back in good spirits. Now he won't beat on nobody tonight."

"Unless he gets into the shine."

"He ain't got any."

"He's always got some, someplace," Luke said.

"Ma' and I found his bottle and poured it out. He'll have t' drink coffee."

"Unless Cunningham's got some."

"If he does, daddy won't drink much. He'll wanna' make a good impression," Robert said.

"C'mon, you two," their dad yelled.

"Better go before he decides one isn't enough to smack around tonight," Luke warned.

The boys ran across the plowed field where the dusty ground coated their feet. After two hours of hauling and organizing, the house was sorted, and beds assigned. The smaller children took turns switching on the light and giggling. Elizabeth familiarized herself with the stove and made coffee for sheer practice. They formed a line, and Elizabeth operated the hand pump while each child washed their hands and face. The water was cool and sweet, and each drip-dried in the warm evening air. Hair brushed and clothes beat clean, they formed a line and walked the steep path up to the farmer's house.

"Look at that," Elizabeth whispered when they reached the gate. "Such a pretty place."

Mr. Cunningham called and gestured for them to approach. "Welcome, supper's almost ready."

"Well, that sounds mighty good," Harley said.

"It's such a nice night. We'll be eatin' outside. If that's okay with you, folks?"

"Fine by us," Harley said.

Mrs. Cunningham came to the door, wiping her hands on a cloth. She smiled wide and extended her hand to the shaken. A young man stood just behind her, and she waved for him to come forward.

"This is our son, Paul," she said.

'How do you dos' were said all around, and Robert and Paul gave each other a once over.

"Robert, I think you and Paul are about the same age."

"Yes," Elizabeth said, "you two lookin' like bookends in height and weight."

"Not much else, though," Harley whispered.

"You hush," Elizabeth warned.

"Just sayin'."

"Well, let's get settled," Mrs. Cunningham urged.

They took a seat around the long table in the yard. Freshly picked flowers overflowed from glass jars, and clean metal plates were with forks and knives.

"This is lovely," Elizabeth offered.

"Thanks for havin' us," Harley said. "D'you always have new tenants up f'supper on their first day?"

"Well, no," Mr. Cunningham said with a smile. "Matter of fact, you're our first. The house used to be a bunkhouse, and this farm had paid workers. The last owners sold off most of their land and moved North, so we bought this place, and this is our second year."

"I see," Harley said, and his eyes almost twinkled. "Then you're in luck. I knows everythin' about tenant farmin', and I can answer any questions ya' might have."

"Good to know," Cunningham said. "We'll muddle through this together, and I'm sure we'll get along fine."

"That we will," Harley said.

Mrs. Cunningham came out of the house with a large platter spilling over with sliced pork and potatoes.

"Can I help?" Elizabeth asked.

"Uh, yes, if it ain't too much to ask."

"Not at all." She jumped up and helped carry a veritable banquet to the table.

Harley barely tasted his food, though Mrs. Cunningham was a good cook. His mind ran amuck with the possibilities of having absolute control of his destiny. Cunningham was no farmer, but a landowner, and that was not the same thing. This man had money and plenty of it.

Cunningham probably cared little for the cash that Harley's crop would collect, and having his family here was no more than a lark. Harley imagined him in church on Sunday, bragging about having a family sharecropping his lower acres.

"Harley?" Cunningham snapped him out of his thoughts.

"Yep?"

"Did you get a chance to see the barn?"

"Fine barn," he said.

"Just know that whatever you might need tools wise, everything is at your disposal."

"Say again?"

"Use whatever you need."

"Thanks."

Harley felt his face flush. That settled it. This man's high and mighty words proved he knew squat about farming. He wondered how a man like Cunningham ever came into the kind of money to buy a spread like this.

"If everybody is ready, I have freshly baked pie," Mrs. Cunningham called.

"Well, hon, that sounds wonderful," Cunningham said.

After supper, the women and girls clean up while Harley and Cunningham walked to the barn. The younger boys ran to the stream while Paul and Robert walked to the fence.

"Where's the school?" Robert asked.

"Down the road about two miles. Not far to walk."

"How old'r you?"

Paul spit over the fence. "Ten."

"Me too."

"We'll be in the same class, then."

"What's your favorite subject?"

Paul spit again. "Reading and writing."

"Mine's math. I love math."

"That's tough for me. Maybe you can help me."

Robert smiled wide. "Sure, I can help."

"That'd be great. Daddy tries, but he just makes it harder."

"Sure. What do you like to read?"

Paul smiled back. "Anything, even the newspaper. And I like making stories up like I read in the books at school."

"Tell you what," Robert said. "I'll help you with math, and you can tell me stories."

"I have some about pirates and buried gold," Paul said like it was a secret.

"We got a deal," Robert said and spat into his palm.

"Deal," Paul said and spat in his.

124

Like the day their fathers made a pact for shared land, the boys made a pact for shared talent and became fast friends.

"Tell me one of your stories," Robert begged.

The boys walked to the shadow of the barn and sat down in the dry grass. Paul took on a serious expression and looked deep into Robert's eyes.

"Once upon a time," he began. "A pirate called Blackheart ruled the oceans like a king."

Paul spun an exciting yarn of bravery on the high seas until Robert's mother called for him to come back to the new house.

"We'll finish tomorrow," Paul promised.

CHAPTER SEVEN ~

Hannah sipped a glass of Cabernet while flipping through her wedding album. She stared at the photo of her and her bridesmaids. Beck stood a head taller than the group and looked exactly like a movie star.

When she asked Becky to be a bridesmaid, she never expected her to agree. Besides, if she did say yes, what would be the harm? Back then, she was just one of the thousands of struggling actresses. Moreover, she didn't want her to feel excluded. But when Beck's latest film, a romantic comedy with a well-known actor, became a runaway hit, she became the new "it" girl. After that, Hannah expected Beck to cancel. But, she insisted on being in the wedding.

"No, really," Hannah offered. "I know your schedule is now so hectic."

Beck insisted. "I wouldn't miss it for the world."

Kyle just smiled and shook his head. "We'll have paparazzi crashing our wedding."

He was right. They had to hire security to keep out the photographers.

"I swear," Beck said, "I didn't say a word to anybody."

Hannah doubted that. By then, the constant attention had gone to Beck's head, and she could not do anything without alerting her publicist.

But it was not the paparazzi or the security that overshadowed the festivities. No, it was Beck herself. How could having the latest Hollywood beauty at the wedding not take away from the importance of what was supposed to be Hannah's day? Many well-wishers ended their hugs with, *"What's it like being the sister-in-law of Rebecca Lee MacAllister?"*

Hannah never answered those rhetorical questions. She only smiled and nodded. By the end of the reception, Beck had a crowd around her. When she left the party, life seemed to leave with her. When it was over, Kyle held her while she cried.

"I told you not to ask her to be in the wedding," he whispered.

When the years passed, and Beck's star faded, Hannah felt sorry for her. The tabloids splashed her latest failed marriage or poor decision across the headlines. Again, a foreshadow of her sister-in-law's troubles. Again, the center of attention.

Now, this. One minute, she was alive and as dramatic as ever; the next, dead. The final story was screaming from the checkout lines at the grocery store. In bold, upper case letters, the headlines screamed.

TROUBLED STAR'S TRAGIC END!

Other shoppers discussed Beck's life as if they had known her. The speculations ran from the sad to the ridiculous.

"Such a shame. She was so talented. I heard she was depressed. I heard she was pregnant. Did you hear her boyfriend was gay?"

Hannah could only shake her head and hoped tha, before it all came crashing down, Rebecca found some peace. But, from the sound of it, she had not.

Hannah held up her glass of wine. "Beck, I hope you have peace wherever you are."

The garage door grumbled open, and she called out to Kyle.

"I'm in the living room."

He came in with a dozen roses.

Hannah smiled. "Are those for me?"

"They are," Kyle said.

Hannah took the bouquet and took in the sweet, floral scent. Then she kissed him.

"You are welcome," he said. Kyle spied the wedding album. "What made you take this out?"

"I was thinking about her. I was at the store and saw the tabloid headlines. I guess I was feeling bad about the fact I never forgave her for stealing our thunder that day."

"It's all over the radio talk shows," Kyle said. "At least she's back in the headlines. I can only imagine what's boiling on the Internet."

"I was trying to make sense of it all. After that, we didn't see her for two years?"

"More like three," Kyle said. "Then her last two movies flopped, and she had that breakdown."

Hannah nodded. "That was when she came down for Christmas."

"And she got drunk and made a scene. So sad," Kyle said.

Hannah closed the album. "Enough. Let the dead sleep."

"I know. Okay, what's next?"

Hannah said dramatically, "After I finish some homework. Then we'll go over my trip itinerary."

"How can I help?"

"Just by understanding. After I get back from this fact-finding trip, we'll start our lives over."

"You know I'm behind you all the way."

Hannah smelled the roses again. "I know. After I track down the traces of my undiscovered family history, Karen wants me to examine the bones, identify the line of behavioral influence and then report my findings and how I've reconciled the whole experience."

"Are you ready for this?" He asked.

"Yeah, I think so."

There was a long silence, and Kyle watched Hannah struggle with her shifting emotions. He touched her face. Hannah smiled, but her eyes betrayed her.

"What do you have to do before you leave?"

"Make some calls learn what I can about the family. Then I'll book the trip."

"How long, do you think?" He asked.

"I figure a week to gather my intel, and then ten days on the road looking under rocks for the Bradley family secrets."

Kyle gave her a supportive smile. "I'll ask again. How can I help?"

"Just love me."

"I can do that."

*   *   *   *   *

Three days after her session with Dr. Gregory, Hannah poured over the Bradley's family records. In those depths, she discovered details regarding transport between Texas and the South American trade routes. Several websites made vague references to the family name and hinted at the historical link to cotton farming in Alabama. When she traced the name's origins, she discovered origins in Ireland and England.

A population search produced the highest concentration of Bradley surnames in Texas and the central Southern states, predominantly in Alabama. She imagined open land and acres of cotton.

"Bingo," she said to herself.

Uncle Matt told her to call anytime, so she did.

"Hello, niece," he said.

"Is this a good time?"

"I'm retired," he laughed. "Anytime is a good time. Except when I'm fishing, then I don't answer the phone. What's up?"

"I'm trying to put the aunts and uncles together. Do you know where they might have lived?"

"I have a few ideas and some old numbers. Unfortunately, most are dead. But I can help you figure out where they were before they passed. How's that?"

Hannah felt an odd excitement, like the first time she felt a fish pull on the end of a line. When was that? She was five, and her father stood beside her and coached Hannah on how to land the fish. It felt odd to remember that now.

"That's wonderful," she said.

"Ready?"

"Shoot."

Matt gave her the list of names, all with the middle name Lee. Even the girls.

"They named one of their kids, Leigh Lee Bradley?"

Matt chuckled. "Hey, welcome to Alabama. I do remember one thing. The name of the last farmer we worked with was Cunningham."

"That's a start."

"I know because my dad ran out on his contract when things went bad," Matt said. "He talked about how Cunningham tried to screw him, so he deserved not to pay back his debt. Mom didn't argue, and we knew not to question, or dad would get the switch."

"I know all about that."

"Come again?"

Hannah cleared his throat. "My dad, your brother, was a lot like that too."

"What do you mean?"

"You know, self-justified, quick to judge, and even faster to hit. My brothers were always quick to duck and not make him angry."

There was an empty quiet on the line. Hannah thought he'd lost him. "Matt, are you there?"

"You're saying Robert was violent with the boys?"

"I, well, yeah," Hannah said. "He loved the belt and didn't say much. When he was on the warpath, you kept your distance. It sounds like his father was the same, and, you know, the apple doesn't fall from the tree. Right?"

Matt said, "That has to be the saddest thing I've ever heard."

"Hey, what doesn't kill you makes you stronger, right?"

"That's crap, and I think you know it," Matt said seriously. "It's sad because I always thought he'd be the one that– oh shit."

"What?" Hannah urged.

"Let's just say that Robert, your daddy, used to say he'd never be like our dad. He swore it. I'm just sorry to hear it didn't work out for him. Or you, for that matter."

"We lived."

"So did we," Matt said, "but not well. He never hit my sisters. He wasn't exactly loving, but he spared them that."

"So, dad repeated the sins of the father."

"Seems so," Matt said softly.

"I'm so grateful for the information," Hannah said. "I'll be going to Alabama soon."

"On purpose?" Matt suddenly sounded jovial again.

Hannah laughed. "Yeah. I was hoping to see some of the family histories."

"Let's see. I know my older brother Clem was a musician, and he went back to the South in the sixties. Check out Muscle Shoals. But I already told you that."

"Go on," she said.

"He played the juke joints and wrote music. The whole hippy thing. I heard he almost made it big. Even recorded one of his songs. But I already told you about this."

"Yes, you did. Muscle Shoals. It'll be my first stop."

"Sorry. It's part of getting old, you can't remember shit," Matt said with a laugh. "Oh, see if you can track down Little Bear Creek. I remember talk about that when I was a kid. I think it's where your daddy was born."

"So that's what that means."

"Come again?"

"My sister said something about Little Bear Creek, but we couldn't put it together. All I could find was Bear Creek Lake. Uncle Matt, thanks so much. This helps a lot."

"Glad to help," he said. "Hannah?"

"Yeah?"

"I am sorry to hear my brother turned out to be like your granddad. That's such a shame. Call anytime and be careful down South."

It made Hannah's heart heavy. "I will."

She went to her laptop and logged on to the ancestry website. She typed in 'Bradley.' Ancient Gaelic, it roughly translated to 'Broad Pasture' or 'Broad Clearing.' That sent a shiver up her spine. Vast tracks of flat ground were cleared in Alabama's lowlands to plant thousands of acres of cotton. Then, under an Alabama sub-category, she discovered breathtaking images of water, people, cities, and color.

"Honey?" She called to Kyle.

"Yes?"

"Looks like I have some focus here."

He came in, drying his hands on a dishrag. "So, your uncle could help?"

Hannah gave him a quick recap, then pointed to the monitor. "Look at this."

Kyle leaned over his shoulder and gazed at the riot of images filled with blue sky and green foliage. "This is Alabama?"

"The new Alabama," she whispered back. "Not much like the historical stuff we looked at before."

"Some of this looks spectacular. How close are you to being done?" He asked.

"Another day or two. My uncle gave me some good nuggets. First, I'll do some searches based on what Matt told me, and then I'll figure out my itinerary."

Hannah suddenly thought of the night the police came to the door.

"You have that look," Kyle said. "Are you okay?"

"Matt was upset when I shared my dad was just like his father. He took that pretty hard."

"What about him?"

"He seems like a good guy. Open and likable, but he did become an alcoholic. He's sober now but admitted he avoided life by traveling for work for thirty years."

Kyle gave her a soft look, almost sympathetic. "Dinner's ready."

Hannah watched him walk away and knew he felt the same trepidation she did. So twice she called Karen and talked out her worries. Both times Karen calmed her down.

"Think of this as a treasure hunt," she said.

"Okay," Hannah said.

"Only there won't be a big red X on the ground marking the spot. Instead, you'll have to sift through plenty of ground to find the gold, I'm afraid."

Hannah shut down her computer and left the sordid past behind for now. Kyle served up a hearty helping of chili and cornbread. Then they walked to town and had frozen yogurt.

Funny, Hannah thought, *that after the initial novelty of financial abundance wore off, how quickly they returned to their old, familiar ways. The only difference was they never worried if they could afford the ordinary. They both found peace in that.*

Hannah's cell rang. "It's Leigh."

"Need to take it?" Kyle asked.

"No, I'll call him back."

Then they walked hand in hand back toward home. When they turned up the driveway, her cell chimed a new text message, followed by a chirp that meant it was urgent. She tapped his screen.

Please call me!!! It read.

"Leigh again," she said.

"I'll be inside," Kyle said.

Hannah tapped the number. Her brother picked up in the first ring. "Hey, what's up?"

"I–," Leigh tried and then lost himself in tears.

"Leigh, what's going on?"

"I need–," he managed.

"Talk to me."

"Not on the phone. I–."

"I'm on my way over. Hang tight."

He said. "I feel so stupid, but –"

"Just breathe. I'll be there as soon as I can." She went into the house. "Kyle, my brother is in some kind of emotional crisis. I better go."

"What's wrong?"

"I'm not sure. He sounds distraught."

"Call me on your way home."

*   *   *   *   *

Leigh met Hannah at the door. He grabbed her around the neck and sobbed. Hannah worked her arm free and called Otis.

"Hey?"

"Get Clem and meet me at Leigh's."

"What going on?"

"That's what I'm trying to figure out."

Soon they sat in Leigh's living room, each with a glass of their favorite liquor.

Leigh gathered his composure. "I have a confession to make."

They all waited.

Hannah finally said. "Talk to us."

"I think I'm the reason Beck killed herself."

Clem said, "What're you talking about?"

Hannah spoke up, "Leigh, you didn't make her kill herself."

"No, listen," he whispered. "When I heard she wasn't coming to Dad's funeral, I called her and gave her a ration of shit. I called her a selfish bitch, and when she tried to defend herself, I hung up. She tried calling me back, and I wouldn't talk to her. She emailed me a couple of times, and I ignored her."

"Look," Hannah said.

Leigh shook his head in agitation. "No, I did it. I know I did. I was so mean, and I think what I said pushed her over the edge. She was already broken up about Dad, and I pushed her too far."

"Uh, buddy," Otis said. "I hate to tell you this, but I had the same conversation with her."

Leigh looked up in surprise. "Bullshit."

"No shit. I've been talking with Hannah's shrink," Otis said. "I just went over this with her. I thought I made her do it. And I said worse than that."

"Dr. Gregory's great, isn't she?" Hannah asked.

"She's saving my marriage."

Leigh sat back. "You're not just trying to make me feel better?"

"No. I tore into her," Otis confessed.

"She also called me," Clem said. "I refused to talk to her. Maybe I pushed her over the edge."

Hannah shook her head. "First her boyfriend and now all of us? Nobody made Beck kill herself. She was a selfish, neurotic, and self-destructive whack job, and nobody made her do anything."

"So, you killed her?" Otis said with a straight face.

Hannah glared at him and then cracked a smile. "You dick!"

They all broke up, even Leigh.

"No. I killed her," Clem said dramatically.

"Holy shit," Leigh said and put his face in his hands.

"You know," Hannah said, "Dr. Gregory called me out on all this guilt-driven bullshit. She's got me understanding that nobody made anybody do anything. So, so that you know what's up. I'm taking my fact-finding trip down to Alabama in about a week."

"No shit?" Otis said. "On purpose?"

"I am. When I talked with Uncle Matt, he told me Dad swore he would never be like his father. Then he treated us just the same. He said our Grampa never hit the girls. Does that sound familiar?"

They all nodded.

"Dad never took the belt to Beck or me," Hannah said. "But he messed her up plenty of other ways. She's dead because she couldn't live with herself. Karen says it's nobody's fault, *and* everybody's fault."

"She told me that, too," Otis added.

Hannah nodded and said, "I've tracked down some family history and have some leads on two of Dad's old farms. I'm going to find some semblance of the truth and bring it back to everybody. Mostly I'm doing it, so I don't hang myself in the shower someday."

"Jesus," Leigh said. "Do you need anybody along for moral support?"

"No, I'll be fine. Just knowing you guys are on the other end of the phone is enough."

Clem said, "So, you're going back to hell."

"Something like that."

"You always were the strong one," Leigh said.

"No," Hannah responded. "I was just the oldest."

"I need another drink," Leigh said and went to the bar.

"Pour me one too," Otis said.

They all agreed that it was a good idea. Hannah called home.

"Hi, is everything okay?" Kyle asked.

"Yeah, it's fine now. We've decided we're going to have a few drinks. Sorry to do that to you, but we kind of need this."

"Don't drink and drive."

"I won't. I love you."

"Love you too."

Hannah put her phone on the coffee table. "Little brother, make mine a double."

*   *   *   *   *

The following morning Hannah's head throbbed. She stood under the shower as hot as she could stand, then full cold. The shock was intense. She stood there until the cold torrent felt tepid. When the cold subsided, so did her headache.

Otis taught her this trick as a 'morning after' remedy. After last night, Hannah suspected he might share an addictive streak like their Uncle Matt. She dried off and swallowed two Advil, dressed, and went downstairs.

"Good morning, sunshine," Kyle teased. "You were pretty plastered last night."

"I remember you picking me up from Leigh's. I hope I wasn't too obnoxious."

"You were just sad. So I put you to bed. I slept in the guest room. You snored like a monster."

"I bet," Hannah said.

"Want some breakfast?"

"Just water, coffee, and some toast."

Kyle gave her a plate. Hannah tapped her phone and checked her texts. Leigh wrote that he was hungover but feeling relieved. He ended his note with the request for Karen's number. Hannah laughed. She would be seeing all of them soon enough.

"So, what now?" Kyle asked.

"Back into the trip research."

"Let me know if you need anything," he said.

She dove into her plans. Hannah found Muscle Shoals tucked into the Tennessee River in the Northern part of the state. The nearest airport was Huntsville. From there, the drive to Muscle Shoals wasn't too bad. By California standards, it was no worse than driving from Los Angeles to Santa Barbara. Then she could meander and hopscotch through the state and eventually end up in the deep Southern region. If she were to leave in a week, Hannah needed to get some more clues.

"Sweetie?" Kyle called.

"Yeah?"

"Are you feeling well enough to take a walk with me?"

Hannah took a fast-physical inventory. "Honestly? I don't think so."

"I'm going to make a loop. I'll be back in an hour."

"Be careful."

Hannah went to the Kitchen and chugged a Coke, belched loudly, and felt better. Then she lost herself in the search. By the time Kyle came home, she had a rough plan. Kyle showered and then joined her at the computer. "How's it going?"

"I've got an itinerary and one more call to my uncle and some historical digging. I should have some destinations."

"When do you think you'll go?"

"A week, maybe ten days."

Kyle gave her a comforting smile. "You're sure you don't want me along?"

"Just to get down there," she said. "Then it's all me."

Kyle nodded and kissed the top of her head.

DETROIT – 1944 ~

When the quitting time whistle blew, Harley Lee Bradley stepped back from his post and watched the monster relax. The clang and bellow of the assembly line wound down into a low growl while waiting for the shift change. After two years on the graveyard, now he heaved along with the never-ending movement while he adjusted to a typical day. A second blast of the horn signaled him to remove his goggles and pull off his gloves. His back hurt, and his stomach growled. Harley hoped that wife of his had a good supper waiting when he got home.

"Hey, Harl," Dan, his replacement, chimed.

A beast of a man from Mobile, Alabama, Dan stood a head taller than Harley. Good-natured and always smiling, Harley liked him.

"Hey."

"Anotha' day anotha' dolla, huh? At least it's quittin' time fo' ya'."

"Thank God," Harley said. "I'm dog tired."

"Well, you got all night t' sleep. I'm still livin' like a ghost. Up all night, and I can't sleep worth a shit durin' the day."

"I hear that," Harley said. "Did it fo' a year. Gotta' pay yer dues."

"Yep," Dan said. "Anotha' few months a' this and I could be standin' next to ya' on the line. Say hey to the missus, wouldja?"

"Sure will," Harley said and joined the exhausted line of workers trudging up the safety zone between the lines. Then into the grey hallways leading to the lockers. After eight hours of tightening bolts on the Chevy frames, his body still vibrated. At this rate, he figured he'd be broke and dead about the time he retired. But the work was steady, and the pay good enough to feed and clothe the family. But on days like this, if asked, he'd say farming was never this hard.

At least he didn't work in the war support division. Day and night, the assembly line rolled out all manner of armored vehicles to supply the military fighting the Germans and the Japanese. Those men worked harder in an hour than he did in an entire day. Not to mention they were sworn to secrecy, often worked swing shifts, and went home looking like they'd come from the coal mines. Harley also knew they made more money with better benefits, but at what cost? Besides, he'd applied and failed the aptitude test. The automotive work was good enough.

He opened his locker, slapped his gloves and goggles on the upper shelf. Then he shrugged out of his jumpsuit. The hours of sweat and toil assaulted his nose, so he patted his underarms with a generous slap of talcum—little good it did. Only a long bath could wash away the smell of machine oil, acrid steam, and welded steel. With a practiced hand, he spun the cap off his Brylcreem and gave his comb a squirt. The smooth slide and stiff teeth of the comb soothed his brow, so he took his time putting his hair back in shape.

A coworker patted Harley's shoulder on the way out. "A little dab'll do ya'."

"That's what they say," he called back.

Harley slipped into his jacket, turned up the collar, then followed the line up the halls. Out they escaped the side exit into the cold night. Harley's breath plumed, and his cheeks tightened. He lit a cigarette to help push off the frigid air. Then he walked the vast campus to the edge of the city street, where he picked up his pace to fight the chill. Harley covered the quarter-mile to Brainard Street as fast as he could.

Streetlamps created pockets of warm light where the brick tenement buildings squatted like mausoleums along the sidewalks. Behind him, the distant thump and grind of the factory was always there. Now faded from two years of sameness. When he reached his building and climbed the stairs upstairs, every light was on. The noise of the family assaulted the air.

"Dammit," he cursed. "They think 'lectricty grows on trees?"

But the smell of frying pork and baked beans pushed back his agitation. His stomach growled. Harley took the stairs two at a time and opened the door.

"Who's makin' all this noise?" he said.

"Hey, daddy," the crowd of children nearly said in unity.

His wife called from the kitchen, "How was ya' day?"

"Honest day's work for a day's pay," he said.

"You always say that daddy," his daughter teased.

"And I always will."

"Supper's almost ready."

"Starvin'."

143

He went to the icebox and pulled a plain brown bottle from behind an ice block.

"Not too much, Harl," his wife whispered. "Not till after supper."

"I'll take some for my hurtin' back. Don' tell me what I can and can't do for my own sake."

"Jest sayin'," she whispered.

He took a slow gulp. "Where's Robert?"

"Ain't back yet. He had a meetin' after school."

Above the sink, the small window reflected his tired face—a draft of cold air leaked through a crack.

"Thought the landlord was goin' to fix that winda'."

"I told 'em at the office and wrote 'em anotha' reminder note."

"Damn Jew, no-good cheapskate."

"Harley," Elizabeth hissed.

"Well, he's a no-good cheapskate. He'd see us freeze than part with his money."

"I'll talk to 'em agin'. Supper's ready."

"That damn boy knows better than t' be late," Harley said.

"I can keep his supper warm. He's in his math group."

"Math?" Harley chided. "Great good goddamn them numbers is gonna' do for him."

He was feeling his whiskey.

"C'mon, let's eat," Elizabeth called.

The girls crowded around their Mother and helped set the table. A platter of beans and vegetables rounded out the feast. Elizabeth prided herself on her ability to stretch a penny to a dollar and make sure her family did not go hungry. Footsteps on the stairs announced Robert's arrival. He entered the kitchen, his face flushed from the cold.

"Bout time, boy," Harley said.

"Sorry, I'm late. My meeting went long."

"Say that again," his father said.

"I'm sorry my meeting ran late."

Harley let out a laugh.

"Listen t' that. That boy sounds like they do," he said.

"Don't start," Elizabeth begged.

"No, I'm jest curious. Everybody in this house sound like they's from Alabama, but this boy sound like he's a born and raised Yankee. Now, how can that be?"

"I'm just trying to fit in," Robert said.

"I hear him practicin' in front of the mirror," his sister teased.

"That right?" Harley barked. "You studyin' to be on th' stage, son?"

"Daddy, I don't see any harm any trying to assimilate."

"Damn boy, what'ja do with my kid? Yankee sittin' here don't look like any son a' mine."

"Harley, stop," Elizabeth warned. "Not at the table."

"No, wait," he said and waved a hand at his son. "So, you ashamed a' bein' from Alabama?"

"No, sir," Robert said. "But we don't live in Alabama anymore, and I'm trying to get the best education I can so I can go to college."

"To be what? Some big shot math professor?"

"Yes, as a matter of fact."

Harley pushed back his chair and stood. The table went quiet, and only the hum of the icebox and Harley's breathing filled the room.

"I said not t' sass me, boy."

"I'm not. You asked me a question, and I–"

"I says not to' sass me!" Harley's voice boomed.

The younger children whimpered. Elizabeth begged her husband to sit down and eat.

"Not til this hoity-toity, disrespectin' son a' mine say he sorry for his lateness and his lip!"

"Just say sorry, Robert."

"No."

"What!" Harley screamed.

Elizabeth begged, "Let's all sit and eat. Please."

"Say you're sorry," Harley growled.

Robert stood in defiance. "No."

The tension grew.

Father and son faced each other across the crowded table. Harley's face went a shade of scarlet, but Robert returned his father's stare. The youngest daughter suddenly cried louder than the silence.

"See wha' you done?" Harley yelled.

"Look at it yourself, Daddy. This is all your fault. You and that whiskey you drink."

"Why I'll–" Harley scrambled to get around the table while pulling his belt from the loops. Robert backed toward the door.

"Harley, no," Elizabeth screamed.

"Stop right there. You gotta' whoopin' comin' to you, boy."

But Robert reached the door and scrambled down the stairs.

"I don't want to hurt you, Daddy."

"Hurt me?" Harley laughed. "That a joke? That wha' yer gonna' do, boy? Be a comedian?"

"No," Robert raised his voice. "I'm going to get away from this low-class, podunk, backward bullshit you call a life and make something of myself."

"I'll–" His father said.

"You'll what?" Robert shouted back. "Go on, Daddy, talk like a hick, think like a hick, act like a hick and remind everybody you're a failed dirt farmer that drinks too much and can't provide for his family. I'm going to do something more with my life."

"Goddamn, you!" Harley screamed.

"Oh, trust me, He already did when he put me in this family. Get drunk, daddy. Go work that line and make me a nice car so I can buy it with the money I earn with a real education!"

"I –," Harley's voice caught in his throat. "Ya' get back here!"

"Or what?" Robert said in his best Southern drawl. "You gonna' whoop me? Gonna' take me to da' woodshed? Come on down here, and let's finish this like men. C'mon, let's mix it up!"

Harley clumped down the stairs with the belt in his hand, then stopped in his tracks. In the dim light of the front yard, he saw something dangerous in Robert's face. For the first time, he had to look up to stare his son in the eye.

Robert chided, "Well, daddy, you want to take the first swing. I swear if you start this, I'll finish it."

"I –." Harley did not finish his threat. Robert's eyes burned with a ferocity he had only seen staring back at himself from the mirror. He realized his oldest son was taller than him, weighed more than him, and was, at that moment, just as angry.

He broke the violent silence. "You ain't welcome here no more."

"Good," Robert said. "Momma?"

"Robert?" she called over her husband's shoulder.

"I'll come to see you tomorrow."

His mother watched him go. The neighbor's door opened, and the sound of a police siren wailed in the distance. "Will you people shut the hell up?"

"You mind yer business," Harley yelled.

"It'll be everybody's business when the police get here."

"Please, Harley," Elizabeth urged. "Come back inside. Your supper's getting' cold, and the police are comin'. If we are all sittin' down to a quiet supper when they get here, we can say it was somebody else makin' all the ruckus."

Harley climbed the steps, still shaken by what just happened. "That boy won't set a foot back in this house."

"Jest come sit an eat," she said.

Harley knew the police wanted no trouble, so he wouldn't give them any. He'd spent a night in jail before for standing up to them. The children sat frozen around the table, and the two youngest cried quiet tears. He dropped back in his seat.

"There now," Elizabeth said and put on a smile. "That's better, ain't it? C'mon, let's all eat."

The Bradley family began the charade of enjoying their meal. Moments later, the siren screamed outside, the red light pulsed like a monster heart, and heavy footsteps clomped up the stairs. Then came the heavy knock.

"I'll get that," Elizabeth said. She splashed on a happy smile, opened the door, and politely greeted the tall, uniformed man.

"Oh, hello," she said in mock surprise. "What can I do for you, officer?"

CHAPTER EIGHT ~

Hannah's back ached. Coach airplane seats were always too small. The problem with last-minute booking, the best seats are already taken. With her second carry-on bag tucked under the seat, she had no legroom, either. The whole ordeal was made worse by a delay in San Diego, and her flight was twenty minutes late for takeoff. Once in the air, the captain said a strong headwind would make them even later. By the time they landed in Dallas, she worried she might miss his connecting flight.

When they finally let them off the plane, Hannah ducked to avoid bumping her head on the overhead bins. There she waited in a hunched position until the forward passengers exited in a chaotic line. Then she ran to her connecting flight while dodging slow-moving pedestrians. The ticket agent looked startled when she handed her the boarding pass.

"My last flight was late," she said breathlessly.

"I'm sorry," the attendant said, "the flight is overbooked." Her accent was pure Texas.

"Where does that leave me?"

"We called three times and gave your seat to a standby."

"But I have a ticket," Hannah argued.

"They've already closed the doors. But I can get you on the next flight. Guaranteed."

"But it wasn't my fault."

"I know," the attendant said. "Tell you what. I'll make sure you get an upgrade to first class."

"How long of a wait will it be?"

"An hour and a half."

"I'll take it."

The ticket change took only a minute. Hannah suddenly felt exhausted. She ducked into an airport restaurant and slipped into a booth. She thought back to the days before she left. Her visit with her brothers to assure them she was on a fact-finding tour for all their sakes.

"And Beck's," Otis said seriously.

That made them all nod.

Leigh furrowed his brow and said, "I'll be curious to see what kind of skeletons you dig up."

"Whatever they are, I'll be back with a full report. I called the recording studios in Muscle Shoals and found where our uncle was a session player. Clem, you'll love this. He was your namesake."

"So that's why I'm so musical," he joked.

"I've got the guy's name and where the studio is," Hannah said. "That's my first stop."

Otis chimed in. "Are you sure you're up for this?"

"We'll find out," she said.

"Call if you need us," Otis said.

"Does that mean you'll come to bail me outta' the prison farm?" Hannah teased.

"You bet. And we'll hire an obese lawyer that wears an all-white suit and a string tie that will shame the court into letting the Yankee go free."

"Let's hope so," she said with a laugh.

Kyle joined her in the sentiment.

That night, her Uncle Matt called again with more information—primarily names and a fact or two regarding where they lived. "I hope that helps."

Hannah assured him it did. In fact, with minimal searching, she was able to track the Cunningham family and a deed of ownership to what she was sure was the last farm her grandfather sharecropped. It sat deep in the state by the gulf, so her itinerary would take her from Muscle Shoals, then a long and wandering trek through Alabama's landscape.

Odd, she thought, *as arduous as that sounds, it is no further than traveling from San Diego to San Jose. Three hundred miles.*

"I could do it in half a day," she told Kyle.

He reminded Hannah to take her time. "It's a journey of discovery, not a race."

"Yes, dear."

The waitress approached and snapped her out of her reflection. "What can I getcha?"

Hannah glanced at a table menu. "A draft beer and a bacon cheeseburger with onion rings."

"Coming right up."

She called Kyle but got his message center. "I'm stuck in Dallas. I have a layover. I miss you. Love you."

She sat back and rubbed her sore neck. When her food arrived, Hannah savored the meal. When done, Kyle had not returned her message. She texted him before she boarded. A short flight, a bit wider seat, and free booze. Next stop, Alabama. That thought made Hannah's gut tighten. She took a deep breath.

The woman beside her asked, "Bad flier?"

"Not usually," Hannah said.

"First time for everything."

Once in the air, the flight attendant came around, and she ordered a drink. It helped a little. Her neighbor gave her a sympathetic smile.

"Relax," she said, "they rarely ever crash."

"It's not that. I'm freaking out about where I'm flying to."

"What's so bad about Alabama?"

"I don't know where to begin," Hannah said.

"Okay, talk to me, and let's get through this. I'm Joan Kellerman. What's your name?"

"Hannah MacAllister."

"What's your business in Alabama?"

"Family stuff. My dad passed away recently and was from there."

"What part?"

Hannah's tension lessened, but her mind raced. "Jackson."

"Beautiful country. Where you from?"

"San Diego."

"I love California. I'd love to move there, but my husband would never do it. He's Southern through and through. Too many family ties. Feeling better?"

Hannah nodded. "Yeah. Thanks. You don't sound like you're from Alabama."

"Canada originally," she said.

"Long way from home."

"New Brunswick.," Joan said. "About as far Northeast as you can get. I met my husband at a convention. Now I'm a citizen by marriage. You still have any family in Alabama?"

Hannah's stomach knotted again at the question. "That's what I'm here to find out?"

"That sounds intriguing," Joan said.

Hannah told the whole story in five minutes.

Joan said softly, "You're in a panic because you feel like you're flying into hell."

"That about sums it up," Hannah said.

Joan handed Hannah a business card, "I am a corporate mental health evaluation consultant."

"Perfect. I couldn't have asked for a more suitable travel companion."

"My recommendation is you have another drink, close your eyes, and breathe deeply."

"I'll try, but I'm pretty sure I won't exhale until we reach solid ground."

"First of all, Alabama is not hell, though it feels like it in August," Joan joked. "It's just a place. Yes, lots of bad things happened there and sometimes still do, but no different than you have in Los Angeles or Oakland."

"Thanks. Keep talking, and maybe I'll make it in one piece."

"What do you do?" Joan asked.

"I was an advertising and marketing writer. Since my dad died, I'm an intrepid traveler in search of his past."

"You better keep my card. Call me if you get into trouble."

"I have a therapist back home."

"Did they ever live in the South?"

Hannah shook her head. "No."

Joan smiled and shook her head.

"Then you better call me instead. Alabama troubles are best discussed with an experienced professional."

"Joan," Hannah responded, "that doesn't make my agitation feel any better."

"You're right. We better order those drinks."

The vodka tonic was just what the doctor ordered.

"Better?" Joan asked.

"Yeah, thanks. Is that offer to talk serious?"

Joan smiled. "I don't give my card to just anybody."

The captain announced they were starting their descent. Hannah breathed a sigh of relief. Out the window, she could see a riot of green and the blue horizon of the gulf. Southern California offered hot spots of manufactured green, but the landscape above was mainly desert once away from populated areas. This looked like they were flying into the Amazon basin.

When the plane dropped and turned to approach the Huntsville airport, the single runway cut through green fields, farms, and rural landscape. Beyond the airport, bodies of water bordered housing tracts. It looked like a city park that ran as far as the eye could see.

"Welcome to Huntsville," Joan said.

"It doesn't look so bad."

"Told you so. Just don't drink the water," she joked. "I wasn't kidding about calling me."

"I'll keep your card handy."

Joan patted Hannah's shoulder, then rolled her carry-on down the plane to the exit.

Once inside, Hannah felt oddly at home. The airport looked so much like San Diego, and she almost knew the way to the car rental counter. An hour later, she tapped Muscle Shoals into the navigation system of the Lincoln SUV. It instructed her out of the airport onto Highway 72. Another wave of anxiety rolled through her. She shook it off.

"It's just a place," Hannah said out loud.

Sure, her inner voice smirked, *the place where racism thrived, and slavery lived. A place where people fought for freedom and people died. The place where Martin Luther King died, marchers beaten, and George Wallace stood at the University of Alabama door to bar black students from enrolling. Sure, it's just a place with a dark and violent past.*

"That was all a long time ago."

Less than your lifetime.

"Things are different now."

We will see.

Kyle finally called back. "Where are you?"

"Driving through the top of the state with a nasty voice in my head reminding me where I am."

"I've always hated that voice," he said. "You okay?"

"Yeah. I sat with a psychologist on the plane. I got her card."

"Funny," he said.

"I'm serious," Hannah said. "I met a corporate culture shrink. She gave me her card."

"That's too spooky," Kyle said. "Other than that, what's it like?"

"You know how green it gets in our mountains after the winter rains? Multiply that by five."

"Sounds pretty. Take some pictures. Call me tonight. I miss you."

"Me too."

She passed through small burgs where shacks leaned in fields, and rusted gas station signs stood like forgotten monuments of another era. The trip took only an hour. When

Hannah rolled into Muscle Shoals, she found just what the Internet and Google Earth promised.

Spread out along a checkerboard of streets and land tracks. The place looked stuck in the last century. Tall Dogwoods and tangled Kudzu blocked the view of what waited ahead. Along the Northern border, the Tennessee River broke free of the trapped waters of Wilson Lake and meandered away in search of greener pastures.

From what she read, Native Americans first inhabited this place. Then the white man pushed in, and everything changed. A musical anomaly was discovered in this quiet burg, a Southern sound found nowhere else in the world. On his drunken sojourn of creativity, her Uncle Clem staggered into this place and met up with his fate in a small honky-tonk in 1968.

Sam Jenkins, a session player, and local D.J. heard Clem playing on a three-legged stool in the corner of the old saloon. Mesmerized by what this ragged man birthed from his battered six-string, Sam listened to Clem's story between shots of whiskey. That meeting lead to an introduction to Mel Harberger of Whispering Water Studios. Clem Lee Bradley suddenly became a professional musician.

Hannah put the studio's name into the navigation system, and the mechanical voice guided her to a bridge that crossed the Tennessee River. There she found a hollow with a smattering of buildings set back from the highway.

"I'm not in Kansas anymore," she joked. "Or maybe, this is what Kansas looks like?"

Under the canopy of trees, a modern gas station filled one corner while an ancient Tasty Freeze, restored to its retro glory, sat nearby. Across the road, a two-story brick building looked rejected amongst the restored antiquity. A simple painted sign on the rough brick façade read,

Whispering Water Music & Recording Studio.

Hannah parked against the building's shady side. Faded graphics of musical notes, a guitar, and a saxophone, flaked in the afternoon sun. One door, no windows. The old brass knob turned quickly, and she stepped into an air-conditioned, cluttered lobby where a bell above the door jingled. A portly, silver-haired man appeared from the back. His cherub face so inviting Hannah could not help but smile.

"Hello. Welcome to Whispering Waters."

"I'm looking for Mel Harberger?"

"You found him," he said happily. "What can I help you with?"

Hannah offered her hand. "I'm Hannah Lee MacAllister. I spoke with you on the phone."

"Yes, the gal from California," Mel said. "You're really Clem's niece?"

"I am."

"I'll be damned. C'mon, I'll give you the nickel tour."

Mel walked her around the lobby and explained the instruments on display. Every manner of musical fare had a place of honor on a counter, a shelf, or a table.

"We used to be a music store," he shared. "But when the sound was discovered, we concentrated on recordin'."

"I was surprised how many recording studios there are here now," Hannah said.

"Dozens of 'em. Once FAME hit it big, and when the Swampers jumped ship, it grew."

"I can imagine."

Hannah stared at an ornate guitar signed by a famous British rock star. "My husband and I watched a documentary about that whole thing. They didn't mention your studio."

"No, we weren't part of the drama," he said. "FAME started it all, and even then, we were third fiddle. I ain't complainin', we had our day. I keep this place open as a museum, mostly. C'mon, I'll show you the studio."

"Thanks."

Hannah followed Mel up a narrow staircase to the second floor. Double doors opened into a studio where a drum kit, microphone stand, and assorted musical instruments sat strategically placed around the set. No windows. The air conditioner blew steadily.

"Here she is," Mel announced.

"This is exciting," Hannah said.

"We still record here," he said. "Locals mostly. Some country and western folks lookin' to cut a record. But since things went digital, we're kinda' retired."

Hannah thumbed the neck of a guitar and ran her finger over the piano.

"You play?" Mel asked.

"Oh, I tried a few times, but I can't carry a tune in a bucket or play an instrument."

"Go figure. Your uncle was the best musician and singer I ever met, and you can't sing a lick?"

Hannah said. "Only in the car. Tell me about him."

"Your uncle didn't end up here 'cause he heard he should. He just stumbled into town and did what he could do to make some spendin' money. I saw him perform and signed him. Fame was pissed, but then Clem showed how unreliable he was."

"How so?"

"He drank like nobody I ever saw before."

Hannah nodded with a smile. "I heard he was pretty bad."

"Like the devil himself," Mel said. "I'd get a few great tracks outta' him, and then he'd disappear. Finally, he just left town and didn't even pick up his last paycheck. After that, I heard he was in Texas and then –?" Mel shrugged.

"Yeah, I heard that too."

"You gonna' tell me what happened to him?"

Hannah rubbed her neck and chuckled. "He went to Detroit and did odd jobs until he met my aunt. She dried him out. He did very well for himself selling insurance."

"All that talent, and he sold insurance?"

"When he got sober, he stopped playing, I guess."

"Well, the world is full of folks that had a dream that never came true. But at least he got to record. Funny thing, after he left town, one of his records became a hit. I still owe him money for that. You gonna' be seein' him?"

Hannah shook her head. "I'm afraid he died last year."

"Sorry to hear that."

"Tell me about this song?" Hannah urged.

"Tell it? I think you should hear it."

"That would be amazing."

Mel went to the control booth and rummaged through a box. He pulled out a .45 record in a yellowed paper sleeve. "Song's called 'Lover's Moon.' I'll pipe it into the studio. The best sound that way."

After the scratch of a needle touching vinyl, a melodic banjo filled the room, accompanied by a soft piano. A simple drumbeat joined the dance. Then a familiar voice broke in. Clem sang an emotional story of heartbreak and drink, loss, and hopelessness.

All Hannah could do was listen until the last word left a desperate longing. Tears came to her eyes.

"Whatja' think?" Mel echoed over the room.

"That is amazing."

"There's a 'B' side."

"Is it as good as that?" Hannah asked.

"No," Mel said, "Just boilerplate country twang."

"Then, no."

Mel carefully slid the record back into the paper sleeve. "He did have another song with us, just the lyrics. Nowhere as deep as Lover's Moon, but real personal. I got it here somewhere." Mel searched through a stack of papers. "Got it."

He left the booth and came back to the studio floor with the folder. "I want you to have this."

Hannah felt genuine surprise. "You sure?"

"As sure as I'm standin' here."

"Thank you."

Mel said, "When we played that on the radio, people went crazy for it. Played it all over the South. I went lookin' to sign him to a contract before somebody else did. But he was just gone."

"Now I have two more of his things."

Mel cocked his head. "What's the other?"

"I have his banjo. My dad left it to me after he died, and I put it in my hall closet."

"Why there?"

"Well, my mother had it hanging on their living room wall for twenty years. I thought it was just something she picked up as a decorator piece. Only after he died did I learn Dad got it from Clem."

Mel put his hand on Hannah's arm.

"Darlin', when you get home, you best pull it outta' the dark and hang it in a place of worship. I never heard a man make a banjo sing the way your uncle did."

"I will," Hannah said and some shame. The day she disparaged the instrument came back.

"You okay?" Mel asked. "Look like a goose just walked over your grave."

"It may have done just that."

"So, what now?" Mel asked.

"It's getting late, so I'll find a place for the night. Any recommendations?"

Mel scratched his chin. "There's all manner of lodgin' over the river in town. There's a Hyatt."

"Thank you for everything, Mel."

"Make sure you take a look at that other page of lyrics when you get settled."

"I will."

Mel smiled. "Can't sing a lick, huh?"

Hannah laughed and shook his hand. As she drove across the river, she pulled over. There it was – FAME Recording Studios. The building reminded her of an upside-down cardboard box with windows cut out. A small yellow and white sign declared it was indeed the famous birth of the Muscle Shoals sound. Next to the studio was a pizza joint and across the street from an auto parts store. It felt like finding Stonehenge in a Walmart parking lot.

Hannah shook her head and drove on. She found the Hyatt at the end of the street. After checking in, she felt exhausted. The ride up the elevator seemed to last forever. Once in the room, she sat on the edge of the bed and opened the folder. With the record, she found two pages of sheet music. 'Lover's Moon' was written in a robust and masculine script. Hannah read it slowly. Without the music, the words stood alone as a beautifully written poem, a real story of one man's lost love.

Her uncle carefully captured his moment of clarity, a profound moment that encompassed the path of a lonely heart, then recorded it with a haunting melody that told the depths of his tortured soul.

Hannah pulled the second sheet from the folder and felt stunned.

"Holy shit," she whispered.

The song lyrics read:

LITTLE BEAR CREEK

I remember as a very small boy
Things were bad, we had no toys
We all lived on Little Bear Creek
Hard times were at their peak

I remember those very hard times
Often down to our very last dime
We had no car or truck to drive
Just an old grey mule for us to ride

We fished a lot in the ole Little Bear
We never had any shoes to wear
I can still hear the dogs chasing prey up a tree
Can still hear Dad calling, what can that be?

We plowed our fields along the creek
We killed our hogs to have fresh meat

We'd haul our cotton load to the gin
We worked hard but never could win

Yes, I remember back to those times
We struggled for life, our bodies, and minds
We hunted and gathered from wild honeybees
To keep us all going and fulfill our needs

With three young girls and five strong boys
We worked those fields but found no joys
We had a had a hard life, and so much was wrong
This story is true. I sing a sad, sad, song.

Hannah could barely finish the words. This simple rhyme spoke volumes to her. Now she understood why Mel urged her to revisit this past. Clem's banjo, his vessel of truth, languished in a closet, ignored, and misunderstood. Much like the man himself.

It was as if Clem found himself, shared his plight with the world, then ran from the awful truth he discovered. To never play music again? Hannah somehow understood why. Her uncle had come so close to the brutal reality of life. At the moment of her death, Hannah wondered if Rebecca also had that moment of awful clarity? Hannah suddenly felt too tired to think. Her head on the pillow, she soon lost herself in troubled sleep.

In her dream, Hannah stepped up to the muddy bank and let the lapping water tickle her toes. Banjo music softly filled the air as the cool tickle of the soothing water beckoned her to step further. She carefully waded out until the current tugged at his legs. A piano joined the banjo, and the music grew louder. A chorus of women's voices softly urged her to wade deeper into the river. With another step, the water bathed her body to the neck. The sun dropped to the horizon, and in that fading light, she could almost see the music in the sky.

"Sing girl," a voice urged.

Hannah turned to see Mel standing on the bridge, his round face glowing in the setting day.

"I can't sing a lick," she said.

"The water will guide you. Just trust the river."

"How do I do that?"

"Lose you'self. Let go, girl."

Hannah took one more step and allowed the current to take her. As the sun dropped behind the trees and the current pulled her along, she heard his uncle's voice singing a heartfelt song. Not of his own life, but of the day Hannah screamed and scared the neighbors. When she looked up, she could see Rebecca's wavering face hovering over the surface of the river.

Beck, she thought, *did you find the exact moment as Uncle Clem? Did you look into the face of emotional clarity and see a truth you couldn't endure?*

She got no answer. Instead, her features broke into a thousand sparkling reflections. Then, all went black, and the choir suddenly stopped. The river drew Hannah along the dark bank as it escaped Muscle Shoals and searched for a quieter place.

Her ringing phone snapped her awake. Kyle's face smiled from the screen.

"Hi," she said, her voice rough and quiet.

"Hey there, you okay?"

"I was sleeping."

"Oh, I'm sorry," Kyle said. "When I didn't hear from you, I got a little worried."

"Sorry. I was going to call you."

"How'd your day go?"

She shared her experience at the museum and his conversation with Mel. Kyle listened and offered no comment. When she finished, he said.

"I wish I were there with you."

"Me, too. Can I read you the words to my uncle's song?"

"Of course."

"Let's see if I can get through this without weeping."

"It's okay if you do," he assured her.

"Lover's moon is the title. Here goes. *In the wind, I hear you calling me to please come home to you. I know your heart is broken and that your love's still true. I ask myself why you care and what you see in me. But I have to find what's good in myself. I must find my soul, you see. Lover's moon, you haunt me. Lover's moon, you light my face. In the shadows cast along the river's edge, I feel a gentle trace. Lover's moon, you light my way.*"

Hannah caught her breath.

"Go on," Kyle urged.

"Give me a second."

She swallowed hard and read. *"On the dark road, my spirit dwells. I see it in the mist. I reach for it with a hopeful heart, but it's gone like a lover's kiss. Beneath my urgent wanderings, my heart begs for rest. Under my desperate ponderings, there's silence in my chest. Can my heart be so cold that I resist your cries? Can my mind be so distant that it hears but still denies?"*

She stopped again to compose herself.

"Is there more?" Kyle asked.

"Last verse," she said. *"Lover's moon, you tease me, to follow down this long and lonesome path. The lover's moon speaks a soft caress to lie down in the grass. And while you cry alone at night, I hear the river's voice. It's the liar's moon, hidden by clouds, that leaves me with no choice."*

Hannah's voice trembled with the last words. "Then the last part repeats."

"That's so sad," Kyle managed, "and so moving."

"It was a hit," Hannah said. "They played this on the radio."

"I can see why," Kyle said. "All the girls would feel the pain of unrequited love, and all the bad boys could feel like their wanderlust had a name."

"Either way, it's a heartbreaker. Mel gave me the record. We'll listen to it when I get home."

"Hannah?"

"What?"

"It reminds me of the poems you write to me for our anniversaries. It really does."

She laughed despite her tears. "If I could sing and play the banjo, I could put my poems to music, and we could take our show on the road."

"How about we don't but say we did. That was beautiful."

"He never recorded again," she said. "He was a drunk, got sober, and then sold insurance until the day he died. Imagine just leaving all that talent behind."

Kyle said, "Maybe that was the best he had. Maybe he recorded his heart and knew he would never be able to do that again?"

"I thought the same thing. Wait till you hear this. He also gave me some sheet music for another song he never recorded titled *Little Bear Creek*."

"Holy shit," Kyle whispered. "Does it reveal the secret?"

"Kind of."

"Read it to me." When Hannah finished, Kyle was quiet for a moment. "That tells a story."

"And gives me some direction," she said. "One step closer to this mysterious place."

"Honey, be honest with me. How're you holding up?"

"Truthfully? I've been better."

"I love you," he said.

"I love you, too."

"Go to sleep, and when you get home, you don't have to wander and to discover yourself. You'll have already done that."

"Okay."

They reluctantly hung up. Hannah reread the last line. *It's the liar's moon, hidden by cloud, that leaves me with no choice.*

She tapped her search icon on her phone and typed in 'Liar's Moon.' She learned a 'liar's moon' is when clouds obscure the full moon, whereas a 'lover's moon' shines bright in a clear sky.

This story is true. I sing a sad, sad song.

That needed no explanation.

She turned off her phone and switched off the light. Outside the window, a sliver of moon lay on its back and settled toward the distant horizon.

"Liar's moon," she said quietly.

Then Hannah let her sudden loneliness lull her to sleep.

REVELATIONS ~

Kyle sat at his laptop and scrolled through page after web page about Alabama. The history inspired and frightened him. So much tumult, so much change, and strength of tradition - though many of those traditions mocked conventional norms. Slavery being the most brutal reality to imagine. Especially taken in the form of Hannah's family history.

He found it ironic that the origins of both their families were of the same region. Hannah's name, Bradley, began in Northern Ireland. His, MacAllister did as well. They were nearly neighbors. Then his people traveled through Canada and down to Utah. From there, they embarked on a western trek of three thousand miles to what is now Napa Valley, California. Hannah's clan boarded ships in Boston and faced over a thousand miles of raging seas.

To his family, slavery was but a distant whisper. Not that picking grapes and tilling the soil was unfamiliar to his ancestors. Though also housed and kept by landowners, but his relatives were paid and treated as humans. Not that sharecroppers in the south were all treated as animals, but the African slaves certainly were. Tenant farming was also common in California, but not with the heavy hand of oppression evident *Down South*. Her research explained that early vineyards populated New York and Virginia used paid labor, while the vineyards of Ohio and Missouri ironically, worked their land with slaves.

That was a harsh contradiction to sort out.

So odd, he thought, *that the origins were so similar, yet the outcome of providence of geography, could affect such a difference.*

* * * * *

As Kyle ruminated, Hannah's sense of place and time left her in her sleep. When she awoke she felt a moment of emotional desperation from a fading dream.

You're in Alabama, she reminded herself. She reflected on a time she almost stepped into Alabama while driving to Disneyworld with her family. On the way back from Florida, they reached the border of Alabama.

"Let's check it out," Kyle suggested.

"Why?" she asked.

"Because your family's from there," he said.

"But it's Alabama," she said.

Kyle must have registered her tone and left it alone. He'd only heard snippets of stories of her family history. Later, he apologized for the suggestion.

"I realized something," he said. "For me to suggest we visit Alabama would be like asking someone that nearly drowned as a child to jump into the deep end of the pool."

Hannah appreciated his understanding but remembered when her grandfather died, and her parents went looking for what was left of the Bradley clan. They even visited the last farm where her Father's family sharecropped.

"If they can do it, so can I," she said.

A shower washed the last of the doubts from her head. After breakfast in the hotel café, she looked over her itinerary: next stop, Lebanon. How odd, Hannah thought, that those that journeyed across oceans to escape religious persecution found comfort by naming new lands after the places in the Bible. Unfortunately, such is the lot of humankind. Wherever you go, there you are.

Hannah programmed the car navigation to take her to Lebanon. Maybe it was the emotional hangover from the stark reality of what she was doing, but she could not shake the dark mood. The lyrics of her uncle's song, the open road's loneliness, and her undefined expectations haunted her like a ghost.

More than once, she checked the rear-view mirror, half expecting to see the specter of her Father sitting in disapproval.

What you doin' down here, girl?

Nothing daddy.

Best be gettin' yourself straight.

I'm doing my best.

Ain't good enough.

Hannah said out loud, "Dad never talked that way."

She called Kyle, and it went to voicemail. "It's me. I'm back on the road. I'll be in Lebanon in an hour. Call me when you get back. Love you."

She tossed her cell on the passenger seat and watched the dusty scenery pass by. Again, she thought of the words of Clem's song. The wanderlust and ache in that melody were so much more than a man making music. It spoke of a loss of direction and confusion in life. Though her uncle may have traveled on his wits, his lack of focus must have mirrored what Hannah now felt. There is an emptiness in feeling rootless. She could see how a man could turn to the bottle to find relief.

"Not at 9:00 in the morning," she said to the road.

The green valleys and old buildings, so quaint and mysterious only yesterday, were now a harsh reminder of his father's story. Ten miles passed, and she finally came to Lebanon. It wasn't much. Like so many small towns down here, it was but a blip on Google Earth's radar. California had small towns in rural areas, but Alabama could fit within Los Angeles County. Yet, the distance between souls outside the significant cities seemed to carry weight as foreboding as the Sahara's endless emptiness.

Hannah stopped for gas and a Diet Coke. Around her, the small town went about its business with a lack of urgency. A fine layer of dust seemed to have taken away the color from the town. When the tank was full, and her drink finished, she tossed the empty can and went back into the station. A tower of a young man stood behind the counter. Thin as a rail with a gentle face, he sported a shock of red hair and alabaster skin.

"Help you?"

"I hope so," she said. "I'm looking for Jasper Road. It doesn't seem to be on the map."

"Jasper's not really a road. It's more like a dirt path through the old fields. Back in the day, old man Jasper owned most of the county. He leased out to the sharecroppers and used to be one of the biggest cotton growers this far North."

"Is there anything out there now?" Hannah asked.

"The road's still there. Not much else."

SECRET of LITTLE BEAR CREEK • THOMAS K. MATTHEWS

"Nobody else farms the land?"

"Nothing grows," he said. "Cotton's tough on the dirt. It kills the soil."

"You seem to know a lot about cotton," Hannah said.

"My grandpa farmed that land, and so did my dad. They told a lot of stories about the life of sharecropping and the death of the ground."

"That's well said," she said.

"Yeah, I can be eloquent. I major in English."

"And you're working here?"

"Summer job, helping out with my mom."

"Then what?"

"In the fall, I go back to working on my Master's and teaching credential."

"Basketball scholarship?" Hannah asked.

He laughed. "No. I never had the coordination. I'm all academics, graduated with a 4.0."

"Sounds like you have a future."

"Let's hope so."

"So, will there be a problem if I wanted to go out there? I mean, will the Jasper's chase me out with a shotgun?"

"The Jaspers are long gone. I'm not sure who owns that land now. There're some old fences and signs, but nobody'll stop you if you drive out there. The kids use it to party on the weekends."

"How do I find it?"

"Go South outta' town. Stay on River Road, and when you come to the four-way stop, the dirt road heading east is Jasper."

"Will my car handle it?" she asked.

"Should. If you bottom out, guess not."

"Thanks. Good luck with school."

"What're you looking for out on Jasper?"

"Ghosts," Hannah said.

"Well, if you're gonna' find them, they'd be there."

Hannah clicked on the radio and found a classic rock station. While The Eagles sang about the Hotel California, she followed the directions. Five miles later, she reached the four-way intersection and came to a stop. Trees clustered around the opening like sentinels down the dirt lane, but the shadowed place looked inviting enough.

Hannah drove the lane until she came to a dilapidated barbed wire fence rusting in the sun. The valley reached out to stream beds and hallows where vegetation still found what it needed to grow. What must have been hold-out cotton plants looked forlorn and sick in the bright sun? The rest of the valley looked windblown and empty. The skeletal bones of abandoned structures stood twisted and beaten down by time and weather.

"Jesus," Hannah spoke to the emptiness.

The further she drove, the less evidence of nighttime festivities littered the open space. Eventually, she found herself on a flat stretch where a rainstorm pushed a torrent that cut a gulley too deep and wide for her to cross. At the bottom, the hulk of an old truck lay half-buried in the ground. The cracked windshield and front-end jutted from the earth like the last struggle of a drowning animal. Hannah shut off the engine and exited the car.

Besides the wind winding through the valley, the only sound came from an occasional bird chirping in the nearby trees. She tried to imagine the land planted fence to fence in cotton, sunflowers, and tobacco. The toil of the farmers and the activity at harvest time must have been a sight. All those people were scratching out an existence, piling cotton into wagons, and then making their way to the cotton gin.

"Well, dad?" She said. "This explains a lot."

Hannah stepped through the rusted fence. Her hand to her brow, she squinted across the emptiness. Beneath her feet, the soil had no heft. She scooped up a handful. It felt like powdered sugar. When she released it, it drifted back to earth in a cloud.

"My God," she said.

Hannah found her pants covered with a coat of dust. When she tried to brush it away, it coated her hands and clothes with a veil of beige. Her earlier impression of the town was correct. Dust concealed the sins of the past, and only the rain could wash it away. Her mood darkened, and suddenly the idea of what she was doing seemed insane.

How could this help her understand the unresolved crap of her father's messed up childhood? Suddenly, this whole venture felt like a waste of time. When she returned to the car, the radio blared a report that a white teenager had opened fire in a South Carolina church.

"The young man had attended the prayer group before his attack," the announcer said in a severe tone. *"There are seven confirmed dead and three survivors transferred to a local hospital."*

Hannah closed her eyes. The tall kid in the gas station may be in school to better himself, but from what she could see, Alabama had no intention of improving anything.

"He'll have to take his master's degree North if he wants to make a difference," Hannah said to the radio. "What a crock this whole trip has been. I guess I figured out why my dad was who he was. Now I can go home and never have to come back to this shit hole again!"

"A hunt is on for the young man," the announcer continued. *"Police have established roadblocks, and witnesses said he*

appeared to be in his late teens or early twenties with a crew cut and wearing jeans and a confederate flag printed T-shirt."

Her phone beeped with a missed call from Kyle. She ignored the message and called back.

"Hey there," Kyle said. "How's it going down there?"

"Oh, not very good."

"Talk to me."

"Did you hear the news about the church shooting in North Carolina?"

Kyle sighed. "I did. It sounded like a terrible tragedy."

"Then, you know how it's going."

"Tell me," he urged.

"I tracked down the area where my dad's family once sharecropped. Kyle, this place is too much. I–," her voice cracked.

"Take a deep breath," he said.

She fought tears and said, "I can't even see this place anymore. All I see is old, lost, and pointless shit that reminds me of why my dad left. And that news story makes me feel like nothing down here has changed. I mean, really? In a church?"

"Listen," Kyle soothed. "Our news reported two police shootings of unarmed people in Los Angeles, an apartment fire that killed a family of seven, and a man in Orange County that killed his ex-wife, took the kids and ran. Bad shit happens everywhere. I think you're way too deep to see the forest for the trees."

"You got that right," she said with a lost laugh.

"Tell me something good. Tell me the last thing you saw of beauty down there."

"The river in Muscle Shoals. Since then, I've been chasing demons, spooks, and haints."

"Haints?" he asked.

"My dad once said that when he was a kid on hot summer days, if he walked through a cold pocket of air, he turned around three times and spit. He said the cold air was what they called a haint. Turning and spitting kept the spirit from taking your soul."

"Interesting. By the way, when was the last time you spoke to one of your kids?"

"Not since I left. I've meant to, but I just keep getting sidetracked."

"That might help you and them," he said. "Keep talking."

"Honestly, after looking at the barren wasteland and hearing about the shooting, I want to stop and come home."

He said softly, "Listen. You're tired, stressed, and homesick. What is next on your itinerary?"

"Montgomery."

"Okay. I'm coming down there."

"Kyle, I –."

He interrupted. "Listen, you haven't seen a city since you landed. The ghosts of your dad's past are all around you. I'm joining you, and we will reboot this thing together. In the meantime, get to a hotel and check in. Call Karen and talk it out."

"Okay," she managed.

"Promise me."

"Okay, I promise."

"Good. Now point your car toward Montgomery. I'll buy an expensive last-minute ticket and be there as soon as I can."

"Thank you, Honey," she said. "I love you."

"Me too," he said. "Now call Karen and call me back after you talk to her."

"I didn't think it would hit me this hard."

Kyle was quiet for a moment. "I can only imagine. But listen, you've come this far, and if you stop now, you'll never be able to put this behind you. I know you need to see this through. And I want you to. You need to do that for you and your brothers."

She closed her eyes and pinched the bridge of her nose. "I know. You're right."

"And us," he said. "I love you, and I'll stay on the phone as long as you need me to."

"I love you too. I better call Karen now."

"Then call back," Kyle said. "Your kids want to know if Mom's okay."

"I will."

Hannah dialed Karen's number. After three rings, she got her answering service. She left a message and suddenly felt more alone than at any time in her life. Then she remembered the card in her wallet. She fished it out and dialed.

"Joan Kellerman."

"Hello, Joan. This is Hannah MacAllister, from the nervous flight into Huntsville?"

"Yes, Hannah," Joan said. "How are you doing?"

"Not good. That's why I'm calling. Do you have a few minutes to talk?"

"Of course."

It came out of her like a flood. The meetings and sightings and feelings tasted bitter on her confessing tongue. Twice she had to stop and fight tears. When Hannah finished, the last of the emotion felt like the final sputter of a deflating balloon.

Joan said, "Wow, girl, you've been down a seriously emotional road. When you told me what you were doing on the plane, I looked you over and figured you'd see the sights, brush off your angst and move on with your life."

"Everybody thinks that," Hannah responded. "Nobody expects me to be so sensitive."

"Oh, Hannah, this goes way beyond sensitive. This is life-changing."

"So, I'm not a lost cause?"

Joan laughed. "Let me put it this way. I go into companies and evaluate the emotional culture and the management style to determine where the cancer is and why a company is floundering."

"Interesting," Hannah said.

"It is. Then I interview the people, not the management. I promise them that their session is confidential and will go no further than our discussion. You'd be amazed at how many of these folks do just what you did. I listen, give support, and in the end, that was all they needed. Then there are the others. Sensitive souls, who want nothing more than to have their work recognized, for their lives to have meaning."

Hannah closed her eyes and nodded to herself. "I know people like that."

"It kills them when their boss treats them like a fixture instead of a contributing human being," Joan said. "You'd be surprised how many of these are women suffering from the same thing you are – they eventually start to believe the shit they feel at work. They silently embrace that the sickness inside the company is as a sickness inside themselves."

"So, what do I do with it?"

"Just what your husband suggested," she said. "It's time to reject that you're in the historical cradle of all the sadness that was your family's past. Open your eyes to seeing the Alabama that is the cradle of the civil rights movement and a place of beauty and culture."

"That's a tall order," Hannah said.

"And you're a compassionate, generous, and brave woman that I believe has the depth and emotional health to find peace in all of this and take it back to her own family."

"Thanks for the vote of confidence," Hannah said.

"I'm a great judge of character. That's why I'm good at what I do. When does your husband get in?"

"Sometime in the next twenty-four hours."

"Then do what he suggested. Go to a hotel, have a drink, and get a good night's sleep. Then call me back and let me know you're doing okay."

"I will."

"Wait, did you read *To Kill a Mockingbird?*"

"Of course. That book was one of the reasons I became a writer. I love Harper Lee."

"Then I suggest you take a detour and head for Monroeville," Joan said. "It's not far from where you are and will do you good."

"Why there?"

"That's where Lee lived. The town she based the book on. Truman Capote grew up there with her. So maybe if you take the time to see Alabama, really see some of it, you'll have a change of heart."

"Thanks, Joan."

"My pleasure and I mean that. Call me back if you need to."

Hannah looked out the windshield. Nothing had changed but her attitude. But the drab landscape looked less forlorn.

She made a slow U-turn and pointed herself Southwest. She tapped the navigation and typed in *Monroeville*. It began the directions to the mythical place where Scout and Jem and Atticus Finch lived a summer of revelations and heartache.

After heading south on Highway 43, she connected with 84 East. Hannah took in the green and crossed *Majors Creek*. She had to chuckle to herself. In California, that body of water would be considered a river. Since the talk with Joan, her attitude was indeed better. Soon she rolled into the small village of legend.

Monroeville emerged from the rural countryside like a movie set. Surrounded by vast stretches of green, it embraced the pure essence of exactly what it is, a small working town of genuine God-fearing people. Eateries with the names like *'The Huddle House'* and *'Dave's Catfish Shack'* called to come in and have a hearty meal. Other storefronts offered everything from hardware to real estate. She imagined each serving a community of folks that she guessed went back generations.

Life by sufficient supply and demand.

Two-story brick buildings wore shutters. The town courthouse was too much to resist. Hannah remembered Hollywood took laborious efforts to replicate the courthouse's interior for the movie adaptation of Lee's classic novel. She parked and strolled up to the building. A plaque read that it was restored to its 1930 appearance and was indeed the courtroom that inspired Harper Lee's fictional courtroom settings in *To Kill a Mockingbird*.

Hannah pushed through the door and instantly felt a wave of wonder. The grandeur and craftsmanship were incredible. Curved railings stood like sentinels, and the upper observation platform called to her. The polished floor gleamed in the late afternoon sun. Hannah allowed herself to feel the quiet grace of the place.

Grace? Her inner voice whispered. *Was there grace here when innocent blacks were lied about, testified against, and found guilty because of their color?*

"Oh, shut the hell up."

Listen, this place is not quiet. The air is filled with the cries of families torn apart by injustice and lives destroyed by ignorance. Reflective nostalgia is the great salve tourist use to close the wound of the reality of the past.

Hannah shook off the sudden invasion, but the voice persisted.

If you want the truth, find the pauper's graves. Put a flower on the mound of a forgotten soul murdered by a lynch mob or shot by corrupt police. Take comfort in recognizing the tragedy of this place.

"I won't listen," Hannah said.

Remember the story you so romantically remember. White trash lied and took the life of a good black man.

"And a good white man tried to save that man's life," she argued out loud.

And he lost.

Joan's words came back to her. *Maybe if you take the time to see Alabama, really see some of it, you'll have a change of heart.*

Hannah closed her eyes and thought, *see what is front of you, not what you've heard or were taught. Allow yourself to see the beauty, even in a place that held so much pain. All places of worship or history have tumultuous pasts. Spilled blood does not stain the time and importance of today.*

She opened her eyes and admired the deep browns and marble white of this historical site. Hanna went upstairs and took a seat in the observation platform. From there, she looked down on the gallery, the judge's seat, and the jury box. Yes, honest men faced false charges and unfair sentences here, but justice did prevail – even if that enlightenment came a hundred years later. Hannah allowed her heart to open to what and where she was.

When she felt at peace, she descended to the main floor. Next to the witness stand, a wooden donation box sat beside the chair. Hannah pulled five dollars and dropped it into the slot.

"My donation to enlightenment," she whispered.

Back in the car, Hannah thought of Truman Capote and the hell that small boy must have endured at the hands of local misanthropes. Even Harper Lee called him a sissy. Did the town eventually embrace him for his achievements? God, she hoped so.

A marker on the side of the road answered that rhetorical question. The headline read: Truman Capote – 1924 to 1984. The inscription mentioned his family and his writing. That he often returned to the community, and it remained important to him throughout his life. A quote from his piece *'The Thanksgiving Visitor'* completed the message.

"We will always be together as long as we are remembered."

Hannah smiled. If Truman Capote could find the grace to forgive and still call this place home, why not Hannah Lee Bradley? She ruminated on this question while she drove away. Her poor mood returned. Despite the need for rationalized acceptance, the family stigma returned.

It's Alabama...

"Jesus, Dad," she asked of the road, "Was it salvation to escape from here, or just a change of venue? Was Detroit so wonderful that the South deserved to be forgotten? If Capote could forgive, why couldn't you?"

Her answer came as a call back from Karen.

"Hello there," Hannah said.

"Hello, back. Where are you, and how are you doing?"

"Honestly?"

"That's a good way to start," Karen teased.

"Well, it's like I jumped into To Kill a Mockingbird, and I'm in Maycomb and chasing the ghost of Atticus Finch. I feel like I found him in the old courthouse still weeping over the loss of Tom Robinson. It made me want to go looking for Boo Radley's house, but I was afraid I'd find they'd replaced it with a gas station."

Karen softly said, "Hannah, you sound sadly cynical."

"I am," she said. "I'm also humorously angry, resentfully hopeful, and wondering if my father was ever happy."

"How can I help?"

Hannah smiled. "How much time do you have?"

"About an hour. That enough?"

"Perfect," Hannah said. That was his estimated travel time to Montgomery.

DETROIT – 1952 ~

Little Otis Bradley woke from a dream where the dark sky suddenly cracked with lightning. Though the new house and new town was now home. The memories of the farm still plagued him. The nightmare was always the same. A ghost stood over him with eyes burning red as coals. He remembered the wood stove in Alabama, the burning red of the fierce embers. It was the only memory he had of the old life. When he sat up in bed, he heard his mother gasp. Had she also had a bad dream? He listened for another cry, but all he heard was a deep cough, then a small whimper. Otis climbed out of bed he shared with his two younger siblings and tiptoed down the hall.

"Momma?"

"Back t' bed, boy," his father said.

He scampered back but did not sleep. Tomorrow was Saturday. He did not have to go to school. Otis lay awake and listened to each labored breath his mother took. He wanted to cry out to Robert, but he lived with another family since the fight

with their father. That made Otis feel all the lonelier. His father's whispers sounded menacing from down the hall. When the sun finally promised morning, Otis heard him on the telephone.

"She can't breathe. Okay. Yep, we'll be heah."

"Daddy?" Otis called out.

"Stay in bed, boy."

"Is Momma okay?"

"I said, stay in bed."

Soon an ambulance arrived, and white-suited men climbed the stairs. Otis cried softly, surrounded by his siblings.

"Does Robby know Momma's sick?" Otis asked. "Since he don't live here, no more?"

"We'll make sure he does," Ruby promised. "It'll be fine."

"What's wrong with Momma?" Otis asked.

"We'll know after the doctor sees her. Then daddy will tell us."

Soon their father appeared in the doorway.

"They's takin' y'momma t'the hospital. I got Mrs. Jenkins comin' ova' to look afta' y'all. I's goin' with y'momma. Be back soon's I can."

He followed the men down the stairs. They wore white masks and spoke carefully. When the ambulance doors slammed, each child jumped. Then the siren screamed and rushed their mother away.

"Let's have breakfast," Ruby said with a smile. "I'll make pancakes."

"With syrup?" Otis asked. "And eggs?"

"Of course. Sunnyside up. Just like you like 'em."

Preparing the food kept Ruby from worrying about her mother. But as she cleaned up after the meal, she feared the worst. She closed her eyes to the rising steam of the wash water.

She imagined herself a movie star on a set in Hollywood, and her adoring fans waited outside to get her autograph.

And they would, one day. She was sure of it. Her angular face was so much like Joan Crawford, and her bosom rivaled Marilyn Monroe. With the right clothes and the right lipstick color, Ruby knew she could get the attention of the best agents in California. Then she could get her mother proper medical care and take her to a warm place where the snow never fell.

Her sister's voice snapped her out of her fantasy. "Ruby?"

"Yes?"

"When we going to go visit Momma?"

"Soon as daddy comes t'get us. Just like he said."

"When?"

A dark sedan rolled up outside, and she watched her father get out of the passenger seat.

"Now, I think."

She watched him climb the stairs slowly. When he opened the door, he asked, "Y'all ready?"

"Yes, daddy."

"Let's get a move on. Y'momma's waitin'. Somea' ya will ride with me in the car. Resta' ya gonna' ride with the man in the sedan. Let's get to it."

Ruby gathered them and urged them down the stairs. Sarah and Matthew held her hands until they reached solid ground and then gave her questioning looks.

"You go with Daddy, and I'll see you at the hospital."

Then she climbed into the back seat of the black sedan with Otis and Clem. The drive to the hospital was surreal, and Ruby watched ordinary life go about their business. They walked and drove and ate their lunches, and none knew that she looked into an unclear future. Ten minutes later, the driver pulled into the round driveway of Detroit Metropolitan Hospital. White and stark, the building stretched high into the afternoon sky.

The driver opened the door for her. Ruby stood with her brothers in the building's shadow. A minute later, the rest of her family joined her.

"Okay, listen up," Harley whispered. "Y'momma is real sick. They got in a place where she's with other folks sick as her. When we go in, they's gonna'' ask us to wear masks ova' our faces."

"Like Halloween?" Otis asked.

Harley shook his head gravely. "C'mon, let's go."

The place was busy with activity and human suffering. People sat waiting for treatment with bleeding heads and injured bodies. The children began whimpering, so Ruby gathered them together. When she heard her name called, she nearly broke into a run at the sight of Robert coming down the hall.

"Didn't think you'd care t'come," Harley sneered.

Robert said with a cold tone, "Hello, father."

Harley gave his son a dismissive nod.

Robert turned to the children. "Momma's very sick."

Sarah began to cry. Robert picked her up. "Shush, everything's okay."

"Robby," Ruby asked, "do you know what's wrong with Mom?"

"I just talked with the doctors. They say she has Polio."

Ruby put her hand to her mouth. "Oh, God."

"You don't know that, boy," his father barked.

"Yes, daddy, I do. They said it's affecting her lungs instead of her body. She's in the containment area, and we can only talk to her through a screen. I was just there."

A pallor fell over the entire family. Sarah hugged her brother's neck. They stood in silent emotional shock until a tall, white-coated doctor approached them.

"Mr. Bradley?"

"Yes'ir," Harley said.

"I'm Dr. Hammond. May I have a word with you in private? Away from the children."

"You can talk plain. They need t' know."

He took a deep breath. "Very well. Your wife's condition has worsened. She is in isolation on the fifth floor. I think it's best we hurry. In these cases, the symptoms can get very bad, very fast. Everybody is welcome to come."

"Lead th' way."

The family followed in a huddled mass, their feet shuffling across the tile floor like drunken people. The doctor stopped at a faded green door and pushed a button. From deep in the wall, a mechanical groan preceded the sound of movement and whining.

"Sound like we goin' in't the cotton gin," Harley said.

The door opened, and the family gawked at the deep box in the wall.

"After you," the doctor urged.

"In'ere?" Harley asked.

"It's an elevator," Robert said. "If we take it, we don't have to walk up five flights of stairs."

"I know's that, boy," Harley snapped. But his expression was of pure untrusting wonder.

The doctor pressed the button, and the box jerked and then began to rise. The children held their breaths while Robert did his best to comfort them.

"It's just like going on a ride at the fair."

"Like a Ferris wheel?" Otis asked.

"Just like that."

Dr. Hammond handed out white cloth masks to cover the mouth and nose. He tied one on himself as an example. "Please put these on, just like this."

"What's that?" Otis asked.

"To keep the germs out," Ruby said. Then she made sure each of the small children had them adequately tied. Harley refused and handed it back.

"Sir, I highly recommend you wear this on level five."

"No'sir," he said proudly. "If'n God means me t' to catch Polio, I figger this little cloth ain't gonna'' do nuthin' fer me."

"Very well. Everybody else ready?"

He got back white-faced nods. When the door opened, all they could see were sheets stretched tight over frames. From behind the undulating cloth wall, it sounded like an inhale and exhale of mechanical breath.

"This way," Hammond said softly.

Otis thought it looked like the sails of great ships that once brought people to America. He had seen pictures in books.

"What's back there?" Ruby whispered.

Her answer came when they reached the end of the room and passed a gap in the partition. What they saw was so foreign that the family struggled with sheer confusion. Lined up down a long room, machines that looked like pipes with windows. Heads protruded from one end where nurses attended to the people while the tubes hissed and coughed.

"My Lord," Ruby nearly cried.

They moved on, and the family held one another for moral and spiritual support. But nothing prepared them for the next room. Many children lay in beds, their legs and arms held in place with straps and metal frameworks. Again, nurses attended to them and offered water and soothing comfort to the ones crying from pain and fear. At the end of the ward, some children struggled to walk with crutches or sat in wheelchairs.

"I don't like it here," Clem cried.

"Hey doc," Harley said softly, "Can I git that mask now?"

He tied it on and took a slow breath through the fabric.

"How many people have Polio?" Robert asked.

"Around here, hundreds. In the country? Thousands, they say. They're working on a vaccine, but nothing so far."

"What causes it?" Ruby asked.

"A virus. That's why we wear masks."

The solemn group entered a hall and was greeted by a rotund nurse dressed all in white. Her cap positioned in a way that looked like she wore a small sail on her head.

"Nurse Langley, they're to see Elizabeth Bradley."

"I'll have her brought up, doctor." She disappeared through a door while they waited.

To the right of the door was a screen backed by cloth. Soon they heard a gasping whine on the other side of the mesh curtain.

"Hello?" a strained voice called.

"That's Mom," Robert said.

"Momma?" Ruby said in a desperate huff and rushed the wall. The rest of the family followed.

"Liz'beth?" Harley asked.

"Ye'es," she managed.

"We's all heah."

"I," she labored, "I can't say much. I'm so outta' breath. I–"

"Put her in a metal lung!" Ruby begged Dr. Hammond.

"I'm sorry," he said. "There's not enough to go around."

"But–" she begged.

"Baby?" Elizabeth called to her daughter.

"Yes, Momma?"

"It's a'right. God's with me. It's so good to hear all your voices. I–" she lost herself in a wheezing cough.

"Momma?" Otis cried.

"I'll be with God. Be good."

Then the wall went quiet.

"Momma?"

"Come with me," Hammond urged. "She needs her rest, and we need to talk."

"What'chu gonna' do fer her?" Harley demanded.

"There isn't anything we can do. Please, come with me."

The family followed Hammond through the labyrinth of suffering to an examination room. Robert watched his father stare out of the mesh-covered window, his hands on his hips. When the nurse finally showed up, Harley was furious.

"What the hell?" he demanded.

"Sir, I need you to sit with your children so we can give you an examination."

"For what?"

"We have to test you for Polio."

"Oh my God," Ruby wailed.

"I ain't takin' no Polio test!" Harley yelled.

The nurse turned suddenly cold. "If you won't sit for the test, then we will be forced to keep you overnight and see if you become symptomatic."

"Meanin' what?"

"We'll watch you and see if you start to exhibit the same symptoms as your wife."

Now the older kids sobbed while Harley yelled in frantic anger. The doctor returned and amid the fray and called for orderlies. The doctor forced Harley to sit. He screamed obscenities and threatened to sue while his family finally succumbed to hysteria and cried silent tears.

Sometime between the scuffle and the forced examination, Elizabeth Bradley took her last tortured breath and exhaled for the last time. Three hours later, the family was released and given the news of her passing. As sad as it was, there were no more tears left to shed. They left the hospital in a state of silent mortification.

That   night   Harley   nearly   drank   himself   to   death.

CHAPTER NINE ~

Kyle's flight landed in Montgomery at 10:45 A.M. He grabbed his bag and joined the others, making their way to the exit. No long airconditioned hallway greeted them. No luxury terminal filled with food courts and gift shops. Instead, they walked across the hot tarmac, then to double doors opening into the main building. At least the structure was modern, with a glass façade and elegant decorating. The motif screamed 'Southern' with colonial columns and embossed wall décor depicting cotton fields and landscapes. Glass boxes and wall displays held remnants of a bygone era. Kyle half expected Scarlett O'Hara to sweep across the polished marble floors and offer him a mint julep.

His cell sang. Hannah.

"Hello there," he said.

"How was your flight?"

"Fine. Where are you?"

"Walking toward you." Hannah wrapped her arms around him.

"Good to see you too." Kyle looked into her eyes. "You look stressed."

"Just lack of sleep," she said.

"Hannah, a kiss in the airport can't hide what's wrong. You sounded so lost."

"I was," she said. "But between talking with Joan and your help, I'm doing much better,"

"Have you had breakfast?" he asked.

She shook her head. "Only coffee."

"Then that's where we start," Kyle said.

"All they have to offer here is sandwiches, booze, and gift shop snacks," she pointed out. "But there's a restaurant at the hotel."

"Then take me there."

Twenty minutes later, they sat in the sterile hotel cafe and waited for the food to arrive. Kyle searched his wife's face and feared that just beneath the brave surface, there lurked the anxiety she shared on the phone.

"Sure you're okay?" He prodded.

"I already talked with Karen. I'm doing better."

The waitress brought steaming plates to the table. "Here you go, folks. Getcha' anythin' else?"

"We're fine," Kyle said with a smile. "This looks good."

"That's one thing about Alabama," Hannah said, "the food is great, and there's lots of it."

She was right, the eggs were delicious, and the sausage tasted better than anything he had in California. Kyle wolfed his meal and then scratched his signature on the tab.

"So," he said playfully, "you gotta' room?"

"I do. Wanna' see it?"

He followed Hannah to the elevator. Ordinary except for the Southern plantation prints on the walls. Kyle dropped his bag, sat on the edge of the bed, and patted the mattress.

"Talk to me," he said.

Hannah sat down. "Like I said, I talked with Karen, and she took me through the whole emotional overload thing. In Monroeville I realized I had enough of this. I've seen this through. Muscle Shoals, the blighted land – I'm ready to come home."

"Honey," Kyle said. "I –."

"I know. They moved to Michigan and then California, and they moved on with their lives. Case closed."

Kyle studied Hannah's mottled cheeks and red-rimmed eyes. Her good humor was as phony as the wood paneling covering the room's walls.

He whispered, "Excuse me for being so blunt, but that's bullshit, and you know it."

"Kyle, I –."

"No," he said. "Don't deny this. That's what your sister did and look where it got her."

Hannah's face flushed, and she fell into his waiting arms.

"I know," Kyle whispered.

Hannah wept until the last shred of her denial and sadness was left on the dusty field she found the day before. Then they slept in a tangle of loving limbs. When they woke up, Kyle pulled Hannah into the shower with him.

"Let's wash away the old, and let's start anew," he said.

"And then what?"

"Then, we're going to discover Montgomery."

"Yes, dear."

He led her to the bathroom.

Kyle rubbed her soapy back, and she breathed in the warm, moist air. It felt as if the dust of the empty field washed away with her fear. Her heart felt drenched in acceptance. What had Karen said? Put on a new pair of glasses and see Alabama as it is today, not through the eyes of your father's youth.

"All clean?" Kyle asked.

Hannah smiled and nodded. Kyle's arms and his gentle scolding assured her she could finish this lunatic mission.

"Let's get moving," he said.

They dried off and dressed for the day.

"Okay," Kyle said. "Let's go find out what this city has to offer."

*   *   *   *   *

Montgomery moved with the tide of humanity. Like any city, it had a business district and a tourist corridor. Hannah and Kyle stood on the corner of the town square while Kyle read the brochure.

"Before European colonization, three tribes of Native Americans inhabited Alabama. The first Europeans to visit were Hernando de Soto and his expedition in 1540. After that, the region was left alone, as the travelers saw no real value to the scrubby land and brackish coastline."

"I can imagine it didn't look like much back then," Hannah said.

Kyle continued, "The next recorded European movements in the area happened well over a century later when an expedition from Carolina went down the Alabama River in 1697. In 1717, the French built Fort Toulouse to the Northeast of the future Montgomery, serving primarily as a trading post with the

Alibamu tribe while the British gained possession of the Mississippi River's eastern territory following the French and Indian War in 1764. After that, what is now Alabama was divided between the Indian Reserve and British West Florida. The boundary line ran just North of present-day Montgomery. The Northern portion later became part of what would later become the State of Georgia, owned then by the French."

"That's quite a history lesson," Hannah teased.

"Hush, this is important stuff."

Hannah chuckled, "Will there be a test later?"

"Yes," Kyle said with mock seriousness. "Then the American Revolutionary War tore through the regions and eventually ended with the Treaty of Paris in 1783. As part of the new country's character, the French gifted Georgia's territory to the new United States. However, Spain still laid claim to the Southern border. Finally, after fierce negotiations, the Treaty of San Lorenzo gave the land North of the 31st parallel to the United States, including the Southern half of Montgomery that became part of the Mississippi Territory in 1797."

"How much more of this do I have to listen to?"

"One page," Kyle said. "You know me and facts about places."

"Go on," she urged.

"Due in large part to the cotton trade, the newly united Montgomery proliferated. Then, in October 1821, the steamboat 'Harriet' began running along the Alabama River to Mobile and opened the area to trade. That started the romance that soon became the riverboat culture."

"That little flier had all that information?"

"No, I memorized all that before I came down."

"Where to now?" Hannah asked.

"Riverfront."

The drive took them down quaint streets lined with trees. Neatly kept small homes and clusters of small businesses filled in the neighborhood. Eventually, they connected with Riverside Drive and found themselves drawn to Powder Magazine Park. They faced the water where the afternoon sun felt tolerable beneath a canopy of trees. Rusted cannons pointed toward open water. Defenses.

"The map says this is called Gun Island Chute," Kyle said.

Hannah smiled. "No prizes for guessing why it's called that."

"You're right. This was a strategic point of defense during the Civil War."

"I can see why."

Kyle said, "Reminds me of Point Loma lighthouse and the tour of the Midway aircraft carrier."

"Yes, but we were defending our country and our way of life during that time," Hannah said.

"They were trying to justify slavery and oppression."

"These people were also fighting for their way of life."

"But that doesn't make it right," Hannah said.

Kyle said. "Our ancestors decimated the Native American culture and illegally grabbed land from the Mexicans. Then we charge ahead with the manifest destiny to forge the great land we call America. These people had their own philosophy, and when the North said they had to give it up, they did what they could to protect their own beliefs."

He waited for her response.

"You think they were right?"

"Of course not," he said. "But *they* did. So much was fought for a place that could fit into the bottom third of California. Where we're standing also became the cradle of the civil rights movement and the foundation of the change we see in our lifetime."

"I know," Hannah said.

Kyle led Hannah to a picnic table. They sat down, and he leaned his elbows.

"I have to say something, and it might sting a little." Kyle took her hands. "I see the scared little girl that grew up under the lash of her father's past and the cold distance of your mother's indifference. Your sister killed herself because of it, and that darkness still surrounds you like a shadow."

She nodded and spoke. "I know, that's why I'm here. I'm just feeling overwhelmed by what I've bitten off. I'm struggling with seeing this through or jumping on the next plane home."

"Listen," he said. "You grew up having to be the strong one. Rebecca got to be Daddy's little girl, and the brothers dodged the fists. But that's all behind you now. I feel it's time you take that little girl in your arms and tell her there's nothing to be afraid of. If you don't, the rest of your life will be a shadow of this past. I know that isn't what you want."

"It's not," Hannah said. "But, I didn't expect this to be so hard."

"Listen," Kyle said. "Now that your parents are gone, it's okay for you to be happy."

Hannah nodded. "Okay."

Kyle smiled. "Now, I think we should go to where Martin Luther King marched and see this place for what it is. Not the Alabama your father tried to escape. Remember, you were born a Yankee, and this place has nothing to do with you."

Then Kyle gave her a long hug while Hannah whispered promises she knew she would keep. There was too much to lose if she didn't.

She broke the embrace. "Okay, let's go and see this bullshit through."

They drove out highway 8 and finally came to the Edmund Pettus Bridge that crossed the Alabama River into Selma. Hannah held her breath when they passed over the center bump of the iconic span. Kyle held her hand when they descended into Selma. They parked and looked back. A metal plaque stood in quiet reverence next to simple, iron fences to the left of the approach. The red brick courtyard displayed a sign that proclaimed the space to be 'Songs of Selma.'

Hand in hand, they approached the corner.

Kyle read the message.

"On Sunday, March 7, 1965, 600 people led by Hosea Williams & John Lewis began a march to Montgomery to take their quest for voting rights directly to George C. Wallace. At the Pettus Bridge, they were met by state troopers who used horses, tear gas, and Billy clubs to break up the march."

Hannah finished it.

"A march on March 9, led by Dr. Martin Luther King, Jr. met the troopers at the same place and turned around without incident. The Federal Court ruled the march was legal & with Federal protection, 4,000 began the march to Montgomery on March 21. Camping along the road, the protesters reached 25,000 in number by the time they reached the State Capitol on March 25. National news coverage of these events secured widespread support and led to the Voting Rights Act's approval on August 6, 1965."

Hannah paused and said, "They reached the capitol the day and year I was born."

Kyle said, "You were born on a day of change."

"I'll be damned."

"I'm starving," Kyle said. "Let's see if Selma has some good grub offered up."

"Something tells me they do. But, first, let's walk to the center of the bridge."

Every step was one of relief for Hannah. Finally, when they reached the top of the curve, she took in the green trees, the blue river, and the depth of the sky. The towns on either side faced each other's character instead of a shared dark history.

"Pretty cool, huh?" Kyle whispered.

"Yeah, it is. Now I want fried chicken and mashed potatoes."

"Just like a Southern gal," he teased.

Selma did not disappoint, and they left with their hearts and their stomachs full.

Back at the hotel, they ended the day with more lovemaking. As they spooned, Hannah said softly, "Thank you for saving my emotional life."

"You're very welcome," Kyle whispered back.

"Are you going to complete this mission with me as my lifeguard?"

He rolled over and smiled. "No, I'm not."

"I was afraid you'd say that."

"You know I can't. This is your discovery, and if I'm there as a distraction, it'll ruin the whole reason for what you're doing. You understand that, right?"

She put her head against Kyle's chest. "Yeah, I do. I guess I was just hoping."

"Listen," he soothed, "I'm only a phone call away."

"I know."

"Besides, you've got Joan and Karen, and you're more than halfway there."

"Wherever 'there' is," she sighed.

"You'll know when you find it. And then you'll be able to leave it here when you come home."

"Do me a favor," she said. "When you get home, will you get the banjo tuned?"

"Sure." He didn't ask why.

After dinner, they strolled the streets. Hannah pointed out a club where good, rocking country soul poured from the open door.

"Let's go in," she said. Kyle obliged.

They ordered a drink and tapped their feet to the band. The leader shook back his loose, long hair and leaned into the microphone. "We're the Water Boys. Homegrown and fully blown. Now here's one for the other locals in the house."

The recognizable opening guitar riff brought the entire crowd to their feet. Hannah smiled at the irony. When the vocal began about the big wheels turning, carryin' him home to his kin, they did indeed sing a song about the Southland. Kyle laughed out loud.

"If I saw this in a movie, I wouldn't believe the coincidence," he yelled into Hannah's ear.

"This is perfect," she said. "Wanna' dance?"

Kyle nodded, and they joined the fray. They let the song draw them in and move their feet. Hannah jerked her head toward the door when the last chord was struck. While the cheers died down, they left the noise and frivolity behind.

"Man, that was fun," Kyle said.

Hannah nodded, a genuine smile on her face.

Maybe, she thought, *I might just get through this.*

She fell asleep with hope in her heart.

In the morning, they made love once more. While Kyle packed, Hannah pulled the record and sheet music from her suitcase.

"Here," she said. "Take this home with you. I'm afraid if I carry it, it might get broken."

He held the record and nodded with a tight smile. They ate breakfast in the hotel café and said little. Hannah knew they were both imagining the next few days. When they reached the airport, she parked and walked Kyle into the terminal. He wrapped his arms around her.

"I love you," he said. "I am so proud of what you're doing. I really am.."

"I love you, too."

"Call me as often as you want," he whispered.

She kissed him hard. "I will, coach."

"So, what's next?"

"I'm going to track down Little Bear Creek," she said. "Then the second homestead. It's somewhere in Jackson. Hopefully, it isn't another dust bowl."

Kyle's eyes glistened with tears. "Promise me something."

"Anything."

"Come home to me with joy in your heart."

"Like last night?" she said. "Dancing and happy?"

"Just happy is enough. I better go."

They kissed like they meant it.

Kyle lifted her off the ground in a promise of physical and emotional strength. Kyle passed through the security check and turned to her before entering the waiting area. She gave him a wave and blew him a kiss. Kyle mouthed, '*I love you.*'

Hannah went back to the car. On her way to the hotel, she called Karen.

"Hello, Hannah. Talk to me."

"I'm doing much better. Kyle came down, and we explored the city."

"How'd it go?"

She told her everything, including Kyle's hope of her letting go of the past.

"It almost sounded like a loving ultimatum," Hannah confessed.

"I can see that," Karen said. "But it also shows strength on his part and faith in yours as well. My guess you'll prove his faith is in the right place."

"I'm sure he'll be happy with the woman that comes home."

"So, what's next?"

"Jackson. Little Bear Creek."

"Deep breaths and an open mind," Karen said. "Call if you need me."

"I will."

Hannah checked out of the hotel and set the navigation for Jackson. When her phone called out again, she expected it to be Kyle. No, her uncle.

"Hello, Uncle Matt," she said with irony. "Guess what? I'm in Alabama."

"Wow. So, you have taken leave of your senses."

"Or I'm looking for them down here."

Matt laughed heartily. "Have you found any answers?"

"One or two. Mostly I've discovered a lot of what I thought I'd find and some interesting surprises. Right now, I'm heading toward Jackson in search of where the Bradley clan hung their hats."

"Can't help you there," Matt said. "I called for another reason."

"Talk to me," Hannah urged him.

"My doctor says things are getting worse. The dialysis isn't working anymore, and, well, I guess they're telling me to get my affairs in order."

"Oh, Matt, I'm so sorry to hear about that," Hannah said. "There isn't anything they can do?"

"Just make me comfortable, I guess. Sorry to call and lay this on you. I know you're dealing with some heavy shit yourself."

"Nonsense, I'm glad we finally connected."

"I just wish I could help you more with the Alabama mysteries."

"Do you feel well enough to answer some questions?"

"Hannah, all I have is time to reminisce about the old days."

"I'm curious about something," she said. "When I was a kid, Dad got a call from Michigan with news that his father died. He didn't seem to care. After that, he never talked about it again."

"I remember that," Matt said quietly. "We were all living with our aunt. Your dad got married and lived with his mother-in-Law. Then they bought a small house, and you guys came like clockwork. Catholics, you know?"

"I know," she said.

"When your grandmother died, they sold the house and told us they were moving to California."

"Just like that?"

"I guess, yeah. I was eight, and we all took it pretty hard. Sarah took it the worst."

"Which one was Sarah?"

"My twin, the smallest of all of us. She died in 1978. Drugs and alcohol. At least that's what we heard. But, as Bradleys do, we just took a moment and went on with our screwed-up lives."

"That sounds frighteningly familiar," Hannah said.

205

"When Sarah graduated high school, she packed her belongings and moved back to Alabama. Ruby, my oldest sister, fell apart, and everybody else began scattering. It was like Robert was the glue that held us together. Our aunt gave us a roof, three hots, and a cot, but Robert was our rock. When he left, Sarah just fell apart. I tried to take Robert's place, but it wasn't the same. Then we all grew up and started going our own ways."

"Families do that," Hannah offered.

"We just scattered to the winds. I hit the road and drank myself into diabetes," Matt said. "Listen to me. I sound like a dime novel. All this doom and gloom."

"Not at all," Hannah offered. "This explains so much. I'm sorry for your health issues."

"Hey, I can only blame myself."

"Matt, would it be too much trouble to have you tell me what you remember? Anything will help, and it'll keep me from climbing back into the depths of despair. Of course, I'm only half kidding."

"I have all the time I got left."

Matt's voice took on a flat, reflective tone, and his words came in a steady stream while Hannah listened with her eyes on the dusty highway.

DETROIT – 1959 ~

Robert adjusted the collar of his shirt and combed his hair. Now eighteen years old, recently graduated with honors, he'd been accepted to the University of Michigan on a scholarship to study mathematics. But this was not a day of sharing accomplishments. Today Robert would announce he was getting married to his girlfriend, Mary. Not because they were so much in love. They were getting married because she was pregnant.

As a student of equations, he knew the mathematical probability that if you have intercourse enough, no matter how careful, the possibility of conception was inevitable. Despite this understanding, Mary loved sex, and he was a young and willing partner. Now they would join in marriage because of her lust, weakness, and probability equation. Her father dead, and an ailing mother, marriage became Mary's refuge. Otherwise, she faced a future of servitude to her mom. At his core, Robert knew the chance that she got pregnant on purpose to snag a young man with a future, was a good one.

After his mother's death, his father had begun a slow and diminishing descent into chronic alcoholism. He soon lost his job, his self-respect, his place in life. Then his sanity. When they lost the flat in Detroit and faced homelessness, his Aunt Shirley appeared like an angel of mercy.

Robert knew the story because his mother told it often.

"She was the pretty one," she said. "And there she was, in town in her best dress and lookin' pretty as a picture. A man watched her from the window of a big, shiny car. A week later, she ran off in the middle of the night and moved North. Now she lives in a big house with a maid."

Shirley's husband died young. Between his life insurance, a pension from his business, and lucrative investments, she was set for life. Shirley moved them all into her rambling three-story Victorian home on Hamilton Avenue in Flint.

"Don't worry," she promised them, "your daddy will snap out of this. But until he does, you'll live with me, and I'll take good care of you."

"All of us?" Little Sarah asked.

"All eight of you."

"But Robert lives with another family," Ruby said.

"Not anymore, I don't," he said.

"That's right. Now he lives here."

The sanctuary of Aunt Shirley's home was like heaven after being raised in poverty. Every child had their own bed with fresh sheets and down pillows. The house wrapped itself around them like Shirley's own massive bosom, and each day promised hot food, love, and hugs – whether you wanted them or not.

Usually, they did.

After a year, they saw less and less of their father. One day, Aunt Shirley called them all to the dining room table. She folded her chubby hands, and her eyes communicated genuine hurt.

"I have some bad news, children."

"Dad's dead isn't he," Robert said.

"No, your father has remarried and moved to Ohio. I spoke with him, and he said he wasn't coming back. But don't worry, this is your home, and I will always love and care for you."

"We're orphans," Ruby said.

"No," Robert said, "we're better off."

Ruby could only struggle to understand.

On that day, Robert's sense of abandonment shifted to dedication regarding the family. Try as he might be the man of the house, it eventually felt like a sore spot of injustice. With that resentment came anger, so he closed his heart and became more focused on his education. Soon he had a wall around his emotions and a head filled with numbers. Numbers were constant, deliberate, and, most of all, numbers never lied.

Four years passed, and his father never called or visited. They heard he started a new family and was still a no-account drunk.

Today, Robert's life was changing once more. When he joined his aunt in the living room, she smiled at him and patted the sofa next to her. He slowly sat down and took a deep breath.

"Now, Robert, what's so important?"

"I —" He faltered.

Shirley touched his hand. "Are you sure she's in a family way?"

He gave her a surprised look.

"I spoke with Mrs. Unger already. I didn't want to pressure you, but I know."

"I'll need your permission to get married," he said softly.

"Then after the wedding. You will continue with your education. I don't want you sidetracking yourself."

Robert gave her a weak smile.

"If I had been able to have children, I would have as soon as David and I got married," Shirley said. "But it wasn't to be. You'll see, it will all be just fine."

Two weeks later, Robert and Mary exchanged vows in St. Bartholomew's Episcopal Church surrounded by friends and family. When Father Ward introduced Mr. and Mrs. Robert Lee Bradley, the crowd cheered, and the party commenced across the street at Bailey's Bar & Grill. Robert got good and drunk and woke the following day beside his new wife.

His old life was over.

The baby came eight months later. A girl, and they named her Hannah Lee Bradley, after Robert's great grandmother. Robert finished his first year of college with a 4.0 GPA.

A month later, Mary's mother died in her sleep. They inherited the house and the little money she had saved. Soon after, Mary announced she was pregnant again. That cycle repeated itself for the next four years. By then, Robert had graduated with a bachelor's degree in education, with a major in Mathematics. That winter, the snow piled as high as the roof. When spring finally clawed its way through the frozen ground, Mary and Robert agreed a warmer climate was in order. They decided to move to California.

"I'll need to tell my family," he said.

When he did, Ruby and Otis took it the hardest.

"I promise I will stay in touch," Robert assured them.

"But I always wanted to go to California," Ruby cried. "My dreams are in California."

"You'll come to visit us. You all can come to visit us."

"Yes, children," Shirley said, "we'll all go visit them in California, I promise."

A friendly young family bought their house. Then, with cash in hand and four boys all a year apart, they loaded everybody into a 1958 Buick station wagon, said goodbye, and drove west. They arrived in San Diego on May 7th, 1965, where they rented a house four blocks from the beach. A week later, they found a small, 3-bedroom house and bought it for $14,000. In June, Robert joined the staff of a school three miles from home. He became an eighth-grade math teacher with a salary of $4,456.00 a year.

Three years later, their daughter Rebecca was born. Robert completed his master's degree and hired to teach Mathematics at San Diego State University. The family settled into their new life.

On the outside, everything looked perfect; their children excelled in school, and their future looked bright. But behind closed doors, there was a culture of brooding silence and bouts of abuse. Nevertheless, the boys became strong and independent, while Rebecca received special treatment and the closest thing to love, Robert and Mary, could muster.

After ten years, two things became evident in the otherwise confusing Bradley home. Secrets had to be kept, and Robert never reached out to those he left behind.

It was as if they had never lived.

Until the day his phone rang.

"Mary?" a voice crackled through the phone.

"Yes."

"This is Shirley, Robert's aunt."

"Oh, hello."

"Is Robert available?"

"He's at work. He'll be home after five."

"Will you have him call me? Please?"

"Of course," Mary said. "What's your number?" She wrote it down.

"How are you, Mary?" Shirley asked.

"We're fine."

"And the children?"

"Fine. All fine. We have a daughter now. Rebecca."

The line was quiet. "Can I ask a question?"

"Of course," Mary said.

"Why haven't we heard from you in the last ten years?"

Mary had to think for a moment. "Well, we've been busy, like all people. I know we talked about reaching out. I left that up to Robert. I'll make sure he calls you back."

"Please. It's important."

"Okay, then." Mary heard the car pull into the drive. "Just a minute, he just got home."

Robert came through the door, and Mary held out the phone. "Your aunt."

He took the receiver. "Hello?"

"Hello Robert, it's Shirley."

"Hello. How are you?"

"Robert, your father is dead. He died last week in Ohio. I just thought you should know."

"How did he die?" Robert asked, his voice devoid of emotion.

"He had a heart attack."

"I understand. Thank you for the call."

An awkward silent hung between them.

"Thank you for the call," Robert said.

She said, "Wait. Your brothers and sisters have missed you. I think that, with what's happened, you should reach out and reconnect. Now is a time a family needs to be together."

"I see," he said. "Well, they could have called me."

She was silent for a moment. "You never called to give us a number. I searched for you but couldn't find you. I finally hired a private investigator who tracked you down. I also want to tell you your sister Ruby is in the hospital. She had a mental breakdown, and they think she's manic-depressive."

"I see," he said with veiled irritation.

"Please, Robert. Things have not been easy for them. Your family feels like they must have done something wrong. I feel like I must have done something to drive you away. Please, talk to me and help me understand."

"I don't know what you want from me."

"Please, what happened?"

"I made a new life. You now have my number. If they want to talk, have them call me."

"I think you should call them."

"Why?"

"So much has happened in the last ten years. Weddings, children, sadness, and so much else."

"Shirley," he said calmly. "I have a life filled with the same things. My father's dead, and that's a shame, but I won't mourn him. He lost that when he left us. Now I have a family and will give my attention to them."

"My God," she hissed in his ear. "What happened to the boy I knew?"

"He grew up," Robert said. "I suggest the rest of my family does the same thing and move on with their lives. Goodbye."

He turned to Mary, who stood holding her breath.

"My father passed away."

"Oh, honey, I'm sorry."

"What's for dinner?"

She lowered her gaze. "Chicken and dumplings."

"Well, I have papers to grade. Let me know when it's time to eat. I'll be in the living room."

Around the corner from the kitchen, crouching in the hall, Hannah sat silently with her brothers.

"Who died?" Clem asked.

"Dad's dad."

"You mean, our grandpa?"

"Yeah."

"Are we supposed to be sad about that?"

"I don't know."

Their mom appeared in the hall doorway. The four boys all gave her a wide-eyed stare.

"Your dad has papers to grade. Go play, and I'll ring the bell when supper's ready."

The boys sneaked away and exited the house through the back door to disappear into the neighborhood. The bell would call them home to a somber dinner. They hoped nobody said or did anything to anger their dad and make him take off his belt.

CHAPTER TEN ~

While Hannah followed Google Maps to her next destination, her phone rang. Andrew.

"Hey there," she said. "Good to hear from you. How're you holding up?"

"I'm getting through the days. Is this a good time?"

"Sure, what's up?"

"I called your house, and Kyle told me you're in Alabama."

"I am. I'm looking for clues," Hannah said. "Doctor's orders."

"Well, I've got something," he said.

"Tell me."

"I found the courage to read Beck's journal she'd been keeping this last year," he said. "I have to say it's hard to read the pain and doubt she was struggling with."

"I can imagine," Hannah offered.

"I came across an entry, and I knew I should call."

Hannah prepared herself for anything. "Go on."

"Six months ago, she hired a private investigator to look into your family's history. She was trying to understand who she was. I guess she tracked down your great aunt in Flint, and she was still alive and living in a home. It says she was 92 years old."

"My uncle in Seattle told me the same thing," Hannah said. "He said she just passed away. Wait, let me find a place to pull over. I want you to have my undivided attention and not crash if you shock me with an emotional sledgehammer."

"Just a second."

She pulled into the parking lot of a small feed store and rummaged for something to write with.

"That's funny," he said. "Rebecca used to say things like that. She wrote that the son of their last landlord, Paul Cunningham, is 84 years old and still lives in Jackson. He still owns the property, and she wrote down his phone number."

"Wait a minute," Hannah said. "Was she seeing a therapist during this time?"

"No."

"When she was young, she used to keep diaries, and one time my brothers and I found one and read it. She was furious."

"I can understand," he said.

"What I mean is, did Becky write about things you knew weren't necessarily factual?"

Andrew cleared his throat and said, "Yeah, I found some of that."

"Well, when we read her diary, it was filled with all the terrible things that she'd experienced and how we tortured her and broke her things. She wrote about boys that broke her heart."

"That sounds like her."

"None of it was true," Hannah said. "She made it all up."

He was silent for a moment.

"I understand," he said. "But a lot of what she wrote *did* happen. Take the number. If it's bullshit, then what have you lost but a few minutes?"

"You're right." She scratched it down on a napkin. "Oh, Andrew. Did she write about if my great aunt were still alive?"

"It doesn't mention her. She wrote about your uncle the day before she–." He lost his voice.

"It's okay, Andrew. Thank you so much for this call."

"I thought it could be important," he whispered, his voice rough with emotion.

"More than you know," Hannah assured him. "Please call if you find anything else."

Andrew said, "It also said she took the banjo the last time she visited your father. She wrote that it was an important piece of her family's past."

"When was that?"

"Six months ago."

"Thank you, Andrew."

"Uh, Hannah?"

"Yes?"

"What you're doing is very courageous," Andrew said in a shaky voice. "I feel like you're doing this as much for Beck as for yourself. In a way, I'd like to think that if you can find some peace with all this, it'll help her heart and soul rest."

"Thank you. I want to think so."

She hung up and dialed home.

"Hey there," Kyle said. "How're you holding up?"

"Listen, I just talked to Andrew. Did he tell you what he had?"

"No. He called the house phone because he lost your number."

"Listen to this." She told him everything.

"Have you called?"

"I wanted to talk with you first."

"Hang up and make the call. If it's nothing, call me back. If it's something, call me after."

"Okay. Talk to you soon."

Hannah slowly dialed. She remembered once when her parents went out, she and her brothers were left to babysit Rebecca. She terrorized them until they all locked her out of the den. She sat outside the door and cussed at them for half an hour. When the car drove into the garage, she collapsed into a whimpering heap, then told a tale of cruelty and hostility.

They believed her, and her brothers took a beating the likes they'd never known before. When it ended, nothing was said. The next day at school, a teacher noticed the strap marks across Clem's lower back and marched him to the nurse's office. His wounds were examined and treated. Then the nurse gave him a sucker.

"Wait here," the nurse said.

An hour later, their Mother arrived to pick him up. She gave him a weak smile and spoke quietly with the school officials. Then she walked him to the car.

"Let's go to McDonald's," she said happily.

Clem later explained how confused he felt. Mom had never taken him to McDonald's before. She insisted he order whatever he wanted and, when they got home, she told him to go to his room.

"I sat in morbid fear of what Dad would do when he heard about this," he said.

Hannah remembered that dinner as a silent and tense ordeal. Later, they all huddled together while their parents screamed in their bedroom. Then, finally, their Mother's voice became a shriek.

"You will never embarrass me like that again!" She shrieked. "I swear, if you lay a hand on those boys again, I'll leave you!"

Their father mumbled something while Beck sobbed on Hannah's shoulder.

"What's happening?" Clem asked.

"I think Mom and Dad are going to get a divorce," Hannah whispered.

They didn't, and their father never used the belt again. Beck's lie had inadvertently helped end the physical abuse in the home, but not the inherent culture of fear. Had Rebecca accidentally solved another part of the puzzle through her manic drive? Hannah could only hope. She dialed the number, and a woman's voice sounded welcoming. "Hello? Cunningham residence?"

Hannah nearly choked in excitement. "Hello. Is Paul Cunningham there?"

"May I ask who's calling?"

"My name is Hannah Lee MacAllister. My maiden name was Bradley. I'm trying to find Paul Cunningham, who knew the son of Robert Lee Bradley. The family sharecropped in the fifties."

"You said, Bradley?"

"Yes."

"Are you the daughter of Robert Bradley?"

"Yes," Hannah said.

"Hannah, I'm Lisa Cunningham, Paul's daughter. Please hold on, and I'll get my father."

Muffled words grew close to the receiver, and then an aged but clear voice came on. "Hello?"

Her heart skipped a beat.

"Hello, Mr. Cunningham. My name is Hannah Lee MacAllister. Daughter of Robert Bradley."

"My God. That's a name I haven't heard in a very long time." There was a pause on the line. "So, you're one of Robert's children?"

"Yes, sir, I am."

"I'll be damned. How is your father?"

"Oh, I'm sorry, he just passed away."

"Oh," Paul said. "That's a shame. He was a good man and a good friend."

Hannah almost flinched. "When was the last time you talked with him, sir?"

"Let's see. That would have been 1944 or 45. Your grandfather gathered the whole family up and told your grandmother to get packed. The next morning, they all left for Michigan."

Hannah was shocked. "1945? What was the last thing you said to one another?"

"I think we said, 'so long.' He was worried about going North. We swore we'd be friends forever. I asked him to write, but he never did."

That sounds like my dad, Hannah thought, *always the social one.*

"Is that why you called? Because you wanted to tell me he'd passed?"

"Not exactly," Hannah said. "My father didn't keep much of a record of his life before Michigan. So I'm putting together an anthology of his early years. He taught college mathematics, and I felt my family and his friends would appreciate knowing more about his childhood."

The lie rolled off her tongue with ease. She knew the truth could destroy a fond memory.

"I see," Paul said thoughtfully. "Well, I'd be happy to tell you what I remember. Or maybe I should write it down. Unfortunately, talking on the phone might take a while. Do you live in Michigan?"

"No, sir, California. I'm in Alabama. Would it be possible for us to meet?"

"Well, of course. Welcome, yes, come see us. Let me give you our address."

Hannah wrote it down on the same napkin. "Should I come straight there or get settled into the hotel, and we can get together when we can plan out the best time."

"My dear," Paul said, "my wife would have me horsewhipped if she found out I allowed a visiting friend to stay at a hotel. So you'll stay with us. We have plenty of room."

"I don't want to put you in any imposition. If it's not a good time."

"Young lady," Paul said. "This is the South. It's not only a 'good time,' we consider it mandatory. My wife will be back from the gym in an hour. Water aerobics, she says it keeps her girlish figure."

Hannah smiled. "I'll be there in less than an hour."

"Do you need directions?"

"No, sir. I have a navigation system in the car. It'll get me there. See you soon."

"Looking forward to it," Paul said. "My wife's name is Hilly. She will be thrilled to have the company. See you soon."

Hannah called Kyle. "It's him, my dad's oldest friend."

"You're kidding?"

He could feel her energy through the phone. "And?"

"I'm on my way there now. When I asked what he and my dad said to one another before they left, Paul said my dad just said, 'so long.' He never heard from him again. Funny thing, he spoke of my father like it was yesterday."

"He and your dad must have been very close for the time they knew each other," Kyle said. "It sounds like you're almost to the end of this thing,"

"You know, it feels like I've been down here a month. I'm looking forward to coming home."

"Me too," he said. "Drive safe and call me later. I'm dying to hear how this one plays out."

Hannah lost herself in introspective contemplation as she drove. After her conversations with Joan and Karen, she felt she had a firm grasp on what she was here to do.

The back-country scrub and bridges over slow-moving water no longer felt sad or oppressive. Hannah sang along with the country-western station. Her phone rang. Clem.

"Hey," Clem sounded almost giddy. "Just talked to Kyle. He said you found the gate to hell."

"What I found is Dad's past. His real past."

"God, I hope you know what you're doing."

"Me too," Hannah said.

"You know what, big sister? I think you're the bravest person I've ever known. I mean that."

"Thanks, buddy."

"Be safe. Don't get lost in the past. We need you here."

* * * * *

The highway pushed through green upon green, with open spaces looking over the lowlands. Streams and creeks ran their courses along the road. Every farm had a pond. The road gave way to turnouts where small gas stations and family-owned markets offered whatever a traveler might need. An occasional driveway led back into the trees. Then, just when Hannah was worried she might be lost, the navigation said to turn left to Jackson. Hannah was surprised at how few miles she traveled.

Maybe it was the lack of traffic or the seemingly endless tree-lined straightaways, but when Jackson finally came into view, it felt like she'd crossed the border into another state. The outskirts became lined with properties, cookie-cutter replicas of each other. A small house on an acre or two. Each with a barn, a garden, and a boat beneath a shade tree. To stand in one yard and look into the other would have been like staring into a mirror.

Jackson suddenly appeared through the trees. Much like Monroeville, the main street offered shops and eateries. From the look of it, trade catered primarily to residents. However, if a tourist stumbled into a place of business, it indeed became a topic of conversation.

Hannah passed a mechanic's shop, where the shell of an old DeSoto perched high on a rusted pole. The name painted on the hulk's door had nearly faded away. A mile down, she made a right on the street lined with two-story houses of varying versions of the same species. Healthy lawns fell to the road. Covered porches offered shady places to relax and wave to the neighbors. Some residents trimmed roses or cut lawns. All of them glanced at her. Some waved.

"You have arrived," the electronic voice said.

"I certainly have," she said out loud. Then she called Kyle.

"Where are you now?" he asked.

"Outside Paul Cunningham's house."

SECRET of LITTLE BEAR CREEK • THOMAS K. MATTHEWS

"So, you've come to the end of this thing?"

"I think so."

"Good luck," he said. "I am so proud of you."

"Clem called and said I was brave," she said.

"You are. I love you."

"Me too. Not quite a Victorian, but it reminds me of those vintage homes in Pasadena."

"Get some pictures."

"Okay, gotta go."

A steep driveway reached back to a two-car garage with what looked like an apartment above. A front yard big enough to hold two of hers, the side yard wandered two houses wide to where a fence divided them from the nearest neighbor. Painted shutters bordered the windows. Lace curtains created a veil between the street and what must have been the parlor.

Hannah parked at the curb, then walked up the brick steps and knocked on the front door. When it opened, she hid her surprise at the couple that greeted him.

"Hello," they said happily. "You must be Hannah."

"Yes, I am." What surprised her was Paul and Hilly Cunningham were African American. "Thank you for seeing me on such short notice."

"Not at all," Hilly said. "I've spent many years hearing this man talk about the days on the farm and his and your father's exploits."

Hannah shook their hands. "So nice to meet you."

"I'm afraid you just missed our daughter," Paul said. "She lives in Mobile and visits when she can. Please, come in."

Hannah took a seat and took in the home. The decorating exquisite. Hannah realized how ordinary and straightforward their home in California was. "This is a great place."

"Thank you," Hilly said. "It was originally built in 1932. We restored it fifteen years ago."

"Beautiful."

"Something to drink?" Hilly asked.

"Please. Thank you."

When she left for the kitchen, Paul gave Hannah a knowing smile. The dark skin around his bright eyes creased like old leather. His nearly white hair gave him the look of a very wise man.

"You didn't expect us to be colored, did you?"

Hannah returned his smile. "No, I didn't."

"What a lot of people don't know is that many blacks owned land and leased to white sharecroppers. I remember when your grandfather first showed up at the farm with the family, even they were surprised."

"I meant no disrespect," Hannah said.

"None taken."

"How long were they with you?"

"One season," Paul said. "Just long enough for your daddy and me to become good friends."

"Your dad didn't mind that?"

"Heck no. We weren't like the other contract farmers. We only had a hundred acres. My father had family money, and farming was just something to keep him busy. Your granddaddy only had twenty-seven acres, hardly enough to make a living and feed a family. But, of course, he had other resources too. But I'm sure you know all that."

"No, actually, I don't."

Hilly came back with tall glasses of iced lemonade, sliced pound cake, and a glass bowl of Pistachio nuts. "Here we go. I hope this is okay."

"Perfect," Hannah said.

They made small talk until Hilly gathered up the empty glasses. "Well, I have some knitting to do."

"That means she wants to give us some privacy to talk," Paul said. "Thank you, honey."

"The guest room is made up if you choose to stay the night. Of course, you'll stay for dinner."

Paul smiled and winked at Hannah. "You noticed that wasn't a question. That was an order."

"Thank you. That sounds wonderful," she answered.

When they were alone, Paul sat back and shook his head.

"What?" Hannah asked.

"It's spooky how much you look like your daddy."

"I've been told that before."

"You know, the last time I saw him, we promised we'd always stay in touch and write when he got settled in Detroit. So before your grandfather got back from town, we sat and talked. When they left, I was sure I'd see him again. I heard from one of your uncles that your Dad came back about thirty years ago and hoped to look me up. But I never heard from him."

"He tried," Hannah said. "It was a trip they took after he heard his father was dead. He tracked down all his brothers and sisters. He visited the farms where he'd lived. I wonder why he didn't visit you?"

Paul's eyes took on a regretful expression. "He did, I think. We were not here then. My daddy was dead, and I was renting the farm to a family. They told me a couple drove up the road and stopped at the gate. They got out of their car and stared at the old bunkhouse. When they asked if they could help them with anything, the couple smiled, got back in their car, and drove away."

226

"That was probably them."

"We still own it and spend weekends there."

"I'd love to see it," Hannah said.

"I'll take you there tomorrow," Paul said. "But, when they didn't find us here, why wouldn't your father try and track me down?"

"Paul, my father was a very private and secretive man. When he got older, he became less social until he finally became a shut-in on his ranch."

"Your father lived on a ranch?"

"They moved us there when we were teenagers. We built a house, and they bought horses, and he grew a half-acre garden every year. He had summers off, and he tended that garden more than he did his children."

Paul could only laugh. "You know, the day your daddy left, he swore to me he would never be a farmer, never dig in the ground ever again and never raise livestock. Instead, he would make something of himself and live in the city and forget he ever lived in Alabama."

"He did all that," Hannah said. "Then one day, he uprooted us, moved us to a small town, and we became country folk. I wore a cowboy hat and boots to school until I went away to college."

"Hard to believe," he said. "I sometimes guess the dreams of the driven can come true. Then the details of their upbringing remind them of who they are."

"Very profound."

"I was a literature professor for thirty years. I also wrote on my summers off but never could seem to finish a book."

Hannah smiled. "Me too."

"So," Paul said and patted her leg. "Tell me more about your Dad. Who'd he become once he moved North of the Mason Dixon line?"

"Oh, well. You want the sugar-coated version or the unvarnished truth?"

"I think the truth would suffice me better."

"Okay, then."

An hour later, Hannah had said it all. Paul's face rose and fell. His eyes laughed and cried. Then, when Hannah went quiet, neither of them said a word for a full five minutes.

"You know?" Paul said. "That wasn't anything like the Robert Bradley I knew. If I hadn't known any better, I'd have sworn you were talking about your grandfather. But without the drink."

"Dad rarely had more than one drink."

"After what he went through with his father and family, I'm surprised he drank at all."

"Yes," Hannah said, "I've heard the stories."

"Then he became a part of that story."

Hilly broke the session. "Are you two done solving all the problems of the world?"

"I think so," Paul said.

"Well, I'm glad to hear that because I suddenly have the urge to get out of this house and have you take me to supper."

"Where would you like to go, dear?"

"I think Hannah would like to sample our Southern Barbecue. How does that sound?"

Hannah gave her a nod. "That sounds great."

The drive there was half the fun.

The place was classic, and the food terrific. Hannah learned Hilly was ten years younger than Paul. They met on campus, married young, and had their daughter.

"We made sure we raised her with God and a sense of challenging strength," Paul said.

Hilly added, "We always told her to do whatever she wanted, and she did. She's a psychologist and has an office in Mobile."

Paul nodded and said, "She married Henry and gave us three grandchildren. We're very proud."

"We certainly are," Hilly added.

"These are the kids," Paul said, pulling a photo from his wallet. A trilogy of girls smiling with their mother and a white father.

"Beautiful," Hannah said.

"She met Henry at school," Hilly said. "He now runs the entire system that services the underprivileged in our county."

Paul said, "A lot has changed down here since your daddy left. They just voted to take down the Confederate flag from the state-building in South Carolina after the tragedy at the church."

"I heard about that."

"That's real change," Hilly said. "When we first met Henry, we were both afraid for them because we were stuck in the old days. But they're strong people, and we couldn't be prouder."

After dinner, Hannah suddenly felt like she hadn't slept in days. She allowed Hilly to march her upstairs and put her to bed. A quick brush of her teeth and a splash of water on her face were all she could manage. When she crawled into the soft, deep bed, the warm and soothing space cradled her in peace. She was asleep in minutes.

If dreams did haunt Hannah that night, her slumber locked the ghosts out of her consciousness.

*   *   *   *   *

While she slept, Kyle lay awake. Hannah's journey was nearly over, and he prayed when she returned home that she could leave the anxiety behind.

A knock came at her door.

"Daddy?" Gwen called softly.

"Yes?"

"Can I come in?"

"Sure, sweetie. What's up?"

"I miss Mom," she said.

Kyle patted the mattress next to him. "I miss her too."

Gwen curled up next to him. "Why hasn't she called me?"

Kyle's heart missed a beat. In the week Hannah had been gone, she'd been vigilant about calling him, but it never dawned on him she wasn't talking to the kids.

"Well, she's been busy." He paused. "No, that's not a good answer. Honey, Mom's been overwhelmed with a lot of stuff. That may not make it any easier, but there's so much on her mind that she probably hasn't thought of it."

"Why is Mom's family so screwed up?" she asked. "I mean, Gramma Mary never remembered my birthday or asked me about school or acted as she cared about us all."

"I honestly don't know," Kyle said. "I often asked Mom the same question, and all she could do was shrug."

"I didn't cry when either of them died," Gwen said. "I felt so bad for feeling nothing at both their funerals."

"I know, sweetie. I felt like that too."

"Why did Aunt Becky kill herself?"

"Oh boy," he huffed. "Well, the best way to answer that is she wasn't well. You know what bipolar is, right?"

"Yeah," Gwen nodded. "We talked about that in health class."

"Then you know when she was up, she could take on the world. When she was down, she couldn't find happiness with both hands."

"But she was rich and famous. So, my friends used to beg me to introduce them to her," Gwen said. "Their parents did too."

"Life is strange," Kyle explained. "The best we can do is take it one day at a time and always remind ourselves to be happy. Mom is trying to let go of all that stuff. I hope that when she gets back, we'll be able to get on with life without the old shit."

"You said shit," Gwen laughed.

A light knock came at the door. "Dad?"

"Come on in, Evan."

He stood at the door wearing pajama bottoms and an old t-shirt. "I heard you guys talking."

Gwen said, "We're trying to figure out why Mom's parents were so screwed up."

He walked over and sat on the edge of the bed. "That's what she's trying to figure out. Right?"

"Yes, she is."

"Is she still mad at me?"

"Oh, Mom was never mad at you. It was never about you. I promise."

"I miss her," whispered.

"I know," Kyle said and gathered his kids together. "We all want Mom to come home."

CHAPTER ELEVEN ~

At first, Hannah was unsure if Paul could drive them to the old farm. But when he pulled his Cadillac onto the street, he handled himself with confidence and pride. Hilly sat in the back seat and looked happily out the window as the neighborhood went by.

"This is a great neighborhood," Hannah said.

Paul smiled. "When first settled, the town wasn't named Jackson. Only after the town was officially founded was it renamed after President Andrew Jackson. Before that, it was 'Pine Level' because the area was full of pine trees. The main business here was timber. Cotton came later. After that, it was called Republicville. No guesses why."

"How'd it fare after the Civil War?"

"Same as most. There's some rumor my family made their money when my great grandfather avoided slavery by getting involved with the traders."

"That's just a myth," Hilly said from the back seat. "They were timber cutters. His grandfather invested through a white man and held stock in Boise Pacific. Then he went North and came back after the war ended."

"She's probably right," he said.

Paul made a right turn down a two-lane highway with pitted asphalt after another stretch of green-sided road. "I think my version would make a better movie."

A stand of pines opened to a sloping valley that settled into a valley along a riverbed. Homes of all shapes and sizes sat in quiet reverence. The river divided large tracks of land. Paul pulled down a single-lane road and then up to a locked gate.

"Here we are."

He got out and opened the lock, draped the chain over the rail, and pushed the gate open. Then, back in the car, he smiled at Hannah and said, "Ready?"

"As I'll ever be."

They climbed the hill and pulled up to a heavy-roofed home with a wide porch. Steps led up to the rough-wood front door. Two rocking chairs moved with the light wind. A rusted milk can filled with dried flowers finished the scene. Hilly was the first out of the car.

"Give me the key. I want to get inside and air things out."

Wildflowers grew in clumps. Trees lined the deep gorge between the main property and a wide, flat piece of land across the way. As bow backed as an old horse, the barn sat on the knoll above the house. Once red, it was faded and chipped to a rustic gray with patches of brown. Hannah thought it looked like it might collapse at any moment, but she followed Paul to a steep drop-off into the creek bed.

"This is where the old bunkhouse was," he said. "Your daddy's family lived here. That flat spot is where they planted, and that barn was where they kept all the tools. We restored the house and rented it out. Then when I retired, we just wanted the place for family and weekends."

"It's beautiful."

"It was a great place to grow up."

Hilly called from the house, "Lunch!"

"Best be getting up there. My wife makes a mean cold beef sandwich."

They ate and sipped sodas. Paul looked at his Coke can and laughed.

"What's funny?" Hannah asked.

"Coca-Cola has a special meaning to this place."

"How's that?"

"You knew your grandfather was a moonshiner, didn't you?"

Hannah gave him a surprised expression. "No, I didn't."

"God Almighty, your daddy really didn't tell you anything. Yes, that's how your grandfather made extra cash. He sold whiskey."

"But, by then, wasn't prohibition over?"

"Yes, but it was still illegal to make and sell homemade whiskey in this county. Town was far away, and your grandpa made the finest whiskey in the valley."

"Why am I not surprised?"

"Enough about that," Hilly said. "Let's finish our lunch, and you can talk later."

"Isn't she a peach?" Paul said.

After lunch, Hilly busied herself with the house while Hannah and Paul walked the property. She marveled at how ambulatory and agile Paul was. Just before his Parkinson's diagnosis, her father could barely walk to the mailbox and back. Paul pointed out where the flood went through the property ten years ago on its high point.

"It took the old bunkhouse and everything that was in it. We came out after the storm, and all that was left was some lumber and the bare electric wire from the main house. It was a sight."

Hannah said. "We don't get a lot of rain in California, but when we do, we have all kinds of problems."

Paul suddenly said, "Hannah, you haven't talked much about your family. You said you're married and have kids. How's all that in your life?"

"Good," she said.

"Then, why're you down here?"

"You don't want to hear my sad little story."

Paul touched her arm. "Of course, I do. You came all the way from Disneyland to track down your father's past. Tell me."

So, Hannah did. From beginning to end, with the final piece of the puzzle still to be found. Paul listened for a full hour as she explained the angst she felt, and the struggle brought on by the family dynamic.

"But you love your family?"

"With all my heart."

"And you don't drink?"

"Only on occasion. But never to excess."

"Has your husband ever beaten your kids?"

"No."

"So, you have a good life." It was not a question.

"I'd like to think so. When I was almost arrested, I was more than happy to see a therapist."

Paul gave her a friendly smile and patted Hannah's shoulder. "Let's go back. Hilly will think we ran off and joined the circus. Besides, I bet she has supper almost ready."

"When my mother had dinner ready, she would ring a bell," Hannah said.

"So did your grandmother."

They walked silently back where the smell of frying chicken drew them to the house like moths to a flame. After dinner, Paul regaled Hannah with the stories of he and Robert as friends.

"We had each other's backs. More than once, your daddy rescued me from trouble. Some folks didn't like a white boy hanging with a black boy, and vice versa. Once, we stood our ground against a group of hayseeds, and when it was over, they were running for home. We were bloodied but victorious."

Hannah smiled. "Hilly, I'm sure you've heard all these before."

"More than you'll know. But hearing them, with you here, makes it all new."

Paul sat back and took in a deep breath. "Your dad was the one who stood up against the injustice. He defended the defenseless. More than once, he took the brunt of your grandfather's wrath to protect the other kids. He was a good person."

"I've heard that from his brother."

"Which one?"

"Matt."

Paul chuckled. "I remember that kid. Big as a house and only four years old."

"He had a twin sister," Hannah said. "Sarah."

Hilly looked away, and Paul frowned. Hannah sensed tension and assumed it was an ancient, lurking memory shared only between them.

"Yes," Paul said. "She was small and fragile. Your dad looked out for her the most."

Hilly said. "Time for bed. Hannah, I have you set up in the room at the end of the hall."

"I'll be right in, honey," Paul said.

She kissed him and left them alone.

"Hannah," Paul whispered, "I am so grateful for you being here. It does my heart good to know my friend made a life for himself and raised a family. I am sorry to hear he became like his father. I have a question for you."

"Ask away."

"Did you hate him for who he became?"

"I never knew him any other way. But hate him? No. I just want to understand him and how he became what he was and why he had such a hard time being happy."

"Good answer. Well, good night."

Paul hugged her and went to bed.

Hannah sat a few minutes longer to reflect on what she had learned. The wind creaked the roof, and the crickets sounded like a concert of out-of-tune violins. Finally, she went to her room and imagined the bunkhouse still sitting by the creek and what it must have been like to make a simple meal and put eight children to bed. She envisioned her grandfather tending a still somewhere on the property and her father standing up to the town's closed-minded people.

"Okay, Dad," she said quietly. "I'll see you in the morning."

Hannah fell asleep with her ears filled with the southern singing night.

* * * * *

Dawn came and the heavy music of a cowbell resounded in the blackness, followed by the commotion of a waking barn. The air felt alive, the city a distant rumor.

Hannah whispered to herself, "This is what dad woke to every morning."

She wrapped a blanket around her shoulders and went out to the porch. There she sat in the rocking chair, careful to be as quiet as she could. Something scrambled beneath the porch, and she imagined critters of all varieties up to forage an early breakfast. An owl pierced the air with a dawn salute, then lifted from a nearby tree to seek daytime slumber. She put her head back.

With a jerk, she snapped awake and wondered how long she'd dozed. Morning inched closer. What had been a shadowed world was now an impressionist painting of the sweeping valley coming alive.

"Morning," Paul called through the window.

"Good morning. I was watching the sunrise. I guess I fell back to sleep."

"I heard you snoring and didn't want to wake you. We'll have breakfast in a bit."

"Sounds great. I'm just going to keep watching the morning arrive."

"Take your time. We get started a little slow around here on Sundays. Coffee?"

"Yeah, great."

A moment later, Paul joined her on the porch with a large steaming ceramic mug. "That'll cure what ails you. Pretty great, huh?"

"Beautiful," Hannah agreed. "I thinking about taking a walk along the creek by the old house."

"I don't know, Paul. You seem pretty capable for somebody in his eighties."

"Guess there's still some spring in the old step. Hilly says breakfast in half an hour."

Hannah raised her mug. "Thanks."

"Don't mention it."

Paul went back into the house, and Hannah heard his simple statement echo in her mind.

Don't mention it.

Hadn't that been the trouble with his father's life from the start? After all, her father and his father embraced that philosophy – don't talk about it, don't whisper it – *don't even mention it.* As if there were too much darkness and too many secrets to let a single word escape the lips. Her Uncle Matt said those exact words, – *we didn't mention it.* Her uncle's song reiterated the sentiment with that same two-sentence declaration.

Beneath my urgent wanderings, my heart begs for rest. Under my desperate ponderings, there's silence in my chest.

And in that silence, the secrets were kept. The fathers' sins festered until they surfaced in loss, drink, lamentation, and sorrow.

"I have to mention it," Hannah whispered to the morning. "I have to shout it from the mountain tops. I am a Bradley, and I cannot afford secrets."

Then Hannah walked to the edge of the creek ravine and looked over the side.

What would a walk down through the last resting place of his Father's youth reveal? Perhaps an answer to all questions. She doubted it. Maybe a sense of understanding? That seemed a stretch too. Whatever waited in that streambed, Hannah prayed it would come to her in a whisper and not a flood.

"Here goes."

The climb looked precarious.

She walked down the steep embankment and picked her way through grass and saplings making a comeback after the deluge. Once under the canopy of trees, she found a large rock and sat down. A light wind rustled the trees, and the trickling water sounded like the soothing whisper of a soft lullaby. Hannah hoped that the wind offered that lullaby to her Father's family. To blow away poverty and fear gave them peace when they lay their heads on the pillow each night.

"Until dear old dad stumbled home from the bar with his banjo," she reminded herself.

She could almost hear her grandfather demanding the family to

get in line. Suddenly the trickle became roaring violence, and she felt the anger rise at the memory of the night she threatened her Father. Hannah took deep pulls through her nose and let the ragged breath out through her mouth. Karen's voice echoed in the back of her mind, and she forced herself to calm down. Then, in that serenity, she heard something.

"Hey," a voice called. Hannah opened her eyes.

A quick look around exposed nobody, so she cocked her head to listen for it again.

"Hey," the distant voice called. It sounded like it was coming from the fields.

Hannah put her coffee cup on the sand and stood to see over the embankment, but the hill was too high. So she carefully climbed out of the gorge and found herself on the edge of the fenced land.

"Hello?" She yelled. Nothing.

As she turned to climb back down to the water's edge, she caught movement from the corner of her eye. A boy stood in the field. He appeared indistinct as if seen through warped glass. He seemed to be looking toward Hannah. But, no, it felt as if he looked past her. The boy's skin copper from long hours in the sun. His cheeks speckled with brown freckles.

Over his thin shoulders, the straps of tattered overalls exposed a torso toned by hard work. Beneath his tussle of auburn hair, he gazed with eyes as blue as marbles. The boy put a callused hand to his brow as though scouting the distant horizon.

"Hey!" the boy yelled, though his voice sounded faint.

"Hello," Hannah yelled back, just in case this wasn't a hallucination.

"Ain't ya' gonna" come out here?"

Hannah laughed and shook her head. Now she was seeing things. Maybe it was the heat.

"C'mon, Paul. We ain't got all day!" The apparition shouted.

Hannah looked back toward the house and saw nothing.

"Wow, I'm finally cracking up. Karen will love hearing about this."

When she looked back to see the weedy field now bloomed with cotton, it moved in the wind like a billowy tide. The ghostly boy stood waist-deep in the bountiful crop, waiting for the harvest. His eyes were so familiar that Hannah held her breath. She knew if she could ask his name, his answer would be Robert Lee Bradley.

She blinked, and the boy and waving cotton were gone.

"My God," she said. "I'm losing my mind."

"Hannah!" a voice cried out, and she looked around for another ghost.

"Hello?"

"Hey," Paul called. "Breakfast is ready!"

"Okay, be right there!"

Somehow the fantasy of her Father's youth filled Hannah's heart with hope. She carefully stepped back down the ravine and traversed the rocks across the trickling water. Smooth stones gleamed in the morning sun, so she carefully stepped across the stream. Her shoe slipped on a flat rock, and she nearly stumbled. When she regained her footing, she spied a curved protrusion in the damp sand. A closer look revealed a pitted edge of something obviously metal. Something old.

"What have we here?"

Hannah dug the object out and brushed it off. She could only stare at the rusted iron oval, set with a worn slot and extruded ridge. Across the face, worn rough by years and flood, the word *COKE* still offered its promise of refreshment. At that moment, Hannah heard another voice, coarse and demanding.

Robert, go-'round the house and fetch a jar.

Hannah whispered, "Oh, my God."

She washed the grit from the heavy opener in the shallow stream, then dried it on her shirt. Here it was, the iron proof of her grandfather's life.

"Did we lose you, Hannah?" Paul called out.

"On my way," she yelled back.

Clutching the relic, she climbed the embankment and nearly ran to the main house.

"Sorry to make you wait," Hannah said breathlessly.

"No worries," Hilly said. "Everything's nice and hot."

"So," Paul said, "what'd you discover out there in the land of the ghosts."

Ghosts. Hannah felt a shiver.

"A spirit or two. But most of all, I found this." Hannah put the opener on the table.

Paul looked from the relic to his wife and then back to the opener. He carefully picked it up and stared intently at the aged hulk. The delicious breakfast waited while Paul sat in solemn reflection.

"Lord Almighty," he said.

"Paul," his wife whispered, "tell me what you're thinking."

"I remember the day Mr. Bradley showed up with that machine. My daddy helped run the cord from the box to the porch and how your granddaddy worked for days to make that thing work. He was good with machines. When he got it working, he showed up with a wooden box of soda bottles. An hour later, we each dropped a nickel and drank a cold Coca-Cola."

"That must have been a treat," Hannah said.

Paul's wrinkled hand shook when he placed the opener gently back on the table. "Like it was yesterday. Hard to believe it didn't wash away with the rest of the past."

"It's heavy," Hannah said. "The water must have torn it free. Then it sank to the bottom."

"You said more than you know," Paul said. "The weight of that piece of metal is enough to drag all of us down below the surface. I --." But he couldn't get the rest out.

"It's okay, Paul," Hilly said. "It's just a part of the past. Let the dead lie, and let's have this breakfast I worked so hard to prepare. We can look back on this after we eat."

Paul smiled sadly. "That's my girl, always the thoughtful one. You're right. Let's eat."

Hannah watched the emotion between these two soulful people and imagined what it must have been like to be raised by parents with so much heart.

"This all looks delicious," she said.

The first bite exceeded her expectation, and they ate in comfortable silence. When the last biscuit was eaten, and the last of the coffee splashed into Hannah's cup, she and Paul went to the porch while Hilly cleaned up. They sat in the rocking chairs while Hannah waited for Paul to gather his thoughts.

"I'm sorry about my little episode at the table." Paul rubbed his hands together, and his face cracked into a wrinkled smile. "When you put that piece of metal on the table, it was like you found the past."

"Believe me. It felt unreal to me as well."

"It's more than that," Paul said. "That machine is a memory of more than what it once was. Your daddy and I circled that machine like flies around honey. It represented something; I don't know, like innocence? But it also had a cloud over it because we both knew there was a darker side to it sitting on that porch."

"Because of the moonshine?"

"There was an innocent promise in it."

"I can see that," Hannah said.

"But the bitter man in charge outweighed the sweet."

"Paul, if this too painful, I–," Hannah offered.

"Do you know why your family went North?"

"My granddad ran out on his agreement with your father. That's what I was told."

"There's truth in that, but there's more to the story."

"You don't have to tell me if it's too much."

"No, no, I've held this inside for too long. It probably burned a hole in my soul. I haven't even told the whole story to my wife."

Hannah waited.

Paul paused, then said, "Your grandfather was honest about his whiskey-making from the beginning, and my daddy allowed it. He'd partake himself some on Saturday nights. Like you pointed out, prohibition ended in 1933, so making shine wasn't illegal. Selling homemade was. Your daddy didn't want any more trouble with the law than he sometimes had, so he used a system. He was great at working out systems."

"I heard about some of that," Hannah said.

"Well, as I said, it all began innocent enough. Then it got serious, and then it went bad."

ALABAMA 1944 ~

Summer arrived like the devil's breath, and Jackson County woke early to do chores, broke after ten in the morning, and was flat out in the shade by noon. Men slept with dogs. Children lay with their feet in creeks and even pails of water. The sky became a heavy shade of blue, and even the flies lazily buzzed through the air, their wings worn out by the scorch. The only man not stopped by the weather was Harley Lee Bradley. His sweat poured like the heat itself. What kept him busy was that goddamn Coke selling machine.

"Goddamn infernal contraption," he growled as he flipped the release switch on the locking mechanism one more time. The spring released, the mechanics began to turn, and then the goddamn thing just goddamn stopped one more time.

"Weepin' Jesus on the cross," he swore.

"Harl," his wife scolded, "mind the children."

"You mind 'em. I's gotta' get this goddamn thing workin'. I paid five dollars for it."

"A sum I coulda' used to buy clothes for our own," she chastised.

"They ain't nothin' wrong with what my young' ns is wearin'. This thing's gonna' make me more than some measly five dollars."

"Too hot to fret," she said and closed the window.

When he found the machine, it was sitting behind Greely's Grocery in town, set aside as broken. While his wife shopped, he stood and stared with his finger to his chin. Then he squatted next to it and tried to look inside it. Greely watched him and laughed, chided him a bit, and finally offered to sell it.

"It don't work?" Harley said.

"Course it don't," Greely said. "That's why I'll sell it for seven dollars."

"Why do n'tcha' fix it?"

"I was gonna', but the Coca Cola man said he's bringin' me a new one and didn't want that one since they got new ones. So, I'll sell it. But if nobody takes it, I'll sell it for scrap."

"No, no," Harley said. "I bet I can fix this Goddamn thing. How's it work, anyway?"

"Well," Greely said in a know-it-all drawl. "You put a nickel in the slot, and that flicks the switch inside that turns on a motor that turns a gear that unlocks the bottle, and the customer opens the glass door and grabs the neck of the bottle. When he pulls it out, it resets the machine for the next customer."

"How many do it hold?"

"Twelve at a time."

"How ya' refill it?"

"The top unlocks, and you load the bottles into the slot. It's a complicated piece of machinery."

"You got the key?"

"Course I do."

"I'll give ya' five fer it? Since it don't work."

"Sho', five dollars."

Harley smiled. When he brought it home, it took two men to carry it. Faded red with cracked glass in the pull door, it was the size of a washtub and looked out of place on the bunkhouse porch.

"I'll get her workin'," Harley promised.

He spliced into the house wiring and ran a cord to the back of the machine. With a flourish, he dropped the coin into the slot and smiled with glee when the machine jumped to life, but then stalled and shut down. A spark test with a nail assured him he had power.

"What's wrong with this goddamn sum'bitch?"

He began tinkering with the inside mechanism.

"Yes' sir, I'll get this sum'bitch workin'."

But he hadn't accomplished that yet. Robert and the farmer's son, Paul, watched from a distance and often sniggered behind Harley's back when he pinched his thumb or cut a knuckle.

"Goddamn. Good fer nuthin' piece a' junk."

Harley worked while the rest of the farm sought shade and quiet. He carefully oiled the gearbox, flipped the switch, and noticed a worn gear housing. He poked around the depths of the motor with his finger. With a hiss, he drew back his hand and glared at the pearl of blood on the tip of his grimy finger.

"Hot damn, I know's what's wrong."

They all paid attention.

He carefully probed with the blade of his pocketknife and soon heard the thin sound of a small shard of metal drop to the bottom of the machine.

"Yeah, I gotcha' sum'bitch."

This time, when he pressed the switch, a small, catching sound followed by the gearbox's full release, and the mechanism completed its revolution.

"Hot damn, and Jesus H. Christ! I got the thing workin'! Momma, I'm going to town for case a' soda pop."

An hour later, the whole family sat in anticipation while ice dumped into the top of the machine and cooled the bottles. Then Harley presented a nickel like a man brandishing a silver dollar. He made a great show of opening the glass door, grasping the bottle's neck, and pulling it free. He slipped the tip of the cap under the opener's tooth and the bottle hissed with released carbonation. He put the bottle to his lips, took a sip.

Then he hollered, "Well, y'all, I'm open for business."

Within the hour, they drank down every bottle of the sweet drink. Mr. Cunningham, his wife, and son each had one, and when it was all over, the day felt less hot. The next day he scraped together enough money to buy two flats of bottles and stashed them in the cellar. A week later, the first man came calling.

"Evening, Bradley," Mr. Smithers said when he climbed the porch steps.

"Evenin' Zack."

"Thought I'd come by for a cold drink."

"Yer welcome to. Jest cost a nickel."

"Thanks, Harl, I'll just help m' self."

Harley smiled and nodded.

Zack Smithers dropped his nickel in the machine and a fiver into a can beside it. Then he sat down and pulled his burlap sack from his pocket. He sipped his cold Coke.

"Robert!" Harley called. "Go 'round t' the corn crib and get Mr. Smithers what he come for."

His son obeyed and returned with the sack, heavy with a Mason jar full of moonshine. Mr. Smithers enjoyed his cold soda pop, shook Harley's hand, and went on his way.

"And if'n the law asks, they's jest comin' over for a cold bottle a' Coke."

And so, it began. Harley kept his still under the house and made sure the law heard nothing of it. If they did, he could douse his fire and cover the small still with a tarp.

If anybody asked, it was all for the Cokes. Word spread, and within a month, every farmer in the surrounding area came by to have a cool soda pop. Harley was doing a service, saving the county's good folks from enduring the embarrassment and scrutiny from the God-fearing folks in town if they wanted to buy a pint. And everybody kept the well-known secret quiet.

The last thing any of them wished for was the sheriff to come asking questions. Even Farmer Cunningham turned a blind eye and took an occasional jar. Besides, the novelty of having a Coke selling machine around brought folk that also paid for his wife's jams and pies. It became a regular cottage industry.

Not that it was all sunshine and roses. Sometimes men came late in the evening, already intoxicated and wanting more. Harley dealt with that sort with a stern word and a threat to cut off the supply if they ever came and bothered his family again. And he would do just that. He kept a list of those men who disrespected the balance and refused to sell to them.

As with any trade, sometimes it brought the wrong customer. Elmer Yarrow was one such man. He was always dirty, hair a mess, and clothes worn as Moses' robes. He began coming with too little money and too big a thirst.

Elmer's wife killed herself two years before, and he hadn't bathed since. More than that, his fields went unplanted, and his reputation went the way of his teeth. Blackened and repulsive. The first time he came by for a Coke, Harley gladly accepted his patronage. After that, his many nickels were followed by empty promises to pay. Harley told him not to come around without proper money.

"You sayin' I ain't got the cash?" Elmer shouted. "I gots mo' cash than allaya!"

"Then ya' come back and show me 'n I'll be happy to let ya' buy a soda," Harley shouted back.

Sometimes Elmer came with money, but most often, he came begging. Harley finally banished him from the farm, but the dusty old man would stand at the road and glared at the family working the acres.

"The man was plain crazy," Harley grumbled.

"Have some charity," his wife said.

"Like I said. Touched in the head. Nuts as a shit house rat."

One day Elmer showed up clean, shaved, and wearing his Sunday best. He walked to the bunkhouse with a five-dollar bill held high, and a smile wide as a river in flood.

"Harley, I'm here for a cool soda pop!"

"That money real?" Harley asked.

"Good as gold."

"Then you best be droppin' a nickel and getting' on yer way."

Instead, Elmer bought his drink, took a seat in a rocking chair and waved his burlap bag.

"I come fer a drink," he announced.

Harley called to his youngest daughter. "Go 'round and bring Mr. Yarrow his jar."

Sarah Bradley did what her father asked. The lid on the crib was heavy, and she struggled to hold it up while she groped for the Mason jar. The sack was a chore for her thin arms, and when she brought it to her father, he waved her toward Elmer.

With her eyes down and her hands up, she handed the heavy sack to Mr. Yarrow.

"Thank you, Miss Sarah," he said with a sick smile.

She blushed. "You' welcome."

"How old are you?"

"Four."

"Well, I'll be. I'd say you's the prettiest little thing I ever laid eyes on. That's a nice dress you got on. Did yo' momma sew that for you?"

Sarah nodded and folded her hands in front of her.

"Yarrow," Harley spat. "You got whachu' come for. Sarah, you get now."

She ran back to the house.

"She is the prettiest little thing," Elmer repeated.

"A'right, ya'll done here. Take yer bag and get goin' now. I mean it, git!"

"Jest as soon as I finish my soda pop."

"Get it done and git!"

"Dammit, Harl, I paid my five and dropped my nickel, and I'll take my time like any other payin' customer!"

Harley hid his anger and until Elmer finished his drink.

Then he grabbed the empty and dropped it into the wooden box.

"Now, git off'n my porch."

"I'll be back," Elmer said. "I'll be back for another drink and another look at that pretty girl a' yours."

Harley spun on his heel and walked up to Elmer. He looked down on the little man and fought the urge to beat him senseless. Instead, he put both his hands on the man's shoulders.

"I says this jest one time, Elmer. Yer n' longer welcome here. You got yer drink, and you got yer sack. That's it. If'n y' show yerself aroun' here agin' I'll run y' off like a cur dog."

Yarrow didn't flinch; in fact, his smile never left his lips.

"I'll be back," he said quietly.

"The hell you say," Harley said.

"Or I'll jest have to have a little talk with the sheriff 'bout what you sellin' here."

"Listen to me. I –."

"No, I'll see you agin'."

Then Elmer slowly walked down the road in his best suit, whistling a tune as he went.

"Damn that cracked mind sum'bitch." Harley growled. "Sarah?"

She came back onto the porch. "Uh-huh?"

"Don't y' ever talk t' that man agin'. Understand me, girl?"

She nodded and ran back in the house.

"Goddamn crazy sum'bitch. He ever calls me out and threatens me again' with the law. I'll kill that sum'bitch."

Harley went back to his still.

Sarah went back to playing with her brother Matthew while Elmer Yarrow returned home to drink his whiskey. He soon lost himself in a drunken fog while thinking of the pretty little girl's vision in the polka dot dress.

That Saturday night, a crowd came to the Bradley porch. Nickels dropped, and jars were passed around. The voices got loud, and the men bragged about younger days and women they'd known. Mrs. Bradley eventually excused herself to see to her children.

"Hey," one of the boys said. "Any a'you heard 'bout all of them boys movin' north for them jobs buildin' cars?"

"Yeah," one said. "I hear a whole messa 'em is packin' up and goin' to work for General Motors. Good pay and steady work."

Another man said. "Good jobs waitin'. Start all over again in a better place."

"Ah," Harley sneered. "Gotta' cousin up and took one a' them jobs. He write and says he can git me one too. Keeps pesterin' me to quit farmin' and come up north."

"Ain'tcha' gonna'' take him up on it?"

"And give up this?" He raised his jar and got laughs all around. "Besides, workin' steady inside all day, I'd go nuts."

"You's already nuts."

That brought more laughs.

What Harley didn't say was Elizabeth often asked if he would consider the offer. He always brushed her off.

Elizabeth still prayed for a sign it was time to leave.

While his father drank and laughed, Robert Bradley stayed out with Paul Cunningham. They sat by the equipment barn and talked about where they would go when they were older.

"Any place but here," Robert said.

"New York City," Paul said wistfully. "Or Paris, France."

"California," Robert said. "Anywhere other than Alabama."

"I heard that the depression has the whole country looking for work," Paul shared. "Daddy said we should be grateful we have land and a crop and food to eat. He says lots of folks have nothing and are starving to death."

Robert nodded. "I heard men are jumping out windows because they lost all their money. Still, we aren't rich, and my mom is always worried about if we'll ever have money."

"Your daddy has money. Playing in the honky-tonk and selling whiskey, he should have enough to get you by. That's what my mom says."

Robert snorted. "My mom says my daddy has holes in his pockets he don't know about. He can't save a dime to put in the church basket on Sunday morning."

"What's he spend it on?"

Robert shrugged.

The bushes rustled near the edge of the creek ravine, and Paul nudged Robert. They both peered to see what was making noise.

Robert whispered, "There's somebody standing by that tree."

"Where?" Robert pointed. "Oh, yeah."

"Looks like a man wearing a hat."

A match flared to light a cigarette. In the quick light, they both recognized Elmer Yarrow.

"Why's he hiding like that?"

Robert shook his head.

"Daddy ran him off. Said if he came back, he'd beat him silly."

"He's a scary man. He used to be a good farmer, and then his wife got sick and died. After that, he just got lost. He used to come by and see my folks. But when he got bad, he smelled like

SECRET of LITTLE BEAR CREEK • THOMAS K. MATTHEWS

an outhouse, so my Daddy had to turn him away. Everybody says he's crazy."

"Well, he's old," Robert offered as an explanation.

"No, he ain't. He's no older than my folks."

"That can't be. He's got white hair and a face like an old glove."

Paul nodded. "Mom says, that's what whiskey and heartbreak will do to a man."

"Hey, Mr. Yarrow," Robert suddenly yelled and waved his hand.

Instead of returning the hello, the dark figure jerked wildly, jumped back, and noisily made his retreat from the property. The porch went silent, and the still night carried the footsteps of the retreating man as he stumbled away.

"Wassat?" Harley yelled from the porch. "That sum'bitch tryin' t' sneak up on us?"

"He just ran off," Robert called back.

"I told that sum'bitch he wasn't welcome!"

"Calm yo' self, Harl," somebody said. "Ain't no harm."

"T'hell it ain't no harm. That damn fool come 'round and threatened me w' the law! He come 'round here agin' I's gonna" take a shovel to his haid!"

"Harl, take it easy –."

But Harley was suddenly too drunk and too angry not to take it easy. He stood and began to shout, and it soon became an ugly scene. Men verbally sparred, and soon, the night was full of cussing and threats.

"That's all, dammit!" Harley screamed.

"Harl, take it easy," somebody said.

"Easy? Damn easy. Off my porch, all you sum'bitches, or I'll take a shovel to y'all."

"I better go," Paul said and scrambled to his feet. "Need me to get my daddy?"

"I'll handle it," Robert said.

"Good luck."

"Yeah, I'll need it," Robert said.

Paul disappeared into the dark.

"Godammit!" his father yelled, and Robert knew what was to come. "Lizbeth, get ya' damn butt outa' bed and get dem kids in a line! Now!"

Robert knew he had to finally stand up to his father. Face the violence to spare his family. Otherwise, this would go on forever. The shouts from the house grew louder, and a light went on at the Cunningham house. Robert went into the shack to find his brothers and sisters standing in a frightened line. Sarah sobbed and sucked her fingers while the rest looked at the floor.

"It twarn't f' me, you'd all be diggin' fer worms t'eat! If it twarn't fer me, you'd be sleepin' in a hole in' da ground'! If it twarn't fer me, you'd all be –."

"We know, Daddy!" Robert stepped in and screamed.

"You –."

Robert approached his father. "We know, Daddy. If it weren't for you, we'd all be dead."

"Ya' betta' back down, boy."

Robert threw the first punch, and his fist bounced off his father's cheek. "We know!"

"What the hell?" Harley screamed.

Robert's next punch struck his father square in the mouth.

What followed was a nightmare of voices and violence.

When the fray ended, Robert was bloody, but so was his father. His mother gathered the children together and tucked them into bed. She washed Robert's face, bandaged a gash on his knuckles, and looked into his eyes.

"That was very brave," she said.

"Momma, I –."

She put a finger to his bruised lips and kissed his forehead. "Sleep. I love you."

"Me, too," he said back.

On the porch, Harley mumbled and slurred, blurting an occasional obscenity. The night grew older, and the family slept in haunted dreams of shouts and threats. Robert woke first at first light, and his body hurt all over. He hoped his father, who slept on the porch, felt just as bad. Robert also knew when the family woke up, not a word would be spoken of the events. He unwrapped his hand and examined the deep cuts. It was worth it. Now, maybe things would be different.

He checked on the family. All slept, and his mother looked peaceful. Then he stopped. Sarah's bed was empty.

"Sarah?" he whispered.

She didn't answer. Robert looked under the bunk, then in the pantry, and finally under his mother's blankets. That woke her up.

"Robert?"

"Momma, I can't find Sarah."

"What?"

"Sarah's not in the house."

"She must have found a dark place to sleep after last night. Did you look around?"

Robert nodded. "I checked everywhere."

"Did you look outside?"

"Just Daddy. I'll look around."

He found nothing. Finally, he went to the farmer's house and quietly knocked on the door. Mr. Cunningham answered and looked in worried surprise at Robert's bruised face.

"Sorry to bother, sir."

"Robert, are you okay? Do you need help?"

"No, sir. Is my sister Sarah with you?"

Mr. Cunningham shook his head. "We worried about you folks. Could she have run away?"

Run away? Why would she run away?

"You alright, Paul? You look pale. Can my wife take a look at those bruises for you?"

"Huh?"

"Your face, son," he said. "You're beat up pretty bad. Maybe you should let Mrs. Cunningham take a look at you."

"So, Sarah isn't here?"

"No, I –."

Robert cut him off. "Thank you. I gotta' go."

When Robert returned, everybody was up, and his father frantically searched the house.

"She's not at the Cunningham's," Robert told his mother.

"Sarah, this ain't funny!" Harley shouted. "C'mon out and stop this. I'm sorry f' yellin' last night. C'mon, stop worrin' yer momma."

But she was nowhere to be found.

"Mr. Cunningham asked if she might 'a runaway."

"Runaway? " Harley growled. "Why'd she do a fool thing like that?"

"She ain't run away," Elizabeth said. "Her nightie's gone, and her shoes still by the bed. None of her other clothes is missin'."

"When was the last time we saw her?" Robert asked.

She gave Harley a sideways look.

"Last night, when w'all finally got t' bed."

"I don't believe she run away," Harley said and left the house. He began calling for his daughter, telling her to stop worrying her mother.

"Momma?" Clem called from the back of the bunks. "The backdoor's open, and there's footprints on the steps.

"What now?" Elizabeth examined the latch and then peered down at the dusty shoe prints on the back porch. They looked like old church shoes with the heels worn to the nails.

"Robert, go fetch your daddy."

"What's all this?" Harley asked and looked closely at the heel print.

"Oh, Harley," Elizabeth now sounded worried. "I gots a bad feelin' 'bout this."

Harley stepped around the footprints and then bent over while he walked down the back path. Twice he dropped to his knees and looked closely at the ground. Finally, he walked to the front of the house and down the footpath toward the road. He came back in long, serious strides. Though the morning was chilly, Harley's face was beaded sweat. His red-rimmed eyes displayed the previous night's drinking, and his hands shook like a palsied man.

"Harley?" Elizabeth pleaded.

"One minute, woman. I gotta' git steady."

He went to the back of the house while they all waited. The corncrib squeaked, Harley coughed, retched, and then went quiet. When he came back, he smelled of whiskey, but his hands were steady.

"Please, Harley," his wife said.

He thumbed his chin and then chewed his cheek. "Them look like Sunday shoe heels to you?"

Elizabeth nodded slowly.

"Worn out Sunday shoes?"

"Uh huh."

"Is Sarah's polka dot dress in'er poke?"

"I'll go see." Elizabeth returned shortly. "It's ain't here."

"Sum'bich," he whispered.

"Harley?"

"Goddamn sum'bitch. I know's who took her!"

"Took her?"

"Goddamn, bastard sum'bitch took my little girl!"

Harley ran to the tool barn and came out with an iron pry bar. "Robert, come with me. 'Lizbeth, keep the children home. No matter what, don' follow us."

"Harl," his wife begged.

"Y'hear me?" he yelled. "Don't say nothin' t' nobody. Let's go, boy."

Elizabeth called her children into the bunkhouse with the promise of biscuits and bacon.

Harley marched down the road, and Robert trotted to keep up. Not a word was mentioned about the fight the night before, though both son and father wore the scrapes and bruises of the terrible struggle. This morning it was all forgotten, though not necessarily forgiven. The dusty road took them over the hill where the overgrown yard of Elmer Yarrow came into view.

"Watch my back," Harley whispered.

Robert could only nod. Maybe it was whiskey or the anger, but Robert's father made no sign of slowing down or knocking at the door. Instead, he climbed the steps, drew his arm back, and drove the pry bar into the door jam. With a single jerk, he nearly knocked the door off the hinges.

"Elmer!" He screamed when they busted in the house.

It all happened so fast.

Robert heard Sarah crying in fear as Elmer Yarrow came stumbling from the back of the house. His eyes wild and his hands up, he babbled nonsense and tried to avoid Harley's advance.

Sarah screamed, and Robert called out to her. When Harley kicked a low table aside and advanced upon Elmer, Sarah came screaming from the backroom to her brother. Naked and weeping, she grasped him like her savior. Robert turned and saw his father's hand slam the bar with unmerciful fury into Elmer's face. Bones broke, and Elmer screamed.

Harley yelled. "Boy! Out, NOW!"

Robert ran blindly from the house, up the road, and raced his sister home to the safety of his mother's kitchen. When he burst through the door, his mother nearly tore his sister from his arms and ran to the bedroom in a state of hysterical relief. Robert stood shaking, his breathing erratic and painful.

"Robby?" Ruby asked.

"Huh?"

"Where's daddy?"

"I dunno," he said.

"Where were you?"

"Nowhere."

"Robby?"

"Huh?"

"What happened?"

"Nothin'," he said and sat down.

His mother sobbed in the bedroom while Robert took long, slow breaths while trying to forget what he'd witnessed. His siblings all sat in silence when he started to cry. Ruby and Rebecca wrapped their arms around him. His brother Matthew began weeping softly, and soon the entire family joined in. Not until the sound of their father's feet approaching the house. did they snap out of their weeping and sit in fearful anticipation.

"Your father's home," Elizabeth whispered and joined them at the table. Sarah, now dressed, clung to her mother. "No, tears now. Just be still."

But Harley did not enter the house. He tossed the pry bar under the porch, stripped off his shirt, and stuffed it in the rubbish barrel. The family watched while he worked the lever of the well pump and washed himself clean. Then he went to the back of the house, gathered up tools, junk, and all he could collect from the tool barn. Harley loaded it all in the truck and came back to the house.

"Gimme' a fresh shirt," he said in cold tone.

Elizabeth pulled one from the laundry basket and waited while the children held their collective breaths.

"I'm goin' t town. Be back in a while. Get us packed."

Elizabeth nodded and watched him drive slowly down the road.

"C'mon," she said to her children. "You heard your father. Pack your things."

*   *   *   *   *

Hannah waited while Paul collected himself. He finally shook his head and gave her a haunted grimace of a smile. "That's the story."

"Jesus," Hannah said softly.

"Hannah, the Lord Almighty had nothing to do with that."

"So, he sold everything, slipped out, and was on the train by morning?"

"That's about it. Before they left, your father came to say goodbye. When I asked what happened, he just shrugged. I'll never forget that. He stood there with his bruised face and bandaged hand, looking like he'd just been through hell. And all he could do was shrug."

"He didn't tell you anything?"

"Oh, I nagged him, and he said a bit, but not much. I knew something had happened. We said a brief goodbye, swore we'd keep in touch, and then away they went. I never heard from him again."

"Until I called," Hannah said.

Paul nodded. "All these years."

"The story got out then?" Hannah asked.

"Oh, they found him dead. Everybody knew what happened that day, but nobody told. Then, finally, they found evidence Yarrow had done this before, and the whole thing dropped. *Good riddance to bad rubbish,* they said."

"Did anybody go looking for my granddad?" Hannah asked.

Paul shook his head. "Wasn't the first time a sharecropper ran out in the middle of the night. My dad was relieved, I think. In the end, we just moved on. Though we never took on another family. It was too much for my parents, and they never wanted to deal with that again."

"Paul, I'm confused about something," Hannah said. "If they ran out and nobody knew, and nobody talked, and my father didn't tell you what he saw, how do you know so much about what happened that night?"

Paul took a full minute to answer. His eyes looked conflicted, though his face remained stoic. "I wondered if you'd catch that contradiction."

"It's kind of a big one."

"I was right when I said you were a good person. I'm right, aren't you, Hannah?"

"My husband and kids seem to think so."

"I think so too."

Hannah waited as Paul was in apparent conflict.

"Well, shit," he said. "Hannah, I know this because your aunt told me herself. Sarah is alive and lives in Mobile. I called her after we first spoke to tell her we were coming. She begged me not to tell you where she was. She made me promise."

"Why?"

"Because she said she never wanted anything to do with another Bradley ever again."

Hannah could only sigh. "It was that bad?"

"The story is her's to tell. She was only four and a half when they left, but some things are too horrible to forget. Or maybe a child has more capacity to remember, especially the worst things. Or maybe your father told her about it later in life. Who knows?"

"I understand. Do you know when Sarah came back?"

"She came back in '56. After she graduated from high school, she came to see my folks, and then I came home from college. We became friendly in 1962."

"All this time," Hannah said.

"Yes,"

"My family was sure she was dead. I remember the day my father got the call about it. I was just a kid. I remember asking him who it was, and all he said was his sister died. Later my parents talked about it, and my brothers and I overheard. I was about six, so that would have been 1971."

Paul nodded. "She didn't want to be a Bradley; that's what she said. Married a man just for his last name, then they went their separate ways. Her name is Sarah Letters now. She said she married the man because she loved that name. Funny thing, she's a writer, so it fits."

"So does this," Hannah said. "Paul, you've been a great help. And so, my journey comes to an end. Jesus, it's been two weeks, and I feel like I've been away forever."

"Did you find what you were looking for?"

"I did. Thanks."

Hilly opened the door and came out with fresh cups of steaming coffee.

"Figured you two could use some refreshment."

"Ain't she the best?" Paul said.

"Knock that off," Hilly scolded. "You know I hate that low-class, redneck slang. Hannah, can I get you anything else?"

"No, ma'am. I do believe I have everything I need."

"Not everything," Paul said and handed her a slip of paper.

"What's this?"

"Sarah's phone number. I couldn't call myself a Christian if I didn't make sure you two could see eye to eye if you chose to try."

"Call her," Hilly urged.

Hannah took a breath

"But she doesn't want to see me."

"No, Hannah," she said, "she doesn't want to relive the past. Don't bring it to her. Show her what the Bradley's have become."

All Hannah could do was nod because his emotion stole her words.

"Bless you, girl," Paul said and patted her hand. "You're so much like your father as I remember."

"Thank you for all of this," Hannah whispered. "Paul, I have another question."

"Okay."

"Do you know where I would find Little Bear Creek?"

He dropped his head a bit and put his hands on his knees. "Your daddy told me about that place. The stories he told."

"I'm sorry," Hannah said. "If I just caused you pain, I–"

"No, it's not that. When they finally found us, times had improved for the Bradley's. Your daddy told me how it was. Years later, I looked it up. I even went there."

"What was that like?"

"Little Bear Creek is now the Little Bear Municipal Reservoir. They dammed the canyon, and now what used to be the creek is under 60 feet of water."

"Ironic," Hannah said. "I came here to find the family secret of what Little Bear Creek stood for. Instead, I feel like Mohammad came to the mountain to find they bulldozed it flat to build tract houses."

"So, you won't go there?"

"What would be the point," Hannah asked.

"That it's still there."

Hannah sat in quiet contemplation and knew he was right.

The journey was not over.

CHAPTER TWELVE ~

Hannah drove the winding rural roads back to the highway. With her elbow out of the window and the radio playing a soft country song, she let the story tumble in her head. Not a catfight or conflict or worry, but like an archaeologist gently brushing away the rubble of a crumbled city, exposing the relics below. Sarah was alive and knowing that changed everything. She pulled back into the Hampton Inn parking lot and took the elevator to her room. Then she lay down on the bed and dialed home.

"Hey, traveling gal," Kyle said, "how'd it go in the heartland?"

"Oh, it was enlightening."

"That sounds cryptic."

"We visited, and I explored the old homestead. Not that there was much left of it. They fed me, and we talked into the night. In the morning, I explored, and I swear I had a vision a young version of my father in overalls."

"Were you drunk?"

"No, actually," Hannah assured him. "But it was powerful. Then Paul told me the story of how and why they finally came north."

"Are you going to tease me or tell me?"

"I hope you're sitting down."

She told him everything. When she finished, there was silence on the other end of the phone.

"Are you still there?"

Kyle sounded shocked.

"That's a serious story. And she's alive?"

"And living a stone's throw from here. There's a part of me that thinks I should leave her alone and come home with what I have."

"Honey," Kyle sweetly scolded, "that would be like driving to the Grand Canyon and not getting out of the car."

"How so?"

"Do you feel that if you left without trying to talk to her, you would have healed the wound you hoped to recover from? Coming home with a coke machine trinket and some horror stories will not end this. Trust me, if you come home now, the 'what ifs' will haunt you."

"I know you're right."

"Your dad stood and watched your grandfather kill a child molester with an iron bar. He carried that with him his entire life. So did she. Call her."

"I will."

"Sweetie, that's the scariest story I've ever heard."

Hannah closed his eyes. "It's a hell of a thing."

"And what does that tell you?"

"Now, I understand his silence and his temper."

"And now what?"

"I'll know the answer to that after talking to my aunt. Oh, and I found Little Bear Creek."

"And?"

"I'll visit it before I leave."

"Closure?" He asked.

"That depends. It's been dammed up and is now a lake. But I'll still go see it."

Kyle said, "Honey, all I can say is I am so proud of you."

"Thank you, sweetheart," she said. "It has been a hell of a journey."

Kyle said, "I have to tell you, I'm shocked by what I heard. I'm sad we didn't know and regretful for the time we could have had if we'd only know how to understand your dad."

Hannah sighed. "But what was my mom's excuse?"

"She probably knew it all. They probably promised him to keep it all a secret. I'm sure she expected to outlive him, and when he was gone, she would have finally told it all."

"I'm not sure that's true," Hannah said. "Maybe they were perfect for each other because she was just like him."

"It's too late to know. All we can do is take solace in letting go of the past."

Hannah sat up and put her feet on the floor. "You're right. I'll call her. I miss you so much. I miss the kids. When this is all over, I want us to come back and see all this through a new pair of glasses."

"That'll be fun."

They both offered their undying love. Hannah hung up. Her phone gleamed back at her. The family portrait desktop photo looked surreal. The innocence compared to the story she just heard. Kyle was right. If she left without trying to see Sarah, the journey would be incomplete. The gnawing pain of it all would be covered but not healed. She pulled the piece of paper from her pocket and slowly dialed the number. A voice answered to say she wasn't available, to leave a message, and she would call back as soon as possible.

This journey, as Kyle called it, was near the end. If her aunt didn't call her back, it would fade to black, leaving the viewer in reflective doubt of whether the story was complete.

Either way, hearing her aunt's voice made the story somewhat complete.

She hoped.

The beep came, and she opened her mouth, and words came out. But, when Hannah hung up, she couldn't remember a single thing she'd said.

"Okay," she said and decided to take a shower.

With her head beneath the pelting streams, Hannah let her mind go blank. She washed the day away. When she stepped out of the shower, her phone was ringing. Naked and still wet, she answered.

"Hello?"

"Hannah MacAllister?"

"Yes?"

"This is Sarah Letters."

Hannah nearly froze. Then she said, "Thank you for calling back. I'm –."

"I know who you are."

Hannah took a breath. "Paul Cunningham gave me your number. He said you didn't want to speak with me. But, after our visit, he thought that, well, maybe we should talk."

Silence greeted her. Hannah waited.

"I heard your father passed away."

"Yes, a month ago."

"How?"

"He had had Parkinson's and Dementia. In his last year, he was in a home and had forgotten who he was. He died peacefully in his sleep."

"And your mother?"

"She died five years ago of a heart attack."

"So, which one are you?"

"I'm daughter number one."

"So, tell me, daughter number one, what do you want from me?" Her voice held a bitter edge.

"Nothing," she said.

"Nothing?"

"I came down here to learn about the family for my own sake," Hannah said. "I was told to find the secret of Little Bear Creek. This may be more than you need to know, but my therapist kind of demanded it. I'm not sure exactly what I'd hoped to find, but I needed to know who he was to figure out who I am. If that makes any sense."

"You're in therapy," she said. It was not a question.

"Yes."

"What precipitated that?"

Hannah nearly laughed. "Well, I freaked out. Cops were called. Then I was ordered to go."

"And?"

"It's been one of the most rewarding experiences of my life, besides my marriage and kids."

"Amazing," she said. "Hannah, can I ask you a question?"

"Anything."

"Have you ever beaten your kids?"

"No."

"Are you an alcoholic?"

"No."

"Have you ever cheated on your husband?"

"No."

"Kids?"

"Two."

"Never berated them, abandon them, or put them in danger?"

Hannah took a breath. "Other than that night, no."

There was another pause. Sarah drew a breath. "You're in Jackson?"

"Yes."

"Got a pen?"

"I do."

"Here's an address. Meet me tomorrow morning at eleven," she said.

"Thank you, Sarah."

"See you soon," she said and hung up.

Hannah slowly walked back to the bathroom and finished drying herself. She brushed her hair and dressed. Then she called home.

"Hey there. Did you call her?"

"I did. Sarah will see me tomorrow at eleven."

"Oh, Hannah, I'm so happy for you."

"We'll see how it goes."

*   *   *   *   *

Like so many historic cities, Mobile is a contradiction of itself. The old town oozed nostalgic charm, and every building thrust its rustic façade onto the thronging tourists. Yet, at the same time, modernized interiors offered food, drink, and trinkets in safe and sanitized commerce bastions.

A central park with a tiered fountain, surrounded by iron benches, invites weary visitors to take a well-deserved break in the shade of a canopy of trees. In the background, towering buildings pierce the blue sky along the waterfront.

"Here we go," Hannah whispered.

If Sarah's goal were to tear her to pieces and send her packing, Hannah would be back with two hours to spare. A tarnished copper sign caught her attention, and she stepped up to read it:

This site marks the Southwestern limit of the city of Mobile in 1711. Known then as Fort Louis de la Mobile, it had been founded by the French at 27 – Mile Bluff in 1702 and moved to its present site in 1711. Mobile has been a city under six flags. The French flag was followed by the English, Spanish, American, Republic of Alabama, Confederate and again American. This is an unusual record.

"That's some history," Hannah whispered.

Her phone offered directions to the address as she walked past people of all colors. Once again, her stereotypes dissolved like sugar in the rain. The once oppressive and closed-minded streets of Alabama were busy with diversity. When she reached the address, she found a coffee shop like none she'd seen before. No hard-edged corporate logos or racks of fresh ground house blend. A blending of two different shops, the line between them blurred by art, drapery, and decor beyond funky. It redefined originality by throwing the definition out the window.

She took a tentative step inside and looked around.

"Hannah?"

She turned to meet an old and smiling woman. No more than five feet tall, her thin build was draped in a riot of color. Her face carried an odd sense of familiarity, and her wrists wore so many bracelets, Hannah wondered if her hands received blood at all. The face, so familiar.

"Sarah?"

"I am," the woman said.

"Thank you for seeing me."

Hannah extended her hand to find Sarah's grip surprisingly firm. "It is so nice to meet you, too. Sit down, dear." Sarah smiled. "I can't get over it."

"What's that?"

"When I heard your message, it was like a voice came out of the past. I had to remember to breathe. It was so spooky."

"I've been getting that a lot."

"Have you seen any old pictures of the family?"

Hannah shook her head. "My parents were never sentimental."

Sarah moved over to allow Hannah to sit beside her. "The best way to put it, we were like a litter of kittens. None of us looked alike. But, you have the family eyes. We all did. Funny thing, my twin brother and I couldn't have more different."

"Matthew," Hannah said.

"Yes, Matt. He was so big when he was born. My mother was exhausted and so glad it was over. Then, according to the story, I came as an afterthought. He was three times my size. They also told me I almost didn't make it. But, then again, that became my motto."

"I heard that story, too."

A waitress approached, and Hannah ordered a large cup of black coffee.

"Careful," Sarah warned. "They make a serious cup of coffee here. So, Paul told you a story."

Hannah nodded. "He did."

"Is it the one you were looking for?"

Hannah said, "Some of it. I guess I'm here for the truth. Or something like that."

"Truth?" Sarah said. "Sometimes, that's a hard thing to come by. Especially in this family. So, what kind of truth?"

"About my father."

"What've you learned so far?"

"Good question." Her coffee arrived, and she took a sip. The robust flavor assaulted her tongue and exploded on her taste buds like nothing she had tasted before. "Wow."

"Big corporate coffee can go to hell, right?"

"Yes. I hope they sell their beans here. My husband would love this. Anyway, to answer your question, I found out he was a good friend and a focused student. I know he hated your father and stood up to him. I know he was there the night you were rescued, and they left Michigan to get away from all that his father represented."

"Funny thing, isn't it?"

"In what way?"

Sarah smiled with ironic humor. "He packed his bags and ran away from Alabama, but had it stuck on the bottom of his shoe. I talked to Paul, and he said he told you what he remembered about that night."

"Yes, that about sums it up."

"The truth is Robert was my savior," she said. "Not just that night. When we moved North, he made sure I was safe. All through school and into high school, he had my back. He helped me get through life despite the tormentors. He protected me from my father even after he moved in with friends."

"I didn't know that."

"Then he met your mom. Your grandmother died of polio, and things fell apart. Your dad tried to keep me safe, but then he graduated from college and, just when I needed him most, he took his wife and kids and left."

"That's a tough story."

"No warning, no goodbye. They just vanished. For the first time, I was alone in that house. Naked and unprotected. Do you know how that feels?"

"I do."

"How's that?"

"When my dad moved us to California, he left us alone, too."

"But he was there."

Hannah laughed. "In body, yes. Let's put it this way; the only time we garnered his attention was when he took off his belt."

"And you hate him for that, don't you?"

"I did, once. I was never beaten, but my brothers were. Then Dad got sick, and when he died, my sister, Rebecca, killed herself."

Sarah raised an eyebrow. "Really?"

"She took a handful of pills and hanged herself the day of his funeral. That's the same day I went nuts, and everybody else went crazy. We all ended up in the pile of human atrocity, mixed up in unresolved shit, then spun in a mixer that left us all feeling lost, angry, and spiteful."

"You're a writer."

"Guilty as charged."

A silence lingered. Sarah broke the tension.

Sarah gave her a questioning expression. "So, Rebecca Bradley, the actress, was your sister?"

"The one and only," she said.

"When I heard about that on the news, I joked with some friends that she was my cousin. I thought I was being a smart ass."

"She was your Niece, actually," Hannah said.

"Can I ask a question?"

"Of course," Hannah said.

"Why did she kill herself? I heard the news and saw it in the tabloids, but nothing said why?"

"In a nutshell, she was bipolar, unhappy, and getting older. That's a tough place to be as a fading actress. But, her will made it clear she meant to do it for a while."

"I guess I can understand that," Sarah said. "I suffer from some of those same things."

Hannah nodded but said nothing.

Sarah's expression softened. "I wanted to hate you, Hannah. I had prepared this speech and wanted so badly to have you be who I hope you weren't so that I could take it all out on a Bradley after all these years."

"If that's what you need, go ahead," Hannah offered.

"No, that's the problem. You're not a Bradley."

"You don't know how happy it makes me hear you say that. Everything I'd heard about what it was to be a Bradley came with a dark and troubling label. The day I lost it with my son, I was afraid I had become what I always hated in my father."

"What did he do to deserve your wrath?" she asked.

"He was drunk and verbally attacked the family."

Sarah smiled, and her eyes moistened. "My God, you are so much of your father. It sounded like when he left Michigan, he forgot to take the best of himself with him. In recovery, we call that an emotional geographic. It generally has a poor outcome. I'm an alcoholic in recovery, by the way."

"I have several friends that are sober," Hannah offered.

"Good for you." Her tone was not sarcastic.

Hannah drank her coffee, and the silence between them was not uncomfortable, more like a break in the conversation so they could both contemplate in silence.

Hannah broke it. "Thanks so much for meeting me today."

"You're welcome. I enjoyed it, too."

"Well, I've taken enough of your time."

"But did you get what you came for?"

"I think so," Hannah said. "Thank you again."

"Bless you, girl," Sarah said. "We have a saying in recovery; *Fuck the past.*"

"What about you?" Hannah asked. "How was your life? If I can be so bold as to ask?"

"Oh, I was a lost and screwed up young woman. Funny thing, I wanted nothing to do with the Bradley men. But for twenty-five years, all I did was chase men exactly like that. The booze and the drugs and the meaner, the better. Then I cleaned up, found myself, and never looked back. Until I heard about you."

"I'm sorry to bring it all up again."

"Don't be. Maybe the advice I'm giving is for me."

"Either way, what you've shared with me has given me some perspective," Hannah said.

"Paul was right. You are a good woman."

Sarah walked Hannah to the street. When they hugged, Sarah gripped her with all her might.

"Don't judge your dad for who he became," she said. "Try and remember him for who he was before. Think of it this way;

he never faced the past and never did the work. He thought if he changed his place and stayed away from booze, that would be enough. He ran away from what he knew but could not get away from who he was."

"Thank you. I have a lot to take home and share with my brothers."

"Hannah, one last thing."

"Sure," she said.

"I asked you questions about your character. I have one about his. You say he was violent and brooding and distant. Was he that way with your sister?"

"No, he never hit us. He gave Rebecca more attention, love, and money than any of us. I was jealous of that. Maybe I should have been grateful that I got to see that side of him. I don't know."

"Did he cheat on your mom?"

"Yes."

"Okay. No more questions. Don't forget to visit the old homestead," Sarah said.

"That's what I'm looking for, Little Bear Creek. But now it's underwater."

"No, what?" Sarah's face looked shocked.

"The old sharecropper plot. I was hoping to visit it. My uncle even wrote a song about it."

"You don't know?" She asked with a smile. "I never thought about you not knowing. Jesus, my brother, really did keep it all to himself."

"Meaning what?"

"Come with me." She grabbed her hand and pulled Hannah down the street.

"Sarah, what's this about?"

"Just follow."

They moved through the foot traffic, an unlikely couple of a tall, young blonde and a short, thin, older woman. Many people passing smiled. Some said hello.

Twice Sarah called out, "This is my niece."

They stopped in front of the *Mobile Cotton Heritage Museum.* Set back from the street, it looked like a former mansion. A short walkway entered a front courtyard, and two-story white columns met the roofline above their heads.

"Impressive," Hannah said. "What does it have to with us?"

"Got a dollar?"

"Yes, why?"

"Donation. Admission is free, but the generosity of visitors supports these places."

Hannah dug in her purse and pulled out a ten. "That'll buy us some time."

Once inside the air-conditioned building, Hannah marveled at the attention to detail in everything from the marble floors to the stained-glass windows. "Amazing."

"Charles Andrew Becker once owned this house. His family helped start the cotton-growing industry in the South."

"And?"

"He took the idea started by one of the first cotton planters in Alabama, Joseph Collins, a surveyor for the Spanish government at Mobile. In 1795, Collins imported ten enslaved African Americans from Kentucky and established a cotton plantation near here. They say Collins's importation of African slaves also demonstrated the importance of slave labor for the cultivation of cotton, and wherever cotton went, slavery followed."

"How does that relate to the Bradleys?"

Sarah smiled wide.

"Follow me." They walked the hall to the next exhibition room.

More impressive than the last, it contained many paintings and old photos of Alabama's early days. She stopped in front of a large painting of a traditional Southern plantation, complete with trees covered with hanging moss and a man on a horse. Slaves worked the fields in the background. An impressive carriage adorned the foreground.

"Amazing, isn't it?" Sarah asked.

"Yes. It looks like many of the paintings in here."

"But this one is different. Read the plaque."

"The Bradley Plantation," she read out loud.

"Ring a bell?"

"What are you saying?"

"Keep reading."

Hannah recited the inscription, *"Once one of the grandest cotton plantations in Alabama, Bradley Acres was a 1000-acre farm and one of the biggest producers of cotton until the Civil War. Union soldiers burned the home and grounds on March 31st, 1865."*

"That's who we once were," Sarah said.

"You know that for a fact? That Bradley is our direct ancestor?"

"I researched it back to the beginning. Then, when I got sober, I had the same nagging need to explain so much and understand where I came from. Even back this far." Sarah jerked her thumb at the painting.

"Jesus," Hannah said.

"We were once rich cotton growers that owned slaves. In fact, we made sure the trade never ran dry."

"I had no idea," Hannah said.

"Not exactly bragging rights," Sarah joked. "So, when the Union boys chased us off and burned the land, the Bradley's wandered lost until they settled into the unfortunate line of work as dirt poor, white trash sharecroppers."

"In a way, it serves them right," Hannah offered. "I'll say it again– Jesus."

"Did I say you were a good woman?" Sarah asked.

"You did."

Sarah smiled wide and took her hand.

They spoke not another word walking back to the car. To a bystander, they looked like a good granddaughter walking her grandmother home. At the car, Hannah turned to her and smiled.

"Thank you for having the trust to see me. I can't tell you how much this has meant to me."

"Not half as much as it has done for me," Sarah responded. "Like you, I had a sore spot on my soul that never quite healed, no matter what I did. But, for the first time in my life, I have a soft spot where that old festering callus used to be."

"It's hard to say goodbye," Hannah said.

Sarah gave her a quiet smile and said, "Little Bear is in Franklin County. Northwest Alabama. Take State Highway 24 west from Russellville, then turn south on Franklin County Road 88, and it'll take you across Little Bear Creek Dam. There's a turnout with a trailhead that goes down to the water. We lived at the base of that ravine, or so I'm told."

"Thank you

"Please stay in touch," she whispered.

"I will. You too."

"Oh, I'm awful at that kind of shit," Sarah said. "You open the line, and I promise I'll do my part. You have my number."

After a moment, Hannah broke the silence.

"So, is there a shopping mall where the old estate used to be? Or a Walmart?"

"Nope, it became a prison."

"A prison?" Hannah asked. "It's still there?"

"No, but they still grow cotton there. The prison shut down when World War II broke out. It's just outside of Andalusia. One of our very own relatives did a stint there. Ain't that an ironic kick in the nuts?"

Hannah laughed. "Aunt Sarah, you're a hoot and a holler."

"Say that again?"

"What? Aunt Sarah?"

Her lip trembled, and she wrapped her arms around Hannah's waist. Sarah cried. Hannah held her and kissed the top of her head.

"Go now before I make a spectacle of myself," Sarah laughed.

"Let's get a selfie so I can show my husband."

Hannah wrapped her arms around her aunt's shoulders and snapped the picture. Then they laughed like teenagers. When they looked at the photo, Sarah leaned into her.

"We look happy," Hannah said.

"I don't just look it; I feel it."

They hugged again, and Hannah climbed into the car. Sarah waved and began her walk back to the coffee shop. Hannah dialed home.

"Hey there," Kyle said. "How'd it go?"

"Amazingly well," she said.

"Tell me."

"By the time she finished interrogating me, we were a long-lost family. She's amazingly sharp and vibrant for her age."

"What a long, strange trip this has been."

"Oh, more than you know. Listen to this." Hannah described the museum and the unknown family history. "Can you believe that?"

"Holy shit," Kyle said softly. "Did your dad know all this?"

"No idea. I doubt it."

"Now what?"

"I'm heading for the creek."

Kyle was quiet.

"You there?"

"Yeah," Kyle said. "Honey, are you feeling overwhelmed by all of this?"

"Well, it's a lot to take in. But I'm doing okay. I'll call Dr. Gregory and say it all out loud."

"Just do one thing for me," Kyle said. "When you come home, leave this all in Alabama."

"That's my plan," she said. "I'm heading for Little Bear to see the old plantation, then home."

"I miss you so much," he said.

"Me too," she said. "Hug the kids. Tell them I love them, and I'll be home in a couple of days."

It felt impossible to hang up, but the silence between them became heartbreaking.

"I better go," Hannah said. "Love you."

The line went dead. Hannah had to sit and weep for a full ten minutes before regaining herself and starting the ignition. She tapped Russellville into the navigation and followed the directions. She had no choice but to follow that artificial voice to an authentic destination.

The reservoir came into view and spread across a wide basin, once a deep valley. The road crossed the earthen dam, where a bridge supported by four concrete columns acted as a structure and spillway. Like many manufactured lakes, the flooded valley became a long and branched body of water.

An information sign explained it to have 45 miles of shoreline and was 85 feet deep in some places. The valley still supported a deep ravine off the side of the dam, where Kayakers drifted like fallen leaves on the current—the last remnant of the place where her family began.

She pulled into a parking area on the southern side where a trailhead offered access to the lake below. Hannah parked and approached a sign. It read:

Little Bear Creek Dam was completed in 1975. The Reservoir (LBCR) was impounded in 1976 as a flood control reservoir and contains 1,560 surface acres of water at full pool. It is one of four Tennessee Valley Authority (TVA) reservoirs operated by the Bear Creek Development Authority (BCDA). Before the construction of the dam, this valley offered fertile ground to many cotton growing farms, as well as wild game and water to small farms and communities. Due to the age and condition of the buildings, Little Bear was abandoned and remains at the bottom of the lake.

"Not to mention, drowning a litany of sins," Hannah whispered.

She imagined the decrepit walls and the forgotten homes moldering in the depths. Hannah thought of the forgotten possessions, and the people's bones sleeping beneath the water.

With three young girls and five strong boys
We worked those fields but found no joys
We had a had a hard life, and much was so wrong
This story is true in this sad, sad, song.

The soul of that rhyme felt like an ache in her chest. Was that the secret of Little Bear? That life held no hope, no love, no joy, and no future? But each member of that very family made something of themselves beyond the lack and pain of this flooded past.

Kyle said it perfectly. *What a long, strange trip it's been.* Literally and figuratively. Hannah stared at the rippling surface and knew there was absolutely nothing beneath that surface that had anything to do with her. Sarah was right, her father ran away from Alabama, and it followed him to California. There it lived as a secret in their home and lives.

"The secret of Little Bear Creek," she said with a small laugh.

Little Bear Creek's secret still lived in her father, and he forced them to live there with him. Hatred and bigotry and violence and lack. All of it created the secret darkness that crept around her father like a specter that haunted all of them.

Hannah said, *"We worked those fields but found no joy."*

Her father's life was joyless.

"BUT NOT MINE!" She yelled across the lake.

Hannah went back to her car and called home.

"Well?" Kyle asked.

"You know that secret of Little Bear Creek?"

"Yes," he said with careful expectation.

"I don't know what it is, and I don't care."

"What did you find?"

"Myself," she said. "I found me."

"Come home," he said.

"Almost there. All I have to do is visit Andalusia."

ANDALUSIA ~

Highway 65 ran a straight line through miles of green. Exits for places like Perdido and Poarch beckoned to leave the main road and explore the hallows and small burgs. London and Castleberry called to her, but Hannah kept her course. When she exited 65, she passed through the appropriately named town of Evergreen. Then Route 31 carried her east on what seemed an endless landscape of trees and water until Hannah dropped slightly South and into Andalusia.

"This is it?"

The intersection offered up a worse for wear JC Penny's across the highway from a newer Rite Aid. Hannah found the road dotted with various tiny stores, auto repair shops, and feed stores. Then she came to another large intersection with a national chain pizza joint, gas stations, and a CVS Pharmacy. Soon she was heading out of town, back into open land.

"What the hell?"

With a name like Andalusia, she was expecting something grander. Instead, it was an ordinary burg offering the usual fare to regular people. Hannah pulled a U-turn, headed up another street, and found herself surrounded by tire stores and auto repair shops.

"I don't think we're in Kansas anymore." She pulled into the nearest gas station and asked the kid inside to find the old prison farm.

"The what?"

"There's supposed to be an old prison farm around here. Now it's just a cotton field, I guess. Is there any place like that nearby?"

"There are some big cotton fields out by West Bypass, take that to Brooklyn Road, and it's down near Peck."

"Thanks," Hannah said, still baffled.

An old man in the back of the store said, "There's nuthin' out there anymore. The prison closed after the war. So now they grow genetically modified cotton out there."

"Thanks. But I still want to find it."

The kid asked, "Where ya' from?"

"California."

"Cool."

"Careful out there," the old man said, "They have signs up warnin' folks to stay away. That's funny as shit considerin' they had t' make it a historical landmark t'git the state to let'm grow that devil cotton."

"I'll keep an eye out," Hannah said. "How do I get there?"

She followed the vague directions. The kid was right. Houses and small enclaves lined the highway until she turned down Brooklyn Road. She passed through hallows and over the Conecuh River. An occasional farm emerged from the trees, planted with cotton and rows of tobacco. Evidence of days long gone materialized as ruins moldering in fields and overgrown with vines. Chimneys jutted like tall grave markers. Then, once again, the trees swallowed the world. Suddenly, the road turned, and Hannah found a vast, table flat valley of cotton—a veritable ocean of white.

"This looks like the place."

She drove slowly, unafraid of blocking traffic. Hannah had not seen another car since leaving town. In the distance, she spotted what looked like an observation tower and headed toward it. When she rounded another bend, a wide driveway exited the road to a state monument sign proclaiming this place an *Alabama Historical Site.* Hannah pulled into a circular parking lot, surrounded by a split rail fence. Plumes of agitated clouds hung in the stark blue sky. When Hannah exited the car, she began to sweat, the humidity nearly unbearable.

She dabbed her brow with a handkerchief. Unseen insects buzzed and clicked in the surrounding foliage while she stared across what seemed an endless sea of powder puff cotton balls. Sarah's voice whispered in her ear, reminding her that every story had a beginning, and this was hers. Hannah pushed the lock button on the key fob, and the chirp echoed over the broad valley like an alien voice. She nearly apologized to the quiet wind.

"Here we go," she whispered to herself.

A stone wall bore a sign stating *No Trespassing Beyond The Barrier, as ordered by the Alabama State Department of Agriculture.*

However, a raised walkway gave the visitor elevated access to a corner of the field and around the base of the tower. Hannah realized it was not an observation outlook but a replica of a prison farm guard tower.

"Holy shit," she whispered. Hannah crossed the lot and climbed the few steps to stare over the cotton. A light breeze lifted over the vast valley, and the stirring air cooled her brow. In that quiet, she could almost hear the voices of slaves in toil, the imprisoned men at hard labor.

Timbers creaked behind her, so she turned to stare at the wooden tower against the deep, blue sky. A sign explained it was indeed a replica of one of the four towers that once guarded the four corners of the prison farm's fenced grounds. The high platform displayed a bullhorn and a spotlight waiting in forlorn uselessness.

Then she turned back to the stretching valley and squinted for any sign of the former old plantation. What she saw was an outbuilding, a water storage tank, and a large metal barn. Hannah stopped to read a brass metal sign anchored to a stone monument.

ANDALUSIA PRISON FARM

Established in 1914, this valley housed one of the largest working penal facilities in the United States. Decommissioned at the start of World War II, the Department of Agriculture farmed the property until its sale in 1966. Before the development of the prison, this land was then known as Bradley Acres, the first successful cotton plantation built and operated so far North of the lower Alabama plains.

Bradley Acres.

As concrete as it was, it still felt impossibly surreal that this was her family's origins, as well the Bradley clan's eventual fall. Now she pondered beginnings. She knew her father's family was Scotch-Irish, her mother German Irish. Long before the first cotton seeds were planted and the South rose to glory, they all came from a different place. When she got home, Hannah would take a new look at the distant past.

The afternoon hurried toward dusk, and she had thirty miles to get back to Mobile. Suddenly she wanted a substantial meal and a good night's sleep. In the morning, Hannah would drop the rental car and fly home.

She turned back and said to the valley, "I've come to know you and have done what I needed to do. Now, I can go home with an understanding I never thought possible. I will come back under other circumstances, and I will see this place for what it has become, not what it was."

She reached over the walkway, cradled a craggy cotton boll in her hand. Then she picked it.

So much like life, she thought. *Inside we want to know the softness and wonder of life, but we become a coarse and prickly shell. We can only see the comfort of fundamental understanding when we break open and expose ourselves.*

Like the bottle opener and the tower behind her, these seeds were symbols of the place where her father fought for his dignity, endured poverty, and ran to find a life where none of that existed. But as Aunt Sarah said, he ran away from Alabama but carried it with him. Hannah walked to the car and checked her cell. No service.

"Of course not."

She looked back over the tower and walked to the fence. Hannah looked down at the boll and carefully plucked the sinewy fiber from the hard boll, then rubbed it with her hands. Five seeds separated from the fiber. She put them in her pocket.

As she pulled back onto the highway, she took one last look at the tower sitting as a hulking reminder of the valley's tumultuous history. She wondered what relative did time in the prison that was once the home of the Bradley family? When she got home, she would make it a point to research that. Why not? They had plenty of time and money.

Night fell, and, in the hollows, the road looked otherworldly. One car passed her going back, and Hannah wondered what could be down that road, other than sad memories and forgotten pasts. When she crossed back over the bridge, the lights of Andalusia looked invitingly good. Less dusty and desolate in the dark. She gave it a wave and turned back onto 84 toward Mobile.

With a sudden thump and a hiss, the car began to sway. Hannah pulled to the side of the road and inspected the damage. A piece of jagged metal protruded from her sidewall. The front driver's side tire sat in sad surrender to its fate.

"Godammit."

She popped the trunk and pulled open the spare tire compartment. Empty. As she walked back to the front of the car, a truck pulled up. The same older man from the convenience store gave her a missing toothed smile.

"Evenin'."

"Hi," Hannah said.

"Gotta' flat?"

"I do. But no spare and no cell signal."

"Lemme' look. I'm Lenny Perkins."

Lenny returned to his truck and came back with a pair of pliers. He grabbed the shard of metal and pulled it from the rubber. He held it up like a trophy fish.

"That's a serious problem."

"Now what?" she asked.

"Well, nobody's open now. You'll have to call the rental agency and tell 'em 'bout yer situation. Lock 'er up, and I'll take you to a phone."

"Just leave the car here on the side of the road?"

"Nobody'll bother it."

Hannah climbed into the old truck. Lenny pulled a U-turn and drove to a small, three-story motel. The worn sign declared it to be the "Welcome Inn."

"They'll putcha' up fer the night. Nice folks. You call yer rental people from the lobby. Jest tell 'em I bro'cha'."

"Thanks, Lenny."

"So, didja' find what ya' was lookin' fer?"

Hannah gave him a sideways glance. "I think I did."

"That's what we're all hopin' to do, I figger. We're all lookin' for some answer t' some question. Best we can hope is that we find it before we die."

"Thanks again, Lenny."

An older woman greeted Hannah at the check-in desk. "Can I help you?"

"And I need to call the car rental, but I have no cell signal," she explained. "Lenny brought me here. He said you could help me."

"No problem, young lady," she said offered her a landline phone.

"Thank you."

The rental company apologized for the inconvenience, assured her a new car would be delivered in the morning. In addition, they offered her a free upgrade.

"But I'm a hundred miles away."

"We have a shop not far from you. They'll be there by 8:00 AM."

"Thank you." Hannah hung up. "Excuse me, is there a place I can get a bite to eat?"

"Right next door. Mabel's. Best food in town."

Hannah checked into a third-floor room that faced the street. Old but clean, it offered a soft bed and a shower. She washed away the day, put her clothes back on, and went to the restaurant next door.

Mabel's menu offered some local favorites and general fare. Hannah ordered a cheeseburger with fries, a draft beer, and peach cobbler. Then she watched the murmuring patrons. Each had a softness about them. The general mood of the room was one of particular focus on the experience.

"Here ya' go," the waitress sang.

"Thanks."

"Where ya'll from?"

"California," Hannah said.

"Long way from home."

"I sure am."

"Enjoy."

The food was excellent, and the pie amazing. She finished her beer, paid the bill, and tipped handsomely. As she walked back to the motel, a tavern echoed with voices set for a good time across the street. What sounded like a local band kicked into a raucous version of Garth Brooks.

"Perfect," She said and went up to her room.

The room phone charged long-distance calls ten cents a minute. She dialed Kyle, but it went straight to voicemail. She called her daughter. She answered in a somewhat suspicious tone.

"Hello?"

"Hey baby, it's Mom."

"Oh, hi Mom, Dad was worried when we didn't hear from you? He's not here right now. Where are you?"

"I'm in Andalusia, Alabama. Where's your dad?"

"He's visiting Uncle Clem," she said. "Guess they had a get-together. His phone must be off."

"Isn't it late?" She asked.

"It's only 9:45."

"Oh yeah, I keep forgetting I'm in a later time zone."

"What's it like down there?"

"That's kind of hard to explain. Just tell Dad I'm fine and going to bed. I'll call in the morning."

"Mom, are you okay?"

"Yes, just dog tired. You have a good night. I love you, sweetie."

"Love you too, Mom."

Hannah lay on the bed and listened to the wall-mounted air conditioner drone out a two-note lullaby of spinning mechanics. Then, without a second thought, she drifted into a fitful sleep.

*   *   *   *   *

In the dream, Hannah stood outside a house so tilted she felt shocked it still stood. Even the glass in the windows had adapted to the leaning structure, taking on the strained trapezoid shape. The chimney leaked a grey wisp, and the light in the windows looked ominously feeble. The frightening thing was not the black night surrounding it, but the soft weeping she heard from inside.

Hannah climbed the creaking front steps carefully. A dull clunk reverberated off her shoe, and she watched a Mason jar roll across the wooden porch. It came to a clinking stop against other jars along the wall. The entire porch was littered with empty Mason jars, the air ripe with the smell of homemade whiskey. Her eyes watered as she stepped close and peered past the tattered lace curtains.

Inside, a small girl sat in frightened loneliness, her head down with arms wrapped around her scabbed knees. A cat brushed Hannah's leg. When she looked down, it gave her a yellow-eyed glare and ran off. When she looked back through the window, the girl was on the other side of the glass. Her eyes looked haunted, her face dirty. Hannah stepped back and bumped into a figure standing behind her.

"Ready?" a voice asked.

A hollow-eyed, older man held a Mason jar in one hand and a heavy iron bar in the other.

"Let's go get 'er."

Hannah jerked awake and gulped air. Then, she sat up, shivering.

"Holy shit."

The dream became a liquid memory, and soon, the only image was the girl's haunted face in the window. She went to the bathroom to splash cold water on her face. Then she stared at her reflection in the mirror.

Let's go get'er.

Sarah.

"Jesus," she said and switched off the light.

Hannah tried to go back to sleep, but it hid from her like a black dog on a moonless night.

"Great metaphor," she said to herself. "This place is inspiring your more creative writer persona. Aunt Sarah would be so proud."

Outside her third-story motel window, Andalusia slept beneath the neon buzz of the closed tavern sign and the flashing red lights of the traffic signal. Not a car drove by, and no voices wafted from the street. At this hour, the good Christian townsfolk were sleeping.

All twenty of them, she thought.

Sarah's voice whispered from the space between the inhale and exhale of her own breath. Could she possibly ingest and accept the stories she told of the father she thought she knew? Nothing, absolutely nothing of the character of the young Robert Bradley fit the man that raised her.

Sarah's voice whispered; *He ran away from what he knew but from who he was.*

What had she called it, an emotional geographic? Sarah's recovery jargon gave it a name, and her own experience gave it a face. *No matter where you go, there you are.*

Hannah rolled over and punched her pillow. At that moment, she wanted nothing more than to get in the car and drive to the airport and pay whatever it cost to go home tonight. Or, should she say, this morning. Had she found what she hoped? Did she finally have the answers she wanted?

Well, not exactly. Yes, she found the truth about Alabama and the family her father tried to hide from. In that discovery, many of her suspicions and fantasies were validated. But there was so much more. In the layers of poverty and ugliness, she'd discovered a sweetness and beauty Hannah never allowed herself to believe could exist *down here.*

She discovered music and hurt faith, fear, and belief - all living within the same walls.

Not just the dilapidated structure decaying in the weeds of an old farm or the rotting stumps that had once been Little Bear. She discovered the walls and roof that were the South.

Sarah was right. She had to break the chain and accept that her father never found the peace necessary to forgive. So, he could never begin again as a new and complete man.

Her mind went quiet, and the trip replayed itself like a tape on fast forward. From a cheerful laugh born in Seattle to Muscle Shoals' smiles and sounds. From the shade of an empty, one-room house where her father once lived, to the painting of the former plantation. All the melting pot of what her father was.

But not who I am, Hannah thought.

Did you find what you were lookin' for?

"Yes, I found myself. The one thing I know for sure is, I am not, and never was, from Alabama. Yes, Dad, you were who you were because this was your life, not mine."

Hannah felt her heart open. Whatever invisible strings that once tied her to her father's past were finally severed. She suddenly felt too tired to think, so Hannah let her mind embrace the stillness of exhaustion. She would return to the cotton field in the morning and say goodbye to her father's past.

DAWN ~

Morning painted the sky with a brush loaded with pinks and grays. Hannah stared out the window of the restaurant and watched the day come alive. She slept soundly and awoke to feel what her mom used to call *'bright-eyed and bushy-tailed.'* She was first into Mabel's and ordered coffee, eggs scrambled with ham, home fries, biscuits, and gravy. Delicious. Now on her third cup of coffee, she watched the day bloom like a flower.

"Can I get anything else for you?" the waitress asked.

"No, I'm just perfect."

"Now, that's good to hear." She left the check and walked away with a sway of her full hips.

Hannah dropped a twenty, checked her watch, and went to check out of the hotel. At the stroke of 8:00, a Lincoln Navigator pulled up, followed by a tow truck.

Hannah met them with a wave.

"Mrs. MacAllister?"

"That's me."

"I just need your signature here. We're so sorry for your inconvenience."

Hannah scribbled her name. "Why wasn't there a spare?"

"We remove them to make sure we don't have any liability issues. Normally we come out and fix them ourselves. We didn't hear about your situation until six this morning."

"Not a problem. By the way, where are you from?"

"Excuse me?"

"You don't sound local."

"I'm originally from Massachusetts."

"How'd you end up down here?"

"I married a Southern belle," he said. "Okay, we're all set."

The rental agent handed her the keys. "Have a nice day and drive carefully."

"Thank you."

Hannah felt at home in the ride.

The luxury SUV sat high above the road. Hannah thought of her new Tahoe waiting at home. When she turned back toward the farm, the landscape looked different. Maybe sitting higher up changed her perspective. But, no, it was more than that. She was different, and her new perspective saw this place as an observer, not somebody emotionally attached. Even the ruins looked like movie sets. When she pulled into the memorial parking lot, she gave the tower a wave and walked to the elevated walkway.

"This is not my life!" She yelled across the valley. "And it never will be!"

No answer came back over the landscape.

"And now I'm going home!"

Hannah's drive back to the hotel was without incident. She checked out and called home.

Kyle answered on the first ring. "There you are. I got your message. I was worried about you."

"Sorry, I had no signal," she said. "I'm on my way to the airport. I had quite an adventure."

"Tell me when you get home. Right now, I just want to talk about happy things and all the crazy plans I've been making for our new lives with money."

"That's exactly what I need to hear right now."

"Now talk to me," he urged.

"I love you more than life itself, and I can't wait to get home."

"We feel the same way. So here are the kids."

They talked for the hour it took Hannah to reach the rental agency.

"Okay, gotta go now," Hannah said in a Southern drawl.

"That's the last time you do that," Kyle said.

"I promise. Love you guys."

"Love you too," they all chanted.

She dropped the Navigator and caught the shuttle to her terminal. Security was a breeze, and when they called her flight, Hannah settled into her business class seat. As soon as they were in the air, she fell asleep. Her layover in Salt Lake City was short, and when they dropped into San Diego, she thought she had never seen anything more beautiful. Kyle met her at the curb. When she climbed into the passenger seat, she kissed him hard.

"Welcome home," he said.

"Happy to be here. Where are the kids?"

"Planning a welcome home celebration." He pulled from the terminal and drove wildly through the shifting traffic. Hannah marveled at how dry and stark Southern California looked compared to the green and wet terrain she traveled over the last two weeks.

"You're awfully quiet," Kyle said.

"I'm just happy to be home."

The kids greeted her with hugs and questions. Then, Kyle surprised her with a dinner of fried chicken, mashed potatoes, black-eyed peas, and cornbread in a gesture of playful irony.

"We wanted to make you feel at home," he said in a terrible Southern drawl.

The meal was delicious, and she regaled the family with stories of what she saw and whom she met. When she finished, Hannah felt a weight of exhaustion like she'd never known. Kyle led her to the bedroom, where they made slow and tender love.

She wrapped herself around him, breathing in his familiar aroma. Then she fell into a deep sleep. In the depths of that unconscious place, the dreams of what she did not tell her family writhed in demanding torment. But Hannah's slumber was too profound for the terrors to reach her. In the morning, she remembered nothing and awoke happily and refreshed.

Kyle still slept, and she carefully climbed out of bed and went to the hall closet. Opening the door was like cracking the seal on a tomb. She stared at the banjo leaning with an attitude against the wall. A tag attached to the neck read 'Alvin Guitar Shoppe.' Kyle had it cleaned and tuned.

Hannah grasped the instrument by the neck and carried it to the living room. She settled onto the couch and dragged her fingers across the strings. A pointless melody birthed from the relationship with a tentative hand.

"Guess I'll have to take lessons," she whispered.

"Hannah?" Kyle said from the doorway.

"Oh, did I wake you?"

"No. I woke up, and you weren't there. Then I heard the music. Are you coming back to bed?"

"Be right there."

She heard the voice of the music man from Muscle Shoals whisper in her head.

When you get home, you best pull that banjo outta' the dark and hang it in a place of worship.

Hannah carefully placed the banjo on the hearth of the fireplace and smiled.

"Lover's Moon," she said.

She returned to bed and snuggled against Kyle. Before she fell asleep, she heard a soft voice call through her heart.

Lover's moon, you tease me to follow down this long and lonesome path. The lover's moon speaks a soft caress to lie down in the grass. And while you cry alone at night, I hear the river's voice. It's the liar's moon, hidden by night, that leaves me with no choice.

"I have a choice," she whispered and fell back to sleep.

CHAPTER THIRTEEN ~

The Bradley boys arrived at Carlo's Restaurant and greeted each other with handshakes and good-natured jibes.

"Did Hannah tell you guys what this little gathering is all about?" Leigh asked.

"Not a bit. Just said to meet her here," Clem said.

"Her car's here. So, let's see if she came back changed by his trip. What'd ya' bet she's wearing a denim jacket with a Confederate flag embroidered on the back."

"A sleeveless denim jacket."

Otis pulled open the restaurant door, and they found Hannah seated at the same table as before.

"Join me, my brothers."

A basket of bread waited in the center of the table, and a shot of Chivas Regal and a tall draft beer waited at each place setting.

"Well, doesn't this look familiar," Leigh said. "You got another big check for each of us?"

"Afraid not. But something more valuable, I think."

Eduardo came to the table and gushed at how good it was to see them again.

"Eddy," Otis called the waiter back. "Can you please take the shot and beer away and bring me a Diet Coke?"

"Of course, sir."

"Diet Coke?" Hannah asked.

"Um, yeah. While you were running around Alabama, I was seeing Karen. She helped me see that I'm probably an alcoholic. I haven't had a drink in two weeks. I'm even going to meetings."

"No, shit?" Leigh asked.

"I shit you not."

"Good for you," Hannah said. "Let's order and eat, and then we'll talk."

Eduardo returned with a tall glass of soda with ice.

"House steaks all around," Hannah said.

"Very good. Be up soon."

An odd silence settled on the table until Otis finally broke the tension. "Uh, Sis, are you going to tell us what happened down there?"

Hannah put a mint tin on the table and tapped it.

"Are you saying we have bad breath?" Clem teased.

Hannah opened the tin and dumped the contents into her hand. "These are cotton seeds. I pulled these from a cotton boll in a field that once held the Bradley past's true legacy. One for each of us. I'll hang on to them until later, then it'll all make sense."

"Jesus," Leigh said, "you're taking this seriously. What the hell happened to you down there?"

"Trust me."

The food arrived. "Eat, then we'll talk."

"Good idea."

They all enjoyed the delicious beef and sopped up the dripping with the hearty bread. Finally, Eduardo collected the plates, and coffee arrived. Hannah downed the rest of her beer and sat back in reflective silence. His brothers all waited patiently.

"First of all, thanks for meeting me. But, it's a story you all have to hear. Then you can decide if it means as much to you as it did to me."

Otis said, "Hannah, enough with the melodrama. Tell us the damn story."

So, she did. From the office of Karen Gregory to the talk with Matt and the emotional struggle with her fear. Hannah told them everything from Muscle Shoals to Montgomery and from Mobile to Andalusia. She shared what she saw, how she felt, and what she discovered. And when she finished, Hannah looked around the table.

"Holy shit," Leigh said.

"Jesus Christ," Otis answered.

"That's a seriously messed up, *oh my God* kind of story," Clem finally said. "And you talked with Sarah?"

"I did."

"Man. That's intense."

"So, Dad wasn't a terrible man," Hannah added. "In fact, he was the hero of the family, in a way. By the time they dragged us to California, he was hell-bent on cutting off all ties with everybody and everything he knew before. But he brought with him because he never faced it."

"Hannah?" Otis said. "Please don't take this the wrong way, but I see a lot of him in you. I remember you as the hero to us, too. I especially remember the day you almost killed Dad."

Hannah shook her head,

"I didn't almost kill him. I just stood up to him. Besides, I think there was a bit of hero in all of us."

"Not me," Otis said. "I remember doing everything I could to avoid anything and everything. Maybe that's why I drank."

That brought silence to the table.

"So, what about this artifact you mentioned?" Clem asked.

Hannah reached into her jacket pocket and carefully placed the Coke bottle opener in the middle of the table. Clem picked it up and turned it over in his hands. Then he passed it to Leigh, who did the same, and then gave it to Otis.

"Take a look and know our past."

"Hard to believe that was the center of the reason that our grandparents uprooted and ran North," Otis said. "Coke and booze and kidnapping and murder."

"You make it sound like the remake of Scarface," Leigh joked. "So, we drank and ate and heard the saga. What now?"

"We go to the cemetery."

"Of course, we do," Otis whispered. "We faced the horror. Now we face the dead."

Hannah paid the bill.

Then the Bradley children left Carlo's in a somber group. Each went to their car and drove in a line, the five miles to Green Hills Cemetery. All were silent when they walked the rolling grassy ground and stood in a half-circle around their father's grave.

"Oh, hi, Mom," Otis said.

"Oh, yeah," Leigh said. "Hi, Mom."

Then they gave their full attention to the low granite marker surrounded by fresh sod.

"It seems a lot longer ago that we stood here and buried him," Clem said.

They all agreed, especially Hannah. She pulled the mint tin from her pocket and opened it. Then she handed each brother a cotton seed.

"What I found in Alabama was a culture trying to find its way in a new world still overshadowed by the old. I saw beauty and heard sorrow, found peace, and faced my demons. And behind it all, there was a single thing that was the driving force behind the oppression. The heartache and the bloodshed." Hannah held up his seed. "Cotton."

Her brothers nodded and held out their seed.

"So, to our father," she said. "He grew up in the shadow of it. Our family grew rich by it, lost all for it, and eventually ran away from it." Hannah paused and caught her breath. "Today, we give these seeds of our father's past to him as an offering of release and salvation. We release everything we had carried for our father's shame and shared misery by planting these seeds. And from this day forward, we're no longer defined by anything from his life and past. Today we surrender it all and declare that were are Yankees, born and bred. Alabama is not part of our story. I say without hesitation that I found nothing down there that had anything to do with us. We are free."

"Amen, sister," Leigh said.

"That was beautiful," Otis said. "How many times did you practice that in front of the mirror?"

"More than I will ever admit to. Now we plant these seeds."

Hannah knelt and dug a small hole between the granite and grass. Then she dropped in the seed and patted it down. Then each Bradley brother repeated the offering. Then they stood in silence.

"So, that's that," Clem said.

"So, we're Californians," Leigh said.

"Great," Otis said, "does that mean I have to take up surfing?"

"Yes," Hannah teased. "It's the law."

They all chuckled.

"We have to make a promise," Hannah said gravely. "If the time comes that any of us feels the old thoughts creeping in, we will call on one another for support. We have to promise we will not allow ourselves to go back there."

"I promise," each said in their turn.

"Then, we're done."

Otis looked down and said, "I forgive you, Dad. I know you were doing the best you could. From what I know now, you made the most of your life as possible. I'm sorry for hating you, and I will do my best to understand this story I've heard and release you with whatever love I can."

Then each brother said his peace. When there was nothing left but reflective silence, the wind came up, and leaves tumbled across the cemetery lawns like circus performers. The walk back to the cars was silent.

Otis pulled Hannah aside. "Hey."

"What's up?"

"I have a question, and it may sound stupid."

"Ask away."

"What about Mom? There's a lot of unresolved shit there too. What do we do with that?"

"Little brother," Hannah said softly, "I have a feeling that when we start letting Dad's stuff go, Mom, may take care of herself."

"But what if it doesn't?"

"One thing at a time, Otis."

"Okay. You're right. Jesus, I sometimes wonder if anybody grew up within a normal family?"

"Define normal?" Hannah said. "Back when Dad was a kid, what I just told you was normal."

"Shit, you're right again."

"Don't overthink it, and don't drink over it."

They hugged, and Otis waved without looking back.

As Hannah drove slowly out of the cemetery, she looked inside of herself to examine whether the ghosts were, indeed, chased away. All Hannah found was a quiet comfort in finding a way to forgive her father and herself. She knew the past might still raise its ugly head, and when it did, she would remind herself it was old and harmless. It was never hers to own. She remembered the last words from his uncle's song.

Lover's moon, you tease me to follow down this long and lonesome path. The lover's moon speaks a soft caress to lie down in the grass. And while you cry alone at night, I hear the river's voice. It's the liar's moon, hidden by clouds, that leaves me with no choice.

Hannah had the choice to embrace the future and count the blessings in her life.

"Karen will be so happy to hear that," she said. "And she will, tomorrow at two o'clock."

She punched the radio on, and a smile broke across his face. Lynyrd Skynyrd blasted in backcountry revelry. She sang along at the top of her lungs. When she arrived at the house, Hannah parked in the driveway.

"Now this," she said softly, "is a sweet home."

THE END ~

Coming soon:

Secret of Andalusia Farm
Book Two of the Bradley Chronicles.

Made in the USA
Columbia, SC
02 December 2021